"I swear you have a death wish. Are you looking for any excuse to use your abilities again?"

The ferocity in his remark drew my back up in defense. He was supposed to be my ally, but I should've anticipated his reaction. "I had no choice."

"Only because you chose to take her in the woods in the first place." The tiny haze of lights ignited around him as his frustration built.

I pushed my hands in my pockets to keep from reaching for him for my own selfish comfort. He had to understand. Griffith was the only one who truly understood me better than myself. He was my rock in this ever-changing town.

"I had to help look for Berta. There isn't a choice in everything. I couldn't let Chance go on his own. Yes, I went because it was my idea in the first place, but also because he's my brother. It's not safe for him."

His gaze locked with mine. "You didn't worry about yourself? Or consider how much worry you've caused me? Damn it, Hope, you, of all people, should realize what lurks undercover in the daylight has little fear at night and outside of town."

Griffith always saw right through me and my petty motives. The trait was what I loved and hated about him.

Praise for Maureen L. Bonatch

"Horror, fantasy, and romance aren't genres I see mixed together very often, but I really liked how Ms. Bonatch handled all three of them." (EVIL SPEAKS SOFTLY) Long and Short Reviews

"Do you like a storyline that's completely different from what you would expect in a Paranormal fantasy, if so then you're going to find putting this down extremely difficult." (DESTINY CALLING) Missy/Michelle's Books, Reviews, Competitions, Blogs

"Overall, I would definitely put this on the TBR list of anyone who likes both fantasy and suspense. It's an excellent combination." (DESTINY CALLING) Book Nerd Paradise

Not a Chance

by

Maureen L. Bonatch

The Enchantlings Series, Book 2

This is a work of fiction. Names, characters, places, and incidents are either the product of the author's imagination or are used fictitiously, and any resemblance to actual persons living or dead, business establishments, events, or locales, is entirely coincidental.

Not a Chance

COPYRIGHT © 2018 by Maureen L. Bonatch

All rights reserved. No part of this book may be used or reproduced in any manner whatsoever without written permission of the author or The Wild Rose Press, Inc. except in the case of brief quotations embodied in critical articles or reviews.
Contact Information: info@thewildrosepress.com

Cover Art by *Debbie Taylor*

The Wild Rose Press, Inc.
PO Box 708
Adams Basin, NY 14410-0708
Visit us at www.thewildrosepress.com

Publishing History
First Fantasy Rose Edition, 2018
Print ISBN 978-1-5092-2284-1
Digital ISBN 978-1-5092-2285-8

The Enchantlings Series, Book 2
Published in the United States of America

Dedication

Thank you, Mom, for introducing me to the joys of reading, inspiring me with your writing to pursue my dreams, and helping me to see the good in everyone with your kind heart.

Chapter One

"Who the hell is that?" My comment went unnoticed by the regular bar patrons engrossed in a hockey game on the old box-style television at Last Call. Luckily, we'd just opened for the day. The customers after dark sought more than cheap tequila and bad choices.

I leaned closer to the smoke-stained windowpane. The dude stepping out of the expensive car was a mortal, but even mortals often harbored cruel intentions. Evil doesn't discriminate. There's a little bit of a monster in everyone, except I was the only mostly mortal freak in this town of misfits that could identify the true monsters.

Men with smooth hands that were foreign to manual labor didn't stop here. They sped by on the rough, unpaved roads of what most referred to as the creepy, little town on the outskirts of Pittsburgh—as if pursued by the devil—which wasn't far from the truth. Unless they wanted something, and usually it was from me.

Everything about this guy didn't sit well with me, even though I couldn't place what filled me with instant dislike. Nor did I understand my newest ability, of foretelling, enough to question my prickly response. Sometimes I just knew. Problem was, I didn't know *what* I knew, or if it was relevant, but gaining my trust wasn't an easy task.

On the outside I looked like an ordinary woman, but both mortals and monsters lusted after my ability to give or take away hope and happiness. There were lots of good and bad people in the world, but not many who could control the balance. When Hecate, the Goddess of the Underworld, attempted to kill me because I refused to join her ranks, it changed me, and not necessarily for the better.

Well, at least no black fog accompanied the newbie. No feelings of hopelessness and despair leaked from a heartless soul intending to invade my thoughts. So he wasn't an Oppressor seeking to nourish itself on the optimism of others—or to cloud that desire with booze.

Alcohol worked its own magic in providing a false sense of happiness, or to at least temper the urge to extract someone else's. Some Oppressors couldn't quite pass as humans this close to their breeding grounds. There were usually a lot here, since this appeared to be one of the hubs of hell. Others might blend in as your surly next-door neighbor.

This stranger in a suit fit in our town like a square peg in a round hole. *Why was he coming to this bar?* Once I arrived and discovered my long-lost family, I knew I belonged. This guy didn't. I stepped away from the window to retreat behind the bar. Perhaps I could reduce my rising tension with routine tasks.

The glass nearly slipped from my slick palm when the animal masks jangled on the door as he entered. His polished shoes echoed and stirred the dust on the wood floor. I choked down my worries with the stagnant air, as I considered and then rejected asking Berta to wait on him. With no justifiable reason to explain my strange reaction, she'd think I was overreacting. Besides, out of the two of us, I was better equipped to deal with him if necessary. Berta was just too nice.

The cagey stranger was wise enough to avoid making eye contact with Andy and Ritchie, the regular bar patrons. After losing interest in the newbie, they returned their attention to the corner mounted television.

My grip tightened on the glass as I took a deep breath. I brushed away the lock of hair hanging in my face to sneak a peek to where he hunched over the counter. My stomach churned. Nothing about his mild appearance validated my apprehension. Wrinkles from an extended car ride lined the pressed suit sagging on his thin frame. Product caked in his professionally styled hair gleamed in the weak lighting fixtures.

"Is there a cost to read my palm?" His nasally voice quivered with excitement.

My racing heart slowed. The inquisitive stranger just raised his poor decision to stop here to a potentially fatal mistake. His comment implied that he already realized this wasn't your ordinary bar, and that I wasn't your ordinary bartender. There might be a lot of secrets in this town, but they were *our* secrets and we liked to keep it that way. I replaced the beer mug under the counter and turned to face him, except the stranger wasn't talking to me.

I hadn't heard Berta emerge from the kitchen. His unwavering attention was locked on to where she battled to cram more napkins in the cheap holder. Never one to neglect the attention of any male, she abandoned her task to saunter over. Berta shot me a narrowed glance to convey disapproval of my lackluster customer service and then bumped me with one of her *assets* as she squeezed by in the narrow space. Unlike me, she looked excited at the prospect of a new customer.

"Bless your heart. Where'd you hear I could do that, Sugar? Word must be getting around about me and my special ability." Berta winked at the creepy dude, eager to flaunt what I thought of as her side show act.

I couldn't read palms, like Berta insisted she could. My touch was for something else, and I paid the price for my so-called gift. I backed away, bracing my hands on my hips and being careful to tuck my fingers under the folds of my shirt. The fog that leaked from my fingertips when my emotions ran rampant was invisible to most, but I remained self-conscious of my unique ability.

Berta giggled and leaned in to whisper to the man. He rested his elbows on the counter. And she dipped her head, huddling close to the stranger. I felt, more than noticed, his gaze sliding to me and then away.

"Hope." Andy startled me when he reached across the counter to poke me with the tip of his finger. He had little interest in the booze. He came here for me, but he knew better than to provoke me. My mood could result in giving—or taking away—the happiness he sought.

I glanced to my arm and then his pockmarked face. His desperate expression and trembling hand begged for pity like an addict looking for a hit. At my glare, he retrieved his hand. Berta's innocent giggle was more indicative of a young girl than an adult woman. She gave our newest customer her best megawatt smile and prattled on about her palm reading skills.

The scrawny stranger studied the bar. His

scrutinizing gaze strayed to the battered, wooden sign hanging cockeyed on the wall behind my head. After lingering on the barely legible etched name identifying the bar, he resumed observing Berta's abundant cleavage.

Despite my unspoken warning, Andy trailed me like a cockroach. "Hope, please, just a quick touch. I've had a rough day."

For the love of tequila. My magic was a whole lot like crack. Once some people get a taste, they get hooked on the drug of hope. Andy behaved like an unrelenting two-year-old tugging at my skirts. No way would I be able to maintain a low profile in front of the stranger with Andy's incessant whining.

I spun to face Andy, bending close so the stranger enamored with Berta's fluttering lashes and pouty lips wouldn't overhear. "Just one time," I muttered through clenched teeth. "Shut up, before someone notices." I inclined my head toward the newbie.

Ritchie glanced our way but quickly lost interest. Andy's begging, and my refusal, had become the daily routine. People in this town accepted or ignored things a little out of the ordinary and most avoided showing too much curiosity.

I shot a glare at Andy and then tilted a mug under the tap. Most people who begged for a hit of hope left empty handed. That's not how my gift should be used, but Andy was on the verge of making a scene. I didn't want the stranger to shift his interest. Right now, neither Berta, nor the man, paid me any attention.

Andy moved his hand closer, and I placed mine over his, gripping his fingers. An icy shudder traveled down my spine when my hope filled energy filtered into him. His mouth gaped, and his eyes hung at half-mast as he basked in the sensation others described as akin to a warm bath, a full belly, or a passionate kiss. While he savored his pleasure, I grimaced with pain.

I released Andy and stumbled back.

He latched onto my arm. "I'm not done."

"I am." Before my rising irritation tempted me to modify my hopeful infusion and withdraw Andy's essence, I jerked away. As much as my body wanted me to succumb to the temptation, I wouldn't act like an Oppressor. The only time I accidently drained the hopefulness from another, six months ago, it changed me. Although none of us had been quite the same since that night.

A quick glance ensured the stranger and Berta remained engaged in a whispered conversation. A horn blew on television, and Ritchie's shout of approval indicated their hockey team had scored. Grateful for an excuse to ditch Andy, I retrieved the Jägermeister from the freezer with a shaky hand. They'd want celebratory shots. The task provided me with a chance to regain my composure.

I slid a basket of crusty peanuts aside to make room for the shot glasses. Ritchie's eyes widened, and he shrunk from the basket. "Don't put them peanuts near me, I'm allergic." He gestured with his hands, concentrating on the peanuts with obvious apprehension. "Take them away."

"Fine." I retrieved the basket and set them under the counter. Normally I'd believe someone about a food allergy, but this was Ritchie. His list of allergies and phobias changed more frequently than Pennsylvania's weather. He wasn't the sharpest knife in the drawer, and I doubted he was truly allergic to peanuts, but when he got an idea in his head he was adamant. Placating him proved easier than challenging him.

Andy glared at Ritchie. "You afraid of a goddamn peanut, simpleton?"

I sighed. My infusion of a little hope should've made him more amicable, but he couldn't tolerate Ritchie. Unfortunately, Ritchie's simple nature made him an easy target. Even though he could be annoying as hell, I had a soft spot for the underdogs of the world—perhaps because I'd been one most of my life.

"Shut up, Andy, or I'll shut you off." My threat included more than the bottle of Jägermeister I tilted in his direction. "Plus, I'll tell your boss you're not playing nice." Andy looked away. I could, since his boss at the liquor store was my boyfriend, Griffith.

For reasons unknown to me, I didn't tell Griffith about Andy's persistent begging. He probably suspected something, but perhaps he wanted to observe how I handled the situation. For me my resistance was like a test. Like a person who quits smoking but keeps one cigarette around to tempt and torment to build resilience. Andy was my cigarette.

As I poured the dark, thick liquor in the shot glasses, I felt someone's gaze—and presence—not far behind me. The stranger must've grown bored with Berta's reading, or was dissatisfied with her claims.

"Can I get you a drink?" I asked while struggling to keep my hands steady with the pour. If it was tequila, I might've been tempted to slip a nip to calm my nerves, but I would pass on the black, licorice-flavored liquor.

"Sure." He slid on the stool facing me, and then

lifted his hand to grimace at the sticky residue of Jägermeister adhering to his palm. "I'll have a soda, you know, a pop. Whatever kind you have with caffeine."

I ignored the liquor droplets on the counter, and hesitated while recapping the liquor bottle. No one ordered pop in this bar—or spoke with a heavy Boston accent. Maybe my brother, Chance, had heard something about this guy on his delivery route. Strangers never blended in well and were regarded with distrust and unease. Kind of how they felt about me when I arrived. How some still felt.

The man lifted the glass I offered while sneaking a glance at Berta's scarcely covered behind encased in cutoff jean shorts. She popped her hip to the side and used her ass to push open the swinging kitchen door. Once it swung closed, he returned his attention to me. "What's your name?"

His question sounded a bit harsh. Perhaps I prompted his insolence because I didn't introduce myself. Berta constantly reminded me how a polite introduction was the first step in Hospitality 101. But I never followed rules well, and I was a shitty bartender.

"Hope." My cheeks ached from the forced smile.

A gust of autumn wind rushed in as Griffith's broad shoulders filled the bar doorway. His intimidating appearance made most men uneasy, but still made my knees weak. Yearning after the man who rejected a position as the Queen of the Underworld's second in command was more hazardous than the bad boys that usually caught my eye. Griffith's rare combination of half-human and half-Oppressor made fitting into either world a challenging task.

Not a Chance

My heart skipped a beat when my boyfriend's gaze rested on me. I winked at Griffith to convey my confidence in my ability to handle the situation. His jaw clenched, emphasizing his striking cheekbones, but conveying his doubt. His gray eyes shimmered with foreboding when he focused on the new guy. After intense scrutiny, Griffith shrugged as if to say, *he's just a mortal man*, and then perched on the edge of a stool.

The newbie paled and choked on an ice cube when he noted Griffith's impressive build and possessive glance. He made an excellent bouncer, but striking terror in any man within a five-mile radius wasn't the best characteristic for a boyfriend. It made acquiring a mechanic to work on my heap of junk car impossible. But this time, it might be a good thing.

The newbie drained his glass and inflated confidence while casting glances at Griffith's muscular arms. He trembled while reaching in his suit pocket to produce a business card to push toward me. The sticky spot of dried Jägermeister halted its progress. "Could I talk to you?"

I used my fingernails to peel the thick card from the counter and hold it at the corners. Avoiding touching him, or the card, so as to evade inadvertently receiving any visions. After a quick glance at the name, Tom Stephens, I sucked in a breath at his title, Neb Knows, Reporter. *Shit.* This couldn't be good. A tingle ran through my fingertips, and I dropped the card. To divert his attention from my odd reaction, I reached for a weak excuse and a rag to wipe the counter. "I'm working. My boss frowns on that."

"He frowns on talking? Or working?" Tom's tight chuckle didn't sound genuine. It sounded like a challenge.

"Yep." It wasn't really a lie. Chief frowned all the time. I rubbed the counter forcefully, and since tossing out the reporter was a bad idea, I took my frustration out on the cheap lacquer coating.

He tilted his head, attempting to project his charm with a professionally whitened smile promising crummy used cars as good as new. "I doubt that. Isn't part of a bartender's job to talk to the clientele, you know, be friendly?"

"Not this bartender." I silently apologized to Berta for another failed lesson in hospitality. Years of caution may have added a little more ice to my smile, but the steel in my spine probably kept me alive this long. Sometimes being nice opened you up to being taken advantage of, or around here—dead.

A trickle of black fog leaked from my fingers. I braced my hands on the bar and turned my fingers underneath. I didn't need a visual reminder about the risks accompanying my unstable emotions. Fear put them in overdrive.

Griffith cleared his throat in warning, cautioning me, and Mr. Tom, reporter, to tread carefully. Since he was the only half-human, half-Oppressor I knew, he was the only one who noticed the black fog.

Maybe it was a coincidence that the reporter stopped here. Perhaps I was overreacting. Time to find out. I cocked my head and raised my brows. "What is it that you want to talk about then, Mr. Stephens?"

Berta popped her head out of the kitchen, closing in on me with narrowed eyes. "Hope? Can I see you for a minute?"

I drew my shoulder blades back at her barely

suppressed dissatisfaction. Perhaps I'd spoken more harshly than I realized. Berta was a formidable bar manager disguised under an exterior of sunshine and happiness—and my brother Chance's girlfriend. Thanks to my brother's big mouth, she should understand the reason for my discomfort with the stranger, but that didn't matter. Not now when she didn't agree.

"I'll be right back," I gestured to the reporter. To limit the length of time Berta detained me to tell me everything I should be doing, I kept my feet planted outside the kitchen. "What?"

"Can't you at least be nice?" Berta rolled silverware in thin, white napkins in preparation for the few that made up the evening crowd.

"I am being nice." As nice as I was prepared to be to a stranger who could expose me to the rest of the world as a freak of nature. It was pretty sad that I felt like too much of an oddity to blend in with an entire town of them. "He's a reporter."

Berta shrugged. "So? Maybe he's going to write a story about Last Call. He asked me a few questions about the bar and how I got this job." Her eyes lit up. "Maybe his story is going to be about me." Now, she positively beamed. "I did do a free reading for him."

I closed my gaping mouth and folded my arms across my chest. She always did revel being in the spotlight. "You've got to be kidding me. A story about the bar? Seriously, have you looked around? The only story he might write would be to recommend the building be shut down or demolished. Plus, he works for Neb Knows."

I frowned and leaned closer to Berta, relieved Aunt Ruthie was outside and wouldn't overhear our conversation. She had enough to worry about. "What did you tell him about Mrs. Shaw?"

"What could I tell him? I never met the last bar manager. He wasn't interested in her anyway. He wanted me to read his palm." She returned her attention to the silverware to stack the rolled napkins in a way-too-optimistic mound. Then she opened her mouth again.

"You don't have to be so cranky all the time. You should try smiling once in a while. Don't you know it takes forty-three muscles to frown and only seventeen muscles to smile? Oh, wait." She put her finger to her chin and furrowed her brow. "Or is it twenty-six to smile and sixty-two to frown? I know it's more. I'm not sure how much more."

I didn't place much faith in the validity of Berta's advice, so I turned to leave. "You're frowning."

The door swung shut on her surprised expression and what would have been one of her all too familiar lectures about how looks made the lady. Something she remained determined to turn me into since she started dating Chance. By now she should've realized that my Aunt Ruthie's creepy porcelain doll collection would be more amicable to playing dress up.

Tom sucked on an ice cube from his drink. The remaining cubes tinkled around his glass as he tilted it to and fro. He fidgeted in his chair while his gaze followed my progress. Outside the bar, the roar of a motorcycle indicated a few more patrons had arrived. It would be best for everyone to get the reporter out of here soon.

"What did you want to talk about?" I tried the smile again. The way he withdrew told me my strained attempt at friendliness didn't go over well.

After clearing his throat, he leaned toward me, eyes wide with excitement. "I heard some things, fascinating things, about this little town." He waggled his eyebrows, a move I envisioned him practicing to draw the viewer into his story. It was wasted on me.

He fidgeted with his jacket pocket and then angled his shoulders even more toward me. "What's the town called, again? The name?"

I'd never told him the name. If it ever had a name it was long forgotten or buried. Most referenced the town in hushed voices or drunken tales as the Crossroads. I narrowed my eyes. The slight bulge in his jacket resembled the shape of a phone. *Was he recording our conversation?*

"Why? What are you writing a story about?" I emphasized the word *story*. A few heads turned at my comment. The people living here either liked to be under the radar of the rest of the world because they chose to become anonymous...or they had to.

Tom lifted his shoulders and let them fall, possibly uncomfortable with the intensity of the stares. "Who said I was writing a story?" His words tumbled out with less confidence, and his attention kept straying to the large men at the end of the bar—particularly Griffith.

"You're a reporter, aren't you?" I lifted the card to point to his title. The force of the vision hit me like a punch in the gut.

I hunched forward, gasping for breath as a fleeting image of this man and Berta flooded my mind. The microphone pressed to her face. Eager words dripped from her lips as the cameras rolled. A cold sweat erupted over my body. I squeezed my eyes shut to regain self-control, but there was no need. The vision passed.

"Is something happening to you now?" Tom jutted his jacket toward me where the phone bulged. "Tell me what is it? Is it magic? Voodoo?" he hissed. "What's your power? Do you call yourself a witch?"

"She said she was busy." Griffith braced one hand on the counter, and the other landed heavily on the reporter's shoulder. His large frame blocked the meager light fixture, casting his handsome features in shadow and boosting his menacing appearance. He loomed over the stool. The reporter shrank into himself.

The murky haze surrounding Griffith revealed just how close he was to losing the control he'd struggled to improve, since the loss of his temper often produced devastating results.

"But…but, I just have a few questions to ask about things I heard she can do," Tom sputtered. No longer able to maintain his ignorant façade any longer, he reached for me with a shaking eager hand.

"Don't touch the lady," Griffith growled through gritted teeth, giving Tom's shoulder a squeeze. The reporter retracted his hand.

I took several deep breaths. Sweat beaded on Tom's upper lip and trickled down his forehead. Panic rose within me. *He didn't see what I did with Andy, did he?* If he did, and he mentioned it, I'd have more than the reporter to worry about. Griffith would be furious.

"It's your touch, isn't it? That's how you do whatever it is you do, right? Amazing, what a story." Tom wiped his sweaty hands across his pants. His eyes shone with excitement. "I could make you famous. The whole world would know your name. The world wants to know all about you. Don't deny them."

I couldn't respond. Saliva had abandoned my mouth and my tongue grew thick and heavy. The sound of my breathing echoed in my ears as I backed up until I bumped the counter—groping for the remote to increase the volume on the hockey game. I had to drown out his words before I was tempted to resort to other means to make him stop talking. *A newspaper?* He wanted to share my secret with the world. Proposing to out me as a freak of nature like it was a good thing. This town was my only refuge in the entire world. He couldn't take that from me. My vision blurred with my mounting alarm. I held to the counter to keep from slumping to the floor.

Griffith's nostrils flared. He clenched his jaw as his anger intensified. The excitement on Tom's face distorted and then faded. His body visibly deflated as Griffith's oppressive nature emerged to project onto the reporter. He took the man's optimism and replaced it with overwhelming emotions of hopelessness. To protect me he was doing the very thing he vowed to never do again, since he banished his brother to save me and mine.

"Griffith, no." Part of me didn't want him to stop. Why not rid the world of someone else who wanted a piece of me for personal profit? Another part of me realized I couldn't be responsible for Griffith bearing another burden of guilt. I'd provided him with enough regret already.

Griffith jerked away from Tom with visible difficulty. His body shook with tremors. I reached out and touched his arm. He lurched away and averted his gaze, but not before I saw the shame flit across his face.

Trying to act like a normal person took a physical and emotional toll on Griffith, but he remained determined to subdue the Oppressor part living inside of him.

Tom slumped over the counter and slid to the ground—landing on the floor with a thump.

The noise prompted Berta to rush from the kitchen. "What happened?"

She looked from me to Griffith and then peered over the counter. "Oh, my word." Her short legs provided her with a limited view of where Tom lay. She ran around the counter, teetering on her heels, and then crouched to cradle the man's head.

Tom blinked a few times and then regarded the room. His furrowed brow and clouded expression wore the confusion that usually followed an abrupt change of thought and depletion of emotion. A gust of wind ushered more customers inside for the upcoming happy hour. The approaching men stepped around the reporter.

Berta's gaze shot to me, the person she blamed for any out of the ordinary occurrences, and often rightfully so. While I sought words to explain what her tight, accusatory expression suspected, Griffith rescued me with an explanation.

"He had too much to drink." The lie flowed with ease from his lips. His expression appeared calm, but I saw what no one else could—the dancing gray lights flickering around him. They sought refuge in a victim as he struggled to willfully ignore his oppressive instincts urging him to consume the joy and pleasure from another.

"But he just got here." Berta patted Tom's back as he grappled to move to a sitting position. The floor housed all manner of litter, cigarette butts, and tobacco spittle. A used drink stirrer dropped from his hair. He brushed at his tan suit splattered with unidentified liquids and trash.

"He had a few drinks before he came here. Must've stopped at another bar," Griffith spoke with force, as if to convince Berta of his certainty, and to stop her incessant questions.

He could persuade Berta to agree if he wanted to. But using his oppressive abilities of persuasion, even once, might renew the temptation to return to the life he rejected.

"He doesn't smell like alcohol," Berta insisted and furrowed her brow.

"Hope smelled vodka on him." Griffith lied with ease, knowing Berta wouldn't challenge my heightened sense of smell. Plus, Tom's disheveled, bleary appearance could be mistaken for an alcohol-induced haze.

She looked to me for confirmation. I nodded, fearful that opening my mouth would ruin the charade. The temptation to reveal the lie and purge my guilty conscience for once again forcing Griffith to behave like an Oppressor was on the tip of my tongue.

Berta studied Tom. "That could be. I did tell him how I used to work at BB's. He seemed somewhat familiar with the bar."

Obviously, the reporter would know she used to work at BB's from his research for the story, but I wasn't about to tell Berta that.

"He needs to go home." Berta tapped her chin.

As she processed the information, I considered reminding her that all that frowning was bound to lead to wrinkles to distract her from thinking too much about what might've happened. Her gaze touched on each person at the bar. I didn't need a vision to follow her line of thought. When she determined no one sober was available, except for me—who she wouldn't trust with the task—and Griffith—who might be responsible for the incident—she said, "I can give him a ride home. He shouldn't be here in this condition before we get any busier."

A steady stream of bikers poured in the door. Even if Berta wouldn't admit it, she knew as well as I did that most of the bikers weren't the real threat. Those people would come later when the darkness helped cloak what most didn't want to see.

Berta lowered her voice, "The guys will give him trouble. Besides, I've watched those television commercials with those lawyers in them, they're just waiting for something like this to happen so they can sue someone."

I worried my lower lip between my teeth. Berta-big-mouth would be the worst possible person to send with a reporter in a car, otherwise serving as a portable interrogation room.

"No, I don't need a ride. I'm fine." Tom stood on wobbly legs and backed away.

His lips quivered, but he must've thought twice about what he'd been about to say. I'd guess that a sense of self-preservation prompted him to withhold his retorts as he studied the size of my muscle-bound boyfriend. He might not know exactly what had happened, but he'd probably hold Griffith responsible.

"Are you sure you aren't hurt? Do you need to go to a doctor?" Berta frowned, most likely visualizing liability claims and lawyers. She brushed ticket stubs and straw paper remnants from his jacket.

I didn't share her legal concerns. No one could successfully pry a dime out of Chief, that is, if he had any remaining after drinking his daily profits.

Tom gripped Berta's shoulders to halt her incessant fussing. "Really. I'm fine." He straightened as he reclaimed his earlier confidence. His gaze locked on mine. "I'm sure Hope and I will have an opportunity to talk another time, when she's not so…busy."

When the door slammed closed at Tom's departure, I anticipated Griffith's next move and grabbed his arm. His thick muscles tensed under my grip.

"It's not worth it," I whispered the soothing words. He once told me he did these things for me, and I certainly wasn't worth the trouble.

Chapter Two

"Like I always say, you'll get more tips if you dress a little better. Couldn't you at least wear something decent to work?" Berta eyed my wrinkled shirt and faded jeans.

"Nope." The familiar banter with Berta helped alleviate the tight knot of unease in my stomach. The large crowd that descended when the reporter departed yesterday left me with little time to process the uncomfortable incident. Perhaps that was enough to scare him off and he'd left town. I had enough to worry about without dwelling on whether the vision of Berta and the reporter would actually happen.

Berta scrubbed the sticky spots lingering on the counter from the prior evening. As she leaned forward, her low-cut shirt dipped. I suspected she dressed this way to distract impatient customers and gain tips. But right now, the only man present was my boyfriend. I scowled. "Couldn't you at least wear a camisole under your shirt?"

Berta beamed. "Camisole? See, you *are* listening to my fashion tips. That's the first time I didn't hear you refer to it as a tank top."

I rolled my eyes.

Griffith pulled his gaze from Berta's cleavage and my withering glare. "I'm heading over to the liquor store. I have an order of tequila coming in. You're getting low."

He stood and stretched his arms out to his sides. The distraction of his T-shirt tightening across his chest made my irritation with Berta flounder. I walked him to the door, clasping his hand lightly. "Just to work, right?"

"Of course." He turned and kissed me, lighting a tingle through my lips and down my arms. My feelings remained tenuous, but I was comfortable enough to admit we were in somewhat of a relationship. Our slow pace was understandable, since initially we weren't certain if we were meant to be together or kill one another.

He ran a hand along my cheek and searched my face. "Are you going to be okay?"

I nodded, leaning into his palm for a moment before he turned to leave. Every cell in my body yearned to ask him to stay. He would, if I asked. Ever since *the incident* with Hecate six months ago, he rarely let me out of his sight. I could take care of myself, but sometimes it was nice to know he wanted the job. Probably why he took the part-time job as a bouncer.

Griffith wanted to live like a normal person, but he'd seen so much of the ugliness of the world that it was hard to deny his Splice tendencies and not guard those he cared about with force, oppression, or intimidation. So I continuously reminded him that normal boyfriends wouldn't linger in my yard, or mope around the bar. I'd explain these were not ways of protecting me, as he insisted, but behaviors most considered weird and stalker-like. The mailman already refused to bring my mail up to my apartment and left it at Uncle George and Aunt Ruthie's. Normal boyfriends didn't generally worry about shielding their woman from the Underworld.

I wasn't normal anyway, but Griffith wanted me to think and act like I was. Acting normal in an abnormal world proved challenging when I realized long ago that sometimes nightmares are real.

As he mounted the motorcycle and slipped on the helmet I insisted he wear, I detected Berta's eyes boring into my back. It was only a matter of time before she complained that I was delaying helping her prepare for the evening shift. Griffith sprayed gravel behind him as he sped from the parking lot.

Griffith leaving right after the reporter yesterday was uncharacteristic. I only hoped he didn't follow him, or hunt him down for interrogation. Unfortunately, I suspected that's exactly what happened. And now, he was leaving again.

I wasn't worried about Griffith. He remained determined to rein in his Oppressor part and bury the evil part of his nature for good. He wouldn't do anything to harm the reporter. I frowned. At least I didn't think he would. I stared out at the empty parking lot and wrapped my arms around my waist. As much as Griffith wanted to mold himself into an ordinary man, there was very little ordinary about him. That's what I loved about him.

"Hope? Are you working or not?"

I winced at Berta's shrill demand and turned from the window, bracing myself for her inevitable lecture. As I returned to the counter, I snatched my apron and tied it around my waist. I only wore the unnecessary, old-fashioned protective fabric to ward off Berta's objections. Most likely she insisted I wear the frilly frock to conceal my tomboyish attire. I froze in front of the bulletin board. "Why did you keep that?" Tom's white business card stood out from the yellowed, worn advertisements.

Berta slid the wrapped dish of sliced lemons in the refrigerator in preparation for the mixed drinks of the evening shift and then turned to study me. "Why are you worried about that reporter? He was just being friendly."

"I'm not." I was. I didn't believe for a second that Tom was just being friendly, but attempting to explain to Berta would be fruitless. As a mortal, she wouldn't understand the things I struggled to understand my entire life and the lengths I endured to keep my secret.

Berta didn't come across as the brightest bulb in the box, but she was persistent.

Her current campaign focused on convincing Chance and I that we were normal people, *with a little more*. Her outward innocence is what drew my brother to her like a bee to honey. He might not realize why, but I did. Berta's trusting nature reminded me of Destiny. Although that was where the similarities ended with the sister I barely got to know before she was murdered. Although proving a murder that looked like a suicide was difficult. I learned that the hard way.

Berta remained oblivious despite living amongst the horrors and weirdoes of the world. That's just who she was. The most optimistic and annoying mortal I ever met. She was worse than Chance.

"You're doing that all wrong. Let me show you." Berta crinkled her tiny perfect nose at my attempt to make a pitcher of Bloody Mary cocktails for the imminent Sunday crowd. They loved Ruthie's mix and it looked easy enough to replicate. Apparently, that wasn't the case. She picked up the bottle of Worcestershire sauce and winked at the guys settling in their usual seats. "You need to add more of this. It's okay, Sugar, lots of people miss that step."

Lots of people—but not Berta. She did everything effortlessly right down to her perfectly proportioned—everything. I stepped aside to set out napkins as she took over completing the pitcher of drinks. At five-foot nine, I loomed like a giant next to her tiny, doll-like frame. Size wise, it was as if the old bar manager, Mrs. Shaw, never left, although the resemblance ended there.

"What's that horrible smell?" Berta grimaced and turned toward the kitchen. Strings of swear words leaked around the door, followed by the clatter of pots and pans.

I replaced the napkin holders and tentatively sniffed the air. It reeked of overcooked something, which was a familiar smell as of late.

The kitchen door flew open and bounced off the wall. My Aunt Ruthie emerged through a cloud of black smoke, waving her arms and coughing. "Gosh darn oven must be on the blink." She quieted when she saw me. Her eyes widened with hopefulness behind the thick lenses of her glasses. "D…Destiny?" Her lips quivered. "I'm sorry, Hope."

I shook my head even though she'd already realized her mistake. It wasn't the first time she'd mistaken me for my dead sister, but it didn't make it any easier. "Don't worry about it. I'm fine." I wasn't, but there was nothing I could do to ease the pain of being a constant reminder of who she lost.

Berta's expression softened as she looked from me

to Ruthie. Before she could try to salve this raw wound with her sympathy or advice, I changed the subject. "The smoke is getting worse. There's a lot this time."

Berta peered at the stained ceiling tiles as a cloud of smoke rose. "Where's the alarm? We better shut it off."

Berta knew there was no smoke alarm, but it was an easy way to extinguish our uncomfortable conversation before Ruthie retreated further into her recent depression.

"Ha." Ruthie examined the end of her singed, long, white braid with a shaking hand. "You think Chief would bother with a smoke alarm in this shack? He'd get more money if the bar burnt than trying to salvage this place." She frowned. "Although I doubt he spent money on insurance."

"You're right," I said.

When Ruthie went silent instead of seizing the opportunity to launch into one of her stories, my heart ached. I agreed to placate her. The oven was fine. Ruthie burnt more food than not lately, and her optimistic mood rapidly went sour. It didn't have anything to do with the oven. It had to do with me.

Ruthie's crestfallen expression made glittery sparks spiral from my hands. The sparkling hope leaked from me and instinctively sought her—but I couldn't help Ruthie. My gift of providing hopefulness never worked on my family. The people I wanted to help the most.

Instinctively I glanced at Berta, fearful, for a second that, she'd see my bizarre, leaking glitter. Yet, even if she wasn't preoccupied with the ceiling tiles, she couldn't see the shimmer accompanying my gift as it flitted from my fingertips. Despite knowing my concern was unnecessary, I remained uncomfortable with my odd ability, since it had only ever brought me pain, or embarrassment. I never lost the desire to just be a normal mortal, even though I knew that could never happen.

I retreated to the kitchen to determine if I could salvage any food and returned with a tray of smoldering unidentifiable lumps. The smoke tendrils curling up from the blistering remnants reminded me of the fog surrounding the Oppressors. "What was it?"

Ruthie slumped in a chair. "They were supposed to be biscuits."

The guys at the bar didn't give Ruthie, or the inedible biscuits, a second glance. They'd become all too familiar with her new habit of burning everything. If she didn't catch the bar on fire, and we kept serving beer, they wouldn't budge.

I touched Ruthie's arm, wishing I could provide her with the comfort she always gave me. "Why don't you go home and spend some time with Uncle George? I'll take over here."

"You? Cook?" Her eyes bulged behind her pop bottle glasses and a glimpse of her old humor peeked through her distress. "You can't cook a hamburger."

I forced a scowl. "I know how to cook a hamburger." Not implying the burger would be any good, or edible, just that I could make one. It couldn't be much worse than the stuff Ruthie made recently. "Nobody is interested in the food anyway, they come for the drinks."

And me. But Ruthie knew that. I drew the Oppressors more effectively than the booze with my brimming hope. Some might have come for the food before, but not in the past six months.

Ruthie's face fell as she watched Berta carry the biscuits outside to toss them in the dumpster. The tray was too warped to salvage. "Yeah, I'm sure you know how to make a burger, I only wish I *knew* why I can't anymore."

After Destiny died, Ruthie's cooking skills had gone to pot. It seemed she no longer knew how to make things delicious. I lost five pounds when she lost that ability, making me appear even ganglier beside curvaceous Berta.

Which was the heart of the matter. Since Destiny's death and Mrs. Shaw's weird disappearance after the Hecate showdown, Ruthie's gift of knowing hadn't been the same. She had almost no magic, while my abilities were bursting to the brim.

My struggle to not infuse hope or take it away from people challenged me enough without visions striking when I least suspected. The vision yesterday featuring Berta and the reporter only fueled my distrust of Berta's true intentions.

Ruthie stood with a sigh of resignation, looking as if she'd aged years in the last months. "You're right. I think I will go home. I'm not doing much good around here. Just let Chief know." She cringed at the word *know*. "Tell him you can handle the kitchen."

"Sure, Ruthie." Most likely Chief wouldn't question her absence. He didn't notice a lot of things anymore. No one realized how much Mrs. Shaw meant to Chief until she was gone. Not even Chief. Though impossible to drown his sorrows more than he already did, he lacked his customary harsh, critical wit.

It seemed that since I arrived everyone had lost

someone close to them, and I couldn't help but feel a little responsible. Perhaps they'd had the right idea when they left me at the orphanage. Perhaps I shouldn't have returned to find them, and then I might be the only one miserable.

Berta returned, catching the end of the conversation. "Who can handle the kitchen?"

I winced at the sugary sweet voice Berta reserved for everyone but me. "Me."

Berta's laugh, light as fairy dust, cut me to the core. "No, I don't think so. Ruthie can go home if she wants, but I'll handle the cooking. Hope can work at the bar, pouring drinks. It's what she does best."

She said the last words with reluctance. We both knew she didn't believe my bartending skills were up to her standards. Nothing I did was. But my job was fairly secure since there weren't many bartenders willing to work at this bar—actually there were none. I kind of had to, but so far I didn't know why Berta did.

When Mrs. Shaw disappeared, Berta had shown up and asked about a job. She used to work at B. B.'s. The acronym supposedly stood for Bob's Bar but most people called it bosoms and booties after getting a glimpse of the bartenders working there. Chief couldn't believe his good fortune in luring her away from his competitor, but I didn't believe in luck. This bar didn't have one thing over B.B.'s...except my brother and me.

"Thanks, Bert," Ruthie called her by the affectionate nickname she and Chance dubbed Berta with, but I refused to use. My sarcastic comparison of her to a doll only upset Chance so I couldn't use that reference anymore. But if she ever took off the heels or her gaudy cowboy boots, I was sure her feet would be stuck in a tiny, permanent arch.

The door swung shut behind Ruthie. She trudged across the parking lot, the gravel crunching under her feet echoed through the open window.

"It is a hot one out there today for October. To be that warm this late in the month it must be like one of them days they call Cherokee summer. Or is it Indian summer? Well, whatever it is, it's gonna be even hotter working in the kitchen." Berta shrugged out of her tiny, pink sweater.

"You might want to put on an apron so you don't accidently burn something in the kitchen." My gaze dropped to her ample cleavage, which was bursting out of the top Berta wore. My guess would be that none of the men could identify her eye color except Chance. He described her eyes as the light blue of a clear sky. I disagreed. I found the blue more like an icy spear that cut through me with a frown of her meticulously plucked eyebrows every time I entered her visual range.

My minimal curves couldn't help me much in that department. That was no surprise. Most women couldn't compete with her external package. I couldn't fill out a top like Berta could. When Chief informed me that he hired Berta, I envisioned an old, grandma-type rivaling Mrs. Shaw in outdated fashion sense. When Berta walked in, she redefined the image of the name. I couldn't pinpoint what made me dislike her on the spot. Griffith thought I was jealous. He commented as much once, but never again after my retaliating argument.

Granted, he might've been right, because at the time Berta was begging for a ride on his motorcycle. When he finally conceded, she clutched him like a spider monkey. She molded against him and ran her hands over his leather coat, gushing over the texture. I admit she may have sparked a jealous cell within me, or perhaps a whole army of them, leaving me craving the opportunity to smash in her cute little face. Once she became my brother's girlfriend, my dislike intensified.

After the vision last night, I couldn't think of any reason I should like her. My gaze strayed to Andy's newspaper and stuck on the small headline that would've been the main story if this town didn't have its share of so-called suicides. I tensed. The suicide should've been the headline and not buried under other irrelevant news. It had been months since one had been reported. It was pretty sad that many had become accustomed to death, but not me. I pulled off my apron. "Since we're not busy yet, I'm going to use my break to find Chance."

"He's down at the river."

My hands stilled. He knew better than to go in the woods alone. It irritated me that she knew where my brother was and that she'd convinced him that there was no need for caution. She'd crammed her perky self between us. "Thanks. I'll be back before the evening rush."

"No hurry, I can handle it," she said with a smile.

I'm sure she could handle it, and everything else. But no one was that perfect. There was more to little miss perfect than meets the eye. I just had to convince someone else to believe me, so it didn't come across like the ranting of a cranky, jealous woman. She might not be responsible for that poor person's so-called suicide, but her big mouth could cause trouble that wouldn't be so easy to ignore.

****

"I didn't expect to find you here," I said. Fishing at the river in the woods wasn't the first place I assumed I'd find my brother, but it was an improvement. Normally he sat at Destiny's gravesite. The sharp snap of a branch had me scanning the heavy foliage in search of signs of an Oppressor, or perhaps the reporter. I hadn't stopped looking over my shoulder since he left.

The suicide had me thinking that the months of relative peace since I banished, vanquished, evicted—or whatever the hell I did to Hecate—seemed to be reaching an end. Many of the Oppressors had left to blend into the slums and outskirts of Pittsburgh. Others lingered, keeping a low profile without a leader.

The calm lasting this long before another impending shit storm surprised me, but I never was the most positive person. I left unbridled optimism to my brother, Chance. Except lately, even he struggled to maintain a cheerful disposition.

My body protested when I lowered myself to the ground to sit next to Chance. A chipmunk started making his way toward me. In addition to my sister's visions, I'd inherited her odd trait of having every living critter follow me around like they expected me to erupt into song and return home to seven short men.

I followed his gaze to the fishing line bobbing in the river. His pole lay propped in the forked middle of a stick. The trees across the river were heavy with branches laden with autumn leaves dipping to sag in the river like fingers trailing through the water's flow. The trees pressed tightly together on the opposing shoreline and hung over the water, making me acutely aware of how they obscured the view into the depths of the woods.

"Did you see the paper today? There was another one." The article could be easily overlooked since it was tucked in the middle of the newspaper. In a town the Internet seemed to have forgotten, news didn't travel as quickly with the lack of sufficient Wi-Fi outside of the local library and limited accessible social media outlets. I doubted that the body discovered this morning, deemed a suicide, would deter the reporter. It would only serve to increase his determination to uncover the town's secrets, specifically mine. "You shouldn't be in the woods alone, it might not be safe."

He shrugged. "Why not? Berta said it's ridiculous to be afraid of the woods. She insists the best way to conquer your fear is to face it head on. The Oppressors don't scare me. Besides, I could be one of them."

Berta said. I rolled my eyes and swallowed my desire to repeat the words in a mocking tone. Hearing Chance recount Berta's wisdom was getting old. "No, you're not one of them, and that's not what I meant."

Everyone avoided going into the woods, and no one with any common sense went alone. It's hard to get rid of something that isn't really alive, which is what all Oppressors really wanted—to be alive. What everyone wants. I hadn't really realized how much until the people I loved started dying.

People were known to disappear because low-level Oppressors bred and grew in the depths of the forest. Chance's increasing recklessness worried me. It was as if he harbored a death wish since Destiny died and he discovered he might have some Oppressor in his blood—since his accidental birth was due to sinister magic. Otherwise Destiny and I would've been twins instead of making us triplets, the Enchantlings. My optimistic, happy-go-lucky brother now spewed cynicism and irritability. It was as if he'd become the male version of me.

Once we came to terms with losing Destiny, I'd hoped Chance and I would have the opportunity to become closer. I'd never had a sibling, and I looked forward to having someone to confide in about the unusual paths our lives had taken. Someone who might not be as quick to judge the abilities I was born with.

He picked at a blade of grass, separating it into three pieces and then discarded each section. "What am I supposed to do now? I never expected to live once we turned twenty-one and came into our abilities."

Chance's words shocked me, but his proclamation brought relief that he was finally opening up. It felt like yesterday, but six months had passed since Destiny's death. I squeezed his shoulder. "You're supposed to live."

I knew he grew up with her, but she was my sister too. Destiny might've looked like me, but I only knew her for a short while. I didn't get to experience what having a sister was like, let alone being a triplet. After searching to find my family, once I arrived I destroyed the peace and harmony in their world.

"For as long as I can remember, I've been told that I have a special responsibility as an Enchantling," Chance said. "That the three of us would help the goodness in the world overtake the evil, or else we would all die. I prepared for that responsibility my entire life." He glanced at me and then returned his attention to the water, reaching to pluck another blade of grass to twirl between his fingers. He sighed. "Then, Destiny was murdered. Evil is still around, and it's even in me. I didn't prepare for anything after you. I didn't think there would be an after."

"You're not just an Enchantling, you're a person." I ignored his grimace of anguish. He needed to hear it. I was tired of tiptoeing around reality and sucked at this whole comforting thing. Being born with some weird abilities wasn't nearly as special as they'd lead Chance to believe. The difference was that I'd always know that. I couldn't face losing another one of my newfound family. "You're not dead. You have a lot to live for, including Destiny. What would she think if she knew you tossed your life away because of her?"

"Do you think she felt any pain?" His eyes remained haunted.

I wished he would see the colorful leaves floating to the ground, instead of picturing the day he found our sister's body as the ground began to thaw from the long winter. Her death appeared like suicide, but we knew it for what it was…murder.

"No." I couldn't let myself believe anything different about Destiny's death or I'd go crazy with grief along with Chance and Ruthie. I had to be the strong one. As the first born of the triplets, that's how it was meant to be. It was my destiny, whether I wanted it or not.

"You have Berta now, too." As much as the woman drove me crazy, she made Chance happy. His sappy smile had disappeared with Destiny. After almost six months of melancholy, Chance's happiness finally began to reemerge. It frustrated me that Berta might understand my brother better than me. "In fact, she told me you were here."

Chance remained motionless, staring at the blades

of grass. Each cracking twig and rustling in the trees drew my attention as I sought telltale signs of an approaching Oppressor, but Chance didn't flinch. "Were you together again last night?"

"Of course, she's my girlfriend." Chance pushed up from the ground. His abrupt movement caused the animals creeping toward me in unexplainable adoration to scurry back to the forest. "Why do you dislike her so much? She's been nothing but nice to you."

I came to discuss the reporter and the vision with Chance, but somehow the conversation had turned back to why Berta and I weren't instant besties. This wasn't going how I planned, but nothing ever did. "I don't know how to have a female friend." That much was true, I never had one, but I also didn't want one. "It's not that I don't like her."

"But you don't like her, I can tell. Anyone can, even Berta said how your obvious dislike upsets her." Chance crossed his arms and stared over the water.

Upset her? I hadn't detected the slightest sign of distress on her perfect little face, but I wouldn't waste my breath arguing with Chance. I reached out to touch him, detecting his underlying tension, but dropped my hand when he stepped away. "I just don't know that I can trust her. She's not like us, you know."

Despite Berta upholding her charade of being a palm reader, that's all it was, a charade. I think she might believe some of what she said, but more than likely she did it to make herself feel like she was a little different to fit in better. It's sad she had to strive to be a freak to fit into our town.

Chance shoved his hands in his pockets. "I'm glad. Why would I want her to be like us? Besides, we're just like everybody else. Mortals with more. That's what Berta likes to say." He smiled slightly when he referred to another one of her goofy expressions.

I couldn't blame them for their uncertainty and unwillingness to fully trust me. I couldn't trust myself. My family always looked at me with a new wariness after that night, as if they were uncertain of my capabilities, and what I might do. Their unease filled me with shame.

"How is Mrs. Dwight holding up now that you're off the market?" I changed the subject to the geriatric jezebel at the police station who adored Chance to try to lighten the mood.

He shrugged.

I stood. Sitting on the forest floor made me feel vulnerable. After a brief internal debate, I decided to share what I saw, even if it might irritate my brother. "I had a vision about Berta today."

Chance turned away from me. His back saying more than his words ever could. "I told you, you don't understand the visions yet. Destiny lived with them her whole life, and she still couldn't separate the truth from fiction half the time. You can't make a judgment from one vision. You aren't giving Bert a chance. I think you're jealous, just like you were jealous of Destiny."

"I wasn't jealous of Destiny, and I'm not jealous of Berta." I was, though. Deep down I recognized this truth, but I'd never admit it. It wasn't because they were both prettier than me. Even Destiny, who was supposed to be identical to me, looked better. It was the way they seamlessly fit in with my family and how people instantly loved them. It was hard to project a personality worth loving when I had trouble figuring out if I loved myself. "She could be a threat to us."

"To you, you mean."

I tensed. Although he spoke softly, the words cut deep because I realized there might be some truth to them. I hadn't realized I'd been so transparent.

Chance touched my shoulder. "Please, sis, give her a chance. She could use a friend, and I think you could use one too. You worry about things a twenty-one-year-old woman shouldn't have to. You're constantly dwelling on evil and death. Stop looking over your shoulder all the time. She's gone."

"Maybe you're right." I would give Berta a chance, for him, not because I agreed with anything else he said. I didn't know how to stop musing on the thoughts of evil and death that consumed me my entire life. It would always be someone—or something—else. I spend my life waiting for the other shoe to drop.

"You have a bite." I pointed to his fishing bobber. The red and white ball dipped in and out of the water as a fish struggled with the bait.

Chance picked up the pole and reeled it in, tilting the line to the side as the fish thrashed through the water. I could see how my brother appealed to Berta, as well as many of the women in town. His lean, muscular build would make most women pause, and with the hint of mischief in his sea green eyes—eyes that looked even greener with his licorice black hair. He just looked so…alive.

I always thought the most appealing thing about my brother was his easy smile, and the one thing absent for months until Berta appeared. She resurrected his smile from the depths of despair. That was the only reason I'd give her a chance.

He knelt as the beautiful trout reached the bank. Even I recognized the fish as a great catch as it flopped about on the grass in its desperation to escape. I sympathized with the fish. Its efforts were fruitless once removed from its natural habitat. I could probably relate to its struggles more than most, but I also learned at a young age that life was about survival.

Chance gently removed the hook from the fish's mouth. Its lips opened and closed in search of water to breathe. He knelt to immerse it in the water and let the fish swim free.

I frowned, watching the speed in which the fish fled deep into the water to recover from his near-death experience. Although despite his narrow escape, it was likely the fish would make the same mistake if a tempting worm was dangled in front of him again. Because we all want to believe in second chances, good fortune, and finding that silver lining in the clouds. We want to believe in the good within people and forget their past wrong-doings. The problem was, despite how hard we tried to forget, our hearts made us prone to repeat the same mistakes.

People like me didn't trust a happy ending. I knew happiness was usually short-lived. That the bad always came with the good. Usually when and where we least expected it. At least that had been my experience. It's why I clung so tightly to those who meant the most to me. "Aren't you going to keep the fish? Why are you fishing if you're going to toss them back?"

His bright smile briefly cut through the cloud of despair surrounding him. "It's not about catching them. It's about letting them go."

Chapter Three

I stroked Tercet's silky fur and then leaned against the door with a sigh. "Did you miss me, sweetie?" She peered at me with solemn eyes. Hordes of admiring critters sought me out in search of Destiny, but Tercet still only provided me with minimal interest. The damn cat gave me a condescending glare with most things I did. I swore the feline strove to increase my self-consciousness, if that was even possible.

Her patient, disinterested regard pleased me immensely. After months of distrust the finicky cat finally accepted me enough to occasionally display a tidbit of affection. It might've been the result of inheriting Destiny's odd ability rubbing off, but I wouldn't question the cat's limited acceptance.

I didn't need a cat to sense the Oppressors like Chance and others did, not when I could see the signs for myself. It was nice to have something love me for who I was, with no expectations. Except for demands of food and the bestowing of endless adoration upon her as most cats required.

I drew the curtain aside and peered through the glass. Tom slumped in the seat, as if I couldn't see him clearly. As I suspected and feared, he wasn't scared off that easily.

Idiot. His was the only car on the other side of the road. Apparently, he didn't consider how difficult it might be to go stealth in a town where everyone knew everyone else and most of the houses were set apart by the dense surrounding woods. I intentionally thought of him as Tom. I refused to give credence to the status he probably believed he deserved as a big city reporter.

I dropped the curtain and turned my back on my transparent stalker, grateful Aunt Tessa didn't decide to pop in the mirror from wherever she resided in the afterlife to lecture me. After I banished Hecate I thought she might move on. Destiny and other people I lost had done so when they felt they'd fulfilled their purpose for this life.

In some ways, I was glad to have Aunt Tessa's spirit stick around. Otherwise it was mostly me and Tercet since Aunt Ruthie hadn't been herself for some time. There was always my Uncle George if I had a few spare hours on my hands to stop downstairs to talk. He was starved for any conversation, especially now that he was desperate to find a way to *bring his Ruthie back.*

Despite my attempt to act nonchalant about Tom's lingering presence, the skin prickled between my shoulder blades, almost as if his gaze pierced me there. I refused be a prisoner in my own home. I spun to peer out the window again. "What the hell is he doing here?"

Tercet tilted her head and blinked once. She fled with her tail held high when she sensed my emotions building within me. Impulsively I turned the doorknob and stepped on the small porch. I folded my arms across my chest and glared at the car parked across the street. Time to let Tom know that he and his slimy presence didn't scare me. His intimidation tactics couldn't frighten me with what I'd faced in the past. Despite the orphanage closing, and me no longer being thirteen years old, we were close enough to Pittsburgh that I still suffered nightmares about the nuns returning to resume their attempts to exorcise the devil from me. But the thought of what he could do with the information he gathered, or concocted on his own, terrified me.

I stormed down the wooden steps, my anger growing with the force of each footfall. *How dare he invade the first place I considered a home?* Even though I'd only lived here for a short time, it was the closest to a home and extended family I'd ever experienced. I wouldn't let him ruin it. I had enough intimidation while growing up in the orphanage.

He startled when I approached. Not in trepidation as I hoped, but excitement. He must not be aware of the risks of getting on my bad side.

"You changed your mind." He unfolded his lanky body and emerged from the car. He stood and smoothed his wrinkled jacket, and sparse hair, as if preparing for the camera.

"How dare you sit outside my house? That's an invasion of privacy." The words poured out. The true source of my anger was the risk of him revealing what I was and exposing me more thoroughly than if I stood naked in front of the world. His claims could secure my spot in the psychiatric ward where the loitering Oppressors would finish me off before the doctors determined a diagnosis.

Tom hedged back, as if realizing there might be more to me than meets the eye. Fear flickered across his face. He probably realized a little too late that there were things he might not want to know about, that sometimes ignorance is bliss. His gaze traveled over me with unease. He couldn't detect the black fog leaking from me to surround me like a cloak, but I was confident that he could certainly determine that something about me had changed.

The vengeful part of me begged to destroy this menacing man trying to wreck the kind of normal life I'd struggled to establish. The evil slumbering inside of me silently pleaded with my conscience to nourish upon his fear and self-loathing and let his emotions destroy him.

Tom's smile was forced, and his chuckle sounded like a futile effort to set me at ease. "Like I said, I just want to talk." He cocked his head, as if we were united in this decision. "What are you doing in this hole-in-the-wall town? You could be so much more. I could help make you more."

"This is my town." When I said the words, it was the first time I believed it was true. I drew my shoulders back. It was my town, whether my long-lost family wanted me here or not, I was here to stay. "This is where I belong, not you."

I leaned toward him, and he cringed away. After skimming my gaze over his jacket, a quick grab snagged the phone from his pocket, confirming my suspicions. The red record button blinked ominously. "What kind of information do you think you're going to gain that you need to record me?"

He pushed me away to regain personal space. I stumbled, still clutching his phone.

"Something good from the way you're reacting." He grabbed my wrist and yanked the phone from my grasp.

At his unwanted touch, I gasped as my powers

hungered for release. I struggled to contain my ability to give or receive hope. I didn't want to validate his thoughts about my abilities. If I released hope, it would deplete me and confirm his accusations. If I retrieved hope from him in my present state of fury, I might accidently kill him.

I tugged my wrist. His grip tightened. My head spun with the fear churning within me. I grimaced as pain seared my skull. My efforts to restrain the emotional anguish from my ability weakened the physical strength needed to free myself. Even though I was considered somewhat of a witch, I didn't have the strength to ward off a male mortal...but Griffith did. The deafening sound of his motorcycle roaring toward us brought relief. This time his uncanny ability to sense my distress proved beneficial.

Mr. Reporter cocked his head and narrowed his gaze on where he held my arm. He had to have felt something from touching me for that extended time. He detected the thunder of Griffith's imminent arrival moments before my boyfriend rode up like a knight mounted on an eight-hundred-pound metal steed, wearing an armor of black leather. Tom's eyes widened, and he released me to fall on my ass before stumbling toward his car. "Later."

He fumbled with the handle on the car door and dove into the seat. The engine started and he sped down the road as Griffith reached me. He stopped to idle the bike, watching Tom's taillights flash in the distance, as they hesitated at the stop sign, before putting on a burst of speed.

My gaze traveled up Griffith's ass-kicking boots, his muscular thighs, and then up to the concerned expression he wore as he dismounted. He examined me. His shimmering gray eyes missed nothing. "Are you all right? What happened?"

"I'm fine. It was nothing." Now that Tom was gone and the threat relieved, heat crept into my cheeks. My temper didn't usually go from one to one hundred in a heartbeat. These erratic mood swings were happening more often.

"No. It was something." Griffith took my hand and pulled me to my feet. "Regardless, it's not something you should get so worked up about. He works for Neb Knows. No one believes the stuff they publish in that shitty tabloid. People think the fake stuff is real, and the real stories are fake. Since you're the real deal, we're safe."

It was more than the magazine, but I didn't know how to explain it. They say some moments change you, while others define you. I had an uncomfortable feeling lately that something was about to change, and not in a good way.

His smile dissolved when he glanced to where he held my hand. Black tendrils of fog poured out to circle his hand and then retreat. Lucky for him, he was immune to my ability, or I might not have been able to stop myself from drawing from him at this point of emotional vulnerability.

I shoved my hand into my pocket. Being with Griffith was wonderful. When I touched him, I didn't have to worry about how it might affect him. Although being with a guy who read your emotions like an open book, when you never anticipated what emotional diarrhea might pour out of you, left something to be desired. Sometimes a little mystery was a good thing.

"He's been recording me on his phone." I studied the vacant road. "You followed him when you left the bar." I stated, challenging him to deny my claim.

He nodded. His expression flattened into a mask of steel, harnessing and hiding the underlying emotions.

"You have to stop worrying about me. I can take care of myself." Although this time, I was glad Griffith showed up when he did, otherwise I didn't know what might've happened.

"I almost lost you before." He smoothed his hand over my wild curls, which grew more defiant with each season.

His touch soothed me. I turned to him, wanting to dispel his fears like he did mine. "But you didn't."

He shook his head. "But I could have. After years of dreaming about you coming into my life, I can't risk losing you."

I gazed into his eyes, waiting for him to confess. He agreed to no more secrets, yet I couldn't be sure he believed he was protecting me by not sharing everything.

He sighed and averted his eyes at my questioning stare. "He's staying at the little hotel on the edge of town. He at least has enough sense not to stay downtown. There's no way he'd last the night there."

He didn't have to elaborate on the dangers Tom unwittingly avoided. We both knew how others in this town functioned, and they wouldn't be as compassionate as us.

Griffith tentatively opened his arms. After a lifetime of being shunned by both mortals and Oppressors, he was always uncertain of how he would be received. I leaned into him, his leather jacket cool against my cheek.

"Why?" I didn't have to explain that I'd changed the subject back to me. Griffith recognized my fears as well as his own.

"People are always curious about anything different." He rested his chin on my head and tightened his embrace. "Someone must have said something."

I tilted my head to study him. "But who? And why would he believe it?" No one else but me saw the Oppressors for what they were. The witches and others gifted with variations of magic outside of my family kept to themselves. Any mortal noticing anything unusual didn't live to tell what they saw. People didn't share secrets here…they kept them.

He shrugged, pulling me in tighter and stroking my hair. "I don't know. Maybe he's snooping around hoping to find something. Those reporter types look for anything to build into a story. Did you tell him anything worth writing about?"

I sifted through my memory but couldn't recall anything. Perhaps I missed something. My life had never been defined as normal. I accepted so much extraordinary as ordinary that sometimes it was hard to differentiate between the two. "I don't think so."

"Then stop worrying." He pressed his lips to mine to dispel my fears.

The tingle of our tongues mingling pushed all thoughts of Tom from my mind. I cupped his face. The rough stubble of his chin scratched against my palms. I slid my hands to link behind his neck, twisting the soft strands of black hair hanging past his collar. When my heart rate rose to catch my breath, it was a good feeling. He made me feel alive.

"I missed you," I whispered against his lips. Those three words were the most I could share about the empty feeling carved in my heart when he wasn't around.

A car horn blared, ruining the moment and reminding us that we stood in the middle of the road. The honk-happy driver behind the wheel was my Uncle George, Ruthie's husband. He beamed at me as he edged by, and then cast a wary glance at Griffith as he drove past us to pull in the driveway. Griffith pushed his motorcycle to the side of the street.

George emerged from the car with considerable effort to hoist himself up with uncooperative knees. He hobbled around to pop the trunk, revealing bags upon bags of groceries. He frowned and rubbed the small of his back as if contemplating how to get all the bags in the house. Being a man, and a stubborn one, there was no way he would ask for our help.

"Why don't you help him?" I nudged Griffith in George's direction.

Griffith never asked why Uncle George didn't like him. He accepted George's instinctive aversion to him. For most of his life, that was the norm for Griffith. I figured George's spontaneous reaction grew from his protective nature. He displayed distrust of anyone encountering his Ruthie.

Griffith insisted he wanted to change that relationship, so he wasn't always looking in from the outside. But he had no idea how. Besides his obliviousness that staring and glowering were often interpreted as a threat even when no words were spoken, he lacked social finesse with the little interpersonal things most people took for granted, like saying "hello," or "please."

Griffith stepped toward Uncle George, lacking his usual confident swagger. I smothered a chuckle at how an elderly, bow-legged man cowed my big, muscle-bound boyfriend who dealt with all kind of monsters on a daily basis. Whether it was the ones formed from hate and despair, or people requiring customer service at the liquor store. Things could turn ugly pretty quick when you get between people and their booze.

Griffith cleared his throat. "Umm, Mister—"

I elbowed his side and whispered, "Call him George."

"Can I help you there, err...George?" Griffith shoved his hands in his pockets and ducked his head, averting his eyes.

"I'm managing." George grimaced as he hoisted the groceries, and his wobbly knees shook. His baggy shorts made his knees appear more prominent. He wore shorts well into the year until he couldn't tolerate the dropping temperature. There was something to be said for long pants when the weather got colder. I told him as much, but he ignored me. Pasty-white, goose-bump-covered legs resembling a plucked chicken didn't bother him.

"Stop being such a *man* and let him help you." I stormed over and took a few bags from Uncle George and handed them to Griffith. "What is all this stuff?"

There were more groceries than he and Ruthie would ever need, even with Chance and I popping in to eat more often than necessary. Those visits occurred less often lately as Ruthie's cooking spiraled into *crapdom*. Even I could make something better—and that said something.

George's ginormous mustache twitched as he abandoned his weak attempt to give Griffith the cold shoulder. His usual beaming smile emerged. His happiness was a ray of sunlight after dealing with all the stress over the past few days.

"It's for Ruthie." He giggled like a small child in his excitement. "I'm going to convince her to open the bake shop she's always wanted. I already checked into renting a small space downtown. I found all kinds of things at the flea markets to furnish it with."

I hesitated, gauging how to respond. If he would've told me this idea six months ago, I would've been ecstatic because Ruthie's baking was legendary. The keyword being—*was*.

Not long after I met Ruthie, she shared her dream with me about having her own bakeshop. She put that dream aside when my mother died with the birth of my siblings and me. Her priority switched to protecting us. As the Enchantlings, we were a heavy responsibility for any witch. With our mother's death, the responsibility went to Ruthie and her sister Tessa, my mother's twin sisters.

Lately, you couldn't pay people to eat Ruthie's baking. Her gift of knowing mysteriously evaporated along with Hecate and Mrs. Shaw. I mentally reworded asking if anyone would want to eat what she might bake, or if he obtained fire insurance with the place he rented. There was no tactful way to say Ruthie's baking had gone to shit. "Do you...do you think she'll still want to?"

George grabbed my hand and squeezed it before releasing it. "We'll just have to convince her. She needs this bakery to give her a purpose for getting up every day. After spending twenty some years worrying about you all only to lose Destiny—" Uncle George glanced toward me. "Umm, well I think she feels she failed somehow."

My smile faltered as I wondered if she'd have felt differently if they'd lost me instead of Destiny. Aunt Ruthie raised Destiny and Chance. Blood or not, they barely knew me.

Griffith returned from depositing bags on the porch, wrinkling his nose as he reached into the trunk to gather more. "What kind of foul smelling plants are those?"

He looked at me with watery eyes. I suspected the plants weren't responsible for the offensive odor. The black cat waddling by confirmed my suspicions. I suppressed a smile. "You must've startled Stinker."

George's excitement rushed undeterred now that he had me and Griffith as his captive audience. "I got all this stuff for Ruthie to practice on." He shrugged. "I don't mind being the one to test what she makes. You know, to get her to bake some at home first, get her to relax, as we prepare the shop. I thought since she's only been cooking at the Last Call the food might turn out different, better, if she resumed cooking where she's most comfortable. You know, with all the bad memories of that night and her not knowing in time to prevent it from happening."

I scowled. Ruthie's gift didn't work that way. It was ridiculous for her or George to infer she was to blame for what happened. She didn't have Destiny's gift of foretelling which I inadvertently inherited. Besides, Destiny was already dead by the time Hecate showed up.

He sighed. "I sure do miss her baking." One look at George's rotund physique wouldn't give me or anyone the impression he missed any meals. Although I'd observed the bottomless depths of Uncle George's appetite, and despite the garlic and onion scent always clinging to him, his mustache appeared free of crumbs.

"We all do," I said, although what I missed more than her baking was Ruthie's cheerful attitude. It was no fun to complain when everyone else joined in. When I started to miss her rambling stories, I realized something needed to be done. George's idea was our best bet at getting our Ruthie back since I lacked any other solution.

"Plus the holidays are coming up. It just wouldn't be the same without Ruthie's cooking," George said.

I had mixed feelings about the upcoming holidays. It would be my first without Tessa physically being here and not just hovering around in a reflection, and my first with my newfound family. I wasn't sure what to expect. I doubted they spent the holidays as Tessa and I did, lounging in pajamas and eating leftover takeout.

Except for Tessa's legendary baked beans, neither of us could cook worth a darn, but I'd heard rumors about Ruthie's legendary holiday meals. Another reason to hope Ruthie's *knowing* mojo returned before Thanksgiving rolled around. Then I could experience a holiday meal that didn't originate from a microwaveable container.

"Okay, let's go convince her." I patted George's back and then reached for Griffith's hand to lead him to the house. His reluctance was evident by his heavy, dragging gait.

George stopped in front of me. He glanced furtively over his shoulder at the closed door and then leaned in as if to whisper, except his hearing loss had his words come out in a shout, "Maybe I should do it."

"No, we'll go with you. You said we needed to convince her. Griffith will help too, if you want." I didn't want to force Griffith upon him if George believed his presence would upset Ruthie. I missed Ruthie too, and would love to have her return to acting like her old self.

George frowned. "Err…I did say we, didn't I? Well, I'll do it. I know you don't like Ruthie's dolls, and she's gotten another one since you last visited." He waggled his thick finger at me. "I bought it when I was in town seeing Joe the barber." He ran a hand over his thin hair that displayed no need for a trim, now, or ever.

"I—"

He kept talking, either because he didn't hear me try to interrupt, or because he chose to ignore it. I was betting on the latter. He enjoyed hearing himself talk.

"Joe told me about an auction at the old Ross Manor, so I bought this big box full of all kinds of antiques. I would've bought it anyway, because I like collecting old stuff. But when I spotted the doll sticking out of the top, I had to get it for Ruthie." He shook his head. "You won't like her. The doll, that is. She's kind of creepy."

I frowned. The dolls were all creepy to me, so if George said this doll was creepy, it must be hideous. I pulled my shoulders back, bracing myself to confront Ruthie and George's army of dolls. "I don't mind." I did, but I tolerated their creepy plastic children for Aunt Ruthie.

Griffith glanced from me to George, sensing George's reluctance to invite us in the house. "Maybe I should go."

"Ruthie doesn't mind you coming here," I insisted. "She said so." Granted she said that a while ago. Griffith never took her up on the invitation, but we'd never determine how she felt about him until we tried.

"Hope. It's not Griffith," George blurted and then averted his attention to a stain on his white T-shirt.

I dropped my gaze to the stain, unwilling to face him and the truth of his words. The smudge on George's shirt looked like drippings of coffee he'd tried to wipe away and only succeeded in making the stain larger and faded at the edges.

"What...what do you mean?" I knew what he meant but I didn't want to accept it. My heart sank. "It's me? She blames me, doesn't she?"

"No, no child, I wouldn't say that. She doesn't blame you, it's just that..." His mustache twitched. He rolled his lips. It must be something exceptionally unpleasant since Uncle George was never at a loss for words. "It's because you look like her."

I blinked. This was something I couldn't remedy.

"Please don't be upset." George touched my arm.

"I'm not upset," I parroted and then swallowed the lump in my throat, hoping George would buy the lie. When my voice cracked on the last word, I knew I hadn't convinced anyone.

He shifted uncomfortably, patting my arm. I couldn't meet his gaze. I didn't want to see the sympathy I knew would be there. The stain on his wrinkled shirt blurred as I stared, hoping if I didn't blink the tears wouldn't start. Griffith retreated a few steps farther into the yard. My elevated emotions had to be distressing him.

George cupped my chin and lifted my head to face him. "I think she'll get past it. It's just that when she sees you, it reminds her of how she failed Destiny. How she failed everyone."

"She said that?" I searched his eyes, desperate for the truth.

He shook his head. "Nah, that's just my theory. That's why I don't want you to take it personally. A little time away from the bar might help her focus on the one thing she loves. That she's always loved, even before…"

His words trailed off. What he meant was before me and my siblings were born and crushed her opportunity to pursue her dreams. More specifically he meant me, because George didn't mentioned Chance. He visited Ruthie and George more frequently than I did. He brought along Berta, his living doll. She probably adored Ruthie's damn creepy-ass dolls.

"Wait, so Ruthie's not going to come back to the bar?" I couldn't conceal my disappointment. Less time with Ruthie meant more time with Berta, just when I thought things couldn't get worse.

George shook his head. "No. Not for a little while until we see if this will help. She needs a break. You'll be fine."

"Oh, no." The strong smell of cinnamon intensified until my eyes watered. My dead relatives hadn't been as courteous with a warning of their imminent intrusion of my mind with the cinnamon aura like they used to. Instead they treated my mind like a revolving door, bursting in whenever they had something to say, no matter how irrelevant. Guess that's what you get when you're the only one who can listen.

"What?" Griffith must've assumed Tom had returned. He peered down the driveway for the source of my distress. He didn't realize the anguish would arrive inside my head.

I hadn't experienced the cinnamon aura in some time. Why did it return now? I grimaced, waiting for the impending migraine. Nothing happened.

"Is something burning?" Griffith sniffed the air moments before the cottage door burst open. Ruthie staggered out coughing in a cloud of black smoke.

"What in tarnation?" Uncle George shuffled up the steps. "Honey, are you all right? What's going on?"

"Goddam oven, I've made that recipe more times than I remember. The oven must be on the blink…" Ruthie's words trailed off when she noticed Griffith and I.

Her face fell. "I was making snicker doodles. I used to know how." She cast her gaze to the woods as her eyes watered from more than the smoke. "I used to make them real good."

Despite Ruthie almost torching the house, I was relieved the cinnamon scent was just that, cinnamon. I glanced at the bags of baking goods lining the rail by the porch and wondered if this was the best time for George to bring up his idea.

"Hope and Griffith were just leaving." George looked pointedly at us, and then the driveway. It seemed Uncle George believed in no time like the present, no matter the circumstance.

"They don't have to go, they just got here." Ruthie's words held little conviction and less of her old enthusiasm. Her face held the warmth of exertion or embarrassment, but none of the welcoming expression I'd taken for granted.

"Yes, we do." It seemed that no matter what I did, or where I went, everything always went to shit.

Chapter Four

"It's fabulous that Ruthie will have the little shop she's always dreamed about." Berta clutched the damp dishtowel against her chest and beamed. "She deserves her bakery after all she's been through."

"She sure does. How can Ruthie stand washing so many dishes all the time? I'm soaking in a grease and lemon scented sauna." The soapsuds trailed my arms to dissipate in the steam surrounding the sink. I reached in, groping until I located the dishes on the bottom of the deep bowl. I used the back of my forearm to wipe the sweat beading and running down my cheeks.

Berta shrugged, ever the optimist. "Think of the steam as getting a free facial." She closed her eyes and leaned over the sink.

Of course, while I bathed in sweat and my skin rivaled a shiny red tomato, Berta was glowing. My skin started to take on a permanent prune-like appearance because I always ended up washing the dishes since Berta couldn't reach the bottom of the sink.

I pulled out the step stool Ruthie kept that enabled Berta to take her fair share of time at the sink. Unless I convinced Berta to change her attire, which was as unlikely as her getting me to change mine, twin crescent moons hung out of her shorts every time she bent over the sink. Sometimes I mentally referred to Berta as an ass, but I had no desire to spend my day staring at hers.

I was happy for Aunt Ruthie, but I couldn't shake my growing irritation with each day I endured with Berta, the five-foot two-inch drill sergeant. Without Ruthie, we had to work more hours. Despite my insistence, Berta informed Chief he didn't need to hire more staff. Berta boasted we could handle the bar ourselves. She smiled and leaned in to me afterward to whisper, *"More tips for us."*

The only tip I usually received was to ask Berta to mix the drinks because hers were better, or to suggest that I wear a lower cut shirt. One guy even had the nerve to advise investing in a push up bra. His next vodka and tonic consisted of mostly tonic and a piece of shriveled up lime skin.

"Chief could spring for a dishwasher with the money he's saving with one less employee. That, or he needs to install a shower." I swiped my arm across my brow, leaving a trail of suds. Sweat trickled down my back. My shirt clung in unattractive splotches of sweat. No wonder I didn't get many tips.

"Speak of the devil, there he is now." Berta inclined her head toward the small window above the sink.

I used the dishtowel to wipe a square on the pane free from steam. Chief rolled into the parking lot in his battered, old boat of a car. Like the bar and the town, no one knew how old Chief was, or his real name. He was just Chief.

The car shuddered to a stop and expelled a gust of black smoke. The door squawked in protest and wedged into the gravel when he opened it completely. He swung out his legs to dangle a few inches from the ground before gripping the door for assistance to climb out.

My boss resembled a miniature Santa Claus minus the belly and good nature. As he wobbled through the gravel he didn't appear to have many years left before choosing a place in the tombstones scattered over the hill behind him.

"What the hell is going on?" Chief strode through the back door into the kitchen.

"We're cleaning up, Chief," Berta bubbled. "Don't worry. We'll be finished and ready for customers before we open in a half hour. We would've been done by now if Hope didn't keep dragging her feet." She winked.

I narrowed my eyes and then splashed her with a handful of soapsuds. Berta squealed in delight. The opposite reaction of what I sought.

"I'm not talking about the dishes." Chief's gaze locked on me. "I got held up for a half hour with that reporter guy who was here the other day. He asked all kinds of questions about you." He pursed his lips and sighed. "What did you do now, Red?"

"Me? I didn't do anything. That reporter is an asshole." I tore the threadbare rag masquerading as a dishtowel from Berta's grasp and dried my hands. "What kind of questions?"

Chief folded his arms. "I dunno, all kind of stupid shit. Like when you started working here and where were you from before. He kept talking and talking. Worse than a woman, cackling on and on about stuff no man in his right mind pays attention to."

"What did you tell him?" More importantly, I wondered why Chief would even talk openly with a stranger. A closer study of his face and a sniff of the air surrounding Chief provided my answer. "He bought you a few drinks."

"So?" When Chief scowled, tobacco dribbled on his chin. He wiped the spittle away with his sleeve, which was stained from repeated use throughout the day. "I had a few questions for him."

"What kind of questions would you have?" The muscle in the side of my jaw twitched uncomfortably. Chief had a limited attention span. I couldn't imagine what interest he would have in someone from the city.

Berta's attention volleyed between Chief and I with a furrowed brow.

Chief shrugged and looked away. "I dunno. Like if he was the one who did the story on the aliens they found living in some guy's basement." His face became animated, and his eyes lit up with excitement. "Or if they really have a ghost working for them like they claim…"

My mouth gaped. "Seriously? You believe that garbage?"

"Hope." Berta jammed her elbow into my side. "I'm sure those stories are fascinating."

Berta would try to spare his feelings. I never paused to think before the words spilled out.

Chief's expression soured, and he stalked past us. "Better get those dishes done."

After the kitchen door swung shut, Berta turned with her hands on her hips and a scowl on her lips. "How can you be so rude?"

I looked to the diminishing suds dissolving in the sink. "I didn't realize I was being rude." Ordinarily I might've found Chief's interest in the tabloid funny, but not when I risked being the headline.

"I thought he was kidding. How was I supposed to know he actually read that tabloid and didn't just laugh at the headlines while waiting to check out of the grocery store? That anyone did?" Although, unfortunately, I knew firsthand how a lot of people lived for such outrageous stories. Stories similar to ones about my family and me.

"Chief loves that stupid magazine. He has a whole stack of those tabloids in the corner of his office. I told him to stop looking, but he won't listen to me. He thinks he's going to find some kind of clue about her." Berta stood on tiptoe to reach for the giant sack of peanuts on the shelf.

"About who?"

"Mrs. Shaw." Berta carefully tugged at the huge bag of peanuts that weighed enough to knock her over. "I told him she probably just left town, to believe anything else is just crazy."

It wasn't crazy, because I was there the night of the ebony moon when Hecate used Mrs. Shaw's body to walk the earth. It was the last time we'd seen either of them. It took me weeks to go to the bar bathroom alone after *the incident*. I kept expecting Hecate and her hellhounds to descend from outside the door. My defeating her was nothing more than pure luck, and I didn't have much of that, so I didn't want to chance another encounter.

Chief wasn't crazy thinking something extraordinary happened to Mrs. Shaw, but I didn't think he'd find answers in a tabloid.

The sack of peanuts thumped to the floor with a cloud of dust, which gathered to settle in the folds of the burlap sack. Judging by the size, and the limited supply we provided to the customers, Chief probably bought the peanuts ten years ago. If he supplied anything for free, he acquired it in bulk to get it super cheap.

Berta pulled at her clinging shirt, fanning herself against the heat. The light glinted off something silver resting against her collarbone. I narrowed my eyes. Her obnoxious cleavage had distracted me from noticing the necklace sooner.

"What is that?" I knew what it was, but I couldn't believe it. Berta had to say it aloud, so I wouldn't think my mind was playing tricks on me. It had before.

I hadn't seen the necklace since that night.

"You like it?" She lifted the necklace, and the three animal heads clicked together. A dog, a horse, and a snake. "Ritchie gave me the necklace. He said he thought I might like it."

"Where did he get it?" I reached for it, but Berta stepped out of my grasp, covering the necklace with her hand.

The last time I saw the hideous necklace, Mrs. Shaw wore it around her neck. There might be something worse to worry about now than the reporter.

Berta shrugged. "I dunno. He said he found it. He's always bringing in all kinds of little odds and ends and trinkets for me. Usually it's junk, so I tell Ritchie I took it home so I don't hurt his feelings when I throw the stuff away. But this…" She smiled as she fingered the creepy critters. "This is pretty. It's like the signs hanging around town."

"You know what they mean—the animals—don't you?" Surely living in this town, she had to have read or heard something.

She twisted her lips to the side and placed her hand on her hip. "Sure, sugar, I heard things. Doesn't mean I believe any of that silly stuff." She waved her hand in dismissal. "I like the necklace 'cause it's pretty, not 'cause I aim to please Hecate." She made air quotes around the name that caused my skin to crawl and then rolled her eyes.

Berta turned and sashayed away, wasting her exaggerated hip swaying on me. "You all overreact about the Hecate stories. I told you before, but none of you all ever take the time to listen." She dumped the little baskets full of broken shells and old peanuts in the trash and then filled them with new peanuts from the sack.

"They're not stories," I muttered under my breath. Arguing with Berta would be fruitless. "You actually fill those baskets each day with new peanuts before you set them out?" That was almost more unbelievable than her not believing in Hecate and then taunting her skepticism by wearing what looked exactly like Mrs. Shaw's old necklace—which she was never without.

"You don't?" She wrinkled her nose. "That's disgusting. Half the time they're filled with empty shells. Who knows how many fingers poked around in the baskets?"

Too many. I learned that the hard way when I inadvertently brushed my fingers against the peanuts and received a multitude of jumbled visions. "Which is why no one in their right mind eats them. If they do, they deserve whatever ailment they get. If Chief knew you were throwing away good peanuts, he'd have your hide."

"Like there aren't more than a few people in this bar who aren't in their right mind?" Berta giggled.

"You have a point." A smile tugged at my lip. Occasionally, Berta came back with a good retort.

"Bert?" Ritchie poked his head in the door. "You got a minute?"

Berta smiled and brushed her hands together. Small pieces of peanut skins floated to the ground. "Sure, sugar, anything for you. What do you need?"

I tilted my head at Berta. We both knew what Ritchie thought he needed. He sought her out continuously for palm readings to the point that he'd begun to expect one everyday. Berta thought she was being nice, but I felt she was taking advantage of his simple nature by misleading him. "We'll be open in a half hour, Ritchie," I said.

"I know." Ritchie slipped in the kitchen with a quick glance over his shoulder to ensure Chief didn't see him and throw him out. "Please, a quick reading. I need to find out how my night will go. I can't wait any longer to find out." His smile reflected the peace of the feeble-minded. He had little else to worry about other than normal daily stressors, not knowing or caring about the Oppressors stalking around seeking people to deplete their joy and hope.

"Okay, sugar, but we gotta be quick before Chief notices you're here." Berta winked. "He doesn't like anyone else in the back."

I stood beside Berta to gain Ritchie's attention. "Hey Ritchie, where did you get the necklace?"

"I didn't steal it. I don't steal." His lower lip protruded in a pout. The childish expression appeared out of place on a large, grown man's face peppered with spots of beard stubble the razor missed. "I found it."

I sighed. "I didn't say you stole it." No matter what I said, he always overreacted. No matter what Berta said, he responded with adoration and a sappy smile.

I forced a smile. "I'm wondering where you got it, 'cause it's so...pretty."

The necklace was ugly as sin, and I wouldn't wear the monstrosity even if someone paid me. Especially considering what people believed the animals stood for. Dead, alive, or banished to who knows where, there was no way I'd support Hecate in any way.

Ritchie shuffled his feet, trying to determine if I was serious or mocking him. His slow wit made him an easy target at the bar. He was accustomed to being ridiculed by the men. Trust didn't come easy to him, and I couldn't blame him. In some ways, we had that in common. Except I hid my hurt from years of being harassed, ostracized, and mocked under layers of sarcasm and witty retorts. Well, at least I thought they were witty. Not everyone did.

He glanced at me. I gave him my most reassuring smile.

"I found it in the woods. I like to collect things. It's pretty. I gave the necklace to Berta 'cause she's pretty too." He hung his head, and a lock of greasy hair fell forward. "Plus, she's nice to me. Not too many people are nice to me."

Ritchie glanced at the baskets lining the counter. His eyes widened, and he swung his head to Berta. "Are those peanuts? I'm allergic to peanuts."

"Okay, I won't feed you any." Berta laughed and scrunched up her shoulders and then let them fall.

I rolled my eyes at Berta's transparent flirting. Long ago I gave up on encouraging her to subdue her oozing damsel in distress performance. It came across more like a desperate ditz if you asked me. Except she never asked me.

Ritchie backed away with his hands raised while rapidly shaking his head side to side. Long strands of greasy hair slapped his cheeks. "No. Too many. There are too many peanuts. I gotta get out of here. Not peanuts!"

He glanced at the large bag on the floor. Beads of perspiration lined his face. "Peanuts everywhere. Berta, can you come out and read my palm after you wash your hands real, real good?" He nodded vigorously.

Berta put her hands on her hips, her expression morphing into unease as Ritchie vibrated with barely suppressed anxiety. "Sure, no problem. Let me finish up with Hope."

Ritchie glanced at me, as if belatedly realizing I was still there. "Oh, okay." He backed out the door while warily eyeing the peanuts.

We watched the door swing shut and then Berta turned to me. "You know he's not really allergic to peanuts."

"He thinks so, that's all that matters." I shrugged. "At least your flirting has one benefit. Makes less work for me. Lately, Richie insists only you can serve him. Guess he prefers you because of your special palm reading ability."

Ritchie was one of the few mortals who frequented the bar who wanted nothing to do with me or my special ability. I kinda liked that about him.

"Ritchie doesn't avoid you because of my palm

reading. It's because you're left handed," Berta said this as if her remark required no further explanation.

"So? I can pour a drink with either hand." Which didn't say much when you compared my drinks to Berta's. She made a career out of bartending. Although I poured a beer as good as anyone, which is the only booze Ritchie drank.

"No, silly, it's because you're a demon, or at least he thinks so," Berta replied without hesitation.

"I'm not a demon." I'd been called a lot of things in my life. Although the only people who'd called me a demon were the nuns at the orphanage. Not a barfly who was afraid of a peanut. My kindness toward Ritchie was taking a nosedive. "Besides, what's that have to do with me being left handed?"

I tensed. *Could Ritchie see the unusual glittery black fog?* I couldn't see how. As far as I could tell, no part of him was Oppressor or witch. He was just simple. His feeble-mindedness enabled him to live under the radar of most Oppressors.

Berta dug in the pocket of her shorts. As she struggled to reach the bottom of its depths, the fabric peeked below the brief length of her cut-off jean shorts. Her fingers strained against the snug cloth. "Here it is." She wielded the crumbled paper like a prize. "I looked the word up at the library 'cause I thought it was fascinating."

"Of course, you'd find people calling me a demon fascinating, thanks." I grabbed the sprayer by the faucet and gave it a quick squeeze, aiming it in her direction. The water sputtered and most of it didn't make it further than down my arm. Berta ducked with a grin as a few residual droplets rained on her shoulder.

"No, not that, silly. It's called—" she unfolded the piece of wrinkled, torn paper— "Sinistrality. It means some folks used to think left-handed people were demons, like you."

"I'm not a demon." I glared at her. It was bad enough how half the time she called me Jane. The name my family made as an alias at my birth to keep the Oppressors from discovering me. As if whisking me away from the only people who might've understood me and then tossing me in an orphanage did any good. But I'll be damned if I'd let Berta start telling people I was a demon.

Berta continued as if I hadn't said anything—enthralled with all the glorious things she'd discovered were housed in the library. "The library is so nice. I got to use one of the computers. I talked with the librarian. I might get myself set up with an email there sometime once I learn to use the computer a little better."

She grimaced. "Did you know they call the little thingy you use to move stuff around on the screen a mouse? I didn't know what she meant at first when she kept telling me to use the mouse." She scrunched up her nose in distaste. "I almost got up and plum left 'cause I don't wanna have to use a varmint to get information. It's ridiculous. But what Ritchie said was true about people thinking lefties were demons. Can you believe that? He's not that stupid. But I already knew that from reading his palms."

I shook my head. "What in the world do you tell him? You surely aren't able to do a palm reading on him every time he asks?" I didn't believe she was doing a real reading at all. If by some miracle she was, and controlled it easily while I suffered from epileptic visions hitting me at unsuspecting moments, it would be one more thing about Berta to irritate me.

She picked up the dishtowel to dry a pan. "No, I don't always have something. Then I simply say things he wants to hear." She giggled. "Okay, sometimes they're things I want to hear, but they're for his own good." Her gaze circled back to me, and she seemed to be waiting.

I sighed. "All right, I'll bite, what do you tell him that's for his own good?" I bent over the rising steam of the sink to tug at the plug at the bottom until it popped free. Unless I missed an elusive piece of silverware on the bottom of the ginormous sink, we were done.

"Well, when I think he's had a little too much to drink—Ritchie can't handle all that much booze." She nodded to me, as if I agreed. "With him being a little…simple, I don't think it's a good idea for him to overdo it. So, when he asks for a palm reading, I tell him something like if he gets home in time to watch the sunset he'll have the best day tomorrow. Or, if he doesn't leave within the next half hour, he'll come down with a bad cold."

"He buys that?" Why didn't I think of something like that when people harassed me for a vision? Perhaps I didn't give Berta enough credit. I shook my head and then swiped at a few strands of hair clinging to my damp, sweaty cheeks.

"I guess." Berta shrugged, and then reached to caress her necklace, lifting and dropping the tiny animal trinkets against each other. "He's never questioned it before. He calls me his angel." She beamed, enamored by Ritchie's attention, and pretty much any man.

"Why don't you tell him he's not going to

combust, or whatever he thinks will happen, if he gets too close to a peanut? I've seen him eating peanut butter candy bars." I undid the tie on my apron. The removal of the light fabric provided little relief in reducing the warmth of the small kitchen.

"I don't think I can convince him of that. His peanut phobia is pretty set in." Her smile faltered, and her gaze cut to me and then away. "I have seen a few things that aren't always pleasant, but I don't tell Ritchie about them. He should be happy. He's had a hard enough life as it is."

I braced my hands on my hips and studied the necklace, wondering just where Ritchie found it and why Berta liked it so much. "Haven't we all."

****

I should stay away like George hinted in his obvious way, but I couldn't help myself. I craned my neck to study the sign above the shop, only to find a blank square where the name of Ruthie's bakery should've been. Peering in the window from the outside, the rest of the bakery looked complete and ready to go. So why didn't they hang a sign up yet?

I touched the door handle and glanced with trepidation around the empty street. I almost expected George to barrel around the corner and tackle me to prevent me from bothering *his* Ruthie. Although the thought of George tackling anyone or anything, other than a cookie, was ludicrous. I pushed the door open, and a tiny bell tinkled as I entered. A tentative sniff of the air didn't prompt me to run for the fire extinguisher. So far so good.

"Who is it?" Ruthie popped up from behind the counter, her expression appearing brighter than I'd seen in some time. "Hope, it's you."

I couldn't discern whether she was happy to see me or not. I hung my head and pushed my hands into my pockets, trying to make myself smaller in the little space.

"Hello." The glass display cases were empty, but the pink doilies lining them looked ready to be laden with all makes of baked goods. The corner shelves lining the walls were filled with the signature clutter of hodgepodge items Ruthie decorated her house with. "This is nice."

My gaze stopped on the middle shelf. I should've expected that Ruthie wouldn't be able to resist bringing in a few dolls from her collection. I cringed.

Ruthie threw her hands in the air and smiled broadly. "Can you believe it? I never thought it would happen. I gave up on the dream of having a bakery a long time ago. I mean, besides all you, there was the cost and all. When I married George." She smiled, her eyes large behind her glasses. "You do realize he's a good ten years older than me?"

She chuckled, clutching her belly as she did so. "People used to say I was snagging myself a sugar daddy. Heck the only sugar daddy in George is his sweet tooth."

"But look at all this now." She gestured to include everything in the little shop. "Look what my sugar daddy got for me."

I let Ruthie babble on. Her enthusiasm proved infectious and I smiled. I never believed it could happen, but I'd missed her rambling stories. Maybe I wasn't responsible for her distress. "Have you tried baking anything here yet?"

Ruthie quieted and her enthusiasm waned. "Not yet."

"Why not?" My smile faltered.

"Well, there's all this preparation to do. There're supplies to stock, and then we needed to decorate the shop to make it look pretty. You know, bakeries need to look pretty. No one gets the urge to eat a donut covered with rainbow sprinkles if the place is dark and dirty. Donuts are happy food. They make you smile, and I say the room should be something to smile about—"

"Are you afraid to try to bake?" I didn't know why I deliberately crushed her happiness with an injection of the truth, but I needed Ruthie to bake something and to *know* how to do it well. Just like she used to. I didn't want to be the one responsible for taking away her happiness and George's cookies. It was bad enough that I shouldered the guilt of Destiny's death. I couldn't add any more on my burden of remorse.

Ruthie turned and busied herself with folding the pink, little napkins. "I wouldn't say 'afraid.' That's a strong word to use when you're talking about baking."

"What word would you use?" My excitement deflated with Ruthie's obvious reluctance to discuss the true problem. If she didn't know how to bake delicious things anymore, it wouldn't matter how cute the bakery was if she couldn't fill it with pastries.

Ruthie's hands stilled, and she sighed. "I didn't name the place yet." She glanced to me. "You might've noticed the empty sign hanging over the door?"

I nodded.

"It's not that I don't have plenty of names in mind. I thought about Baked Goodness, or You Know You Want a Cookie, so part of the delay is narrowing that down, deciding...but that's not all."

We stared at each other in silence, sharing the unspoken truth until Ruthie slumped in the chair. She leaned against the wrought iron scrolls which didn't look the least bit comfortable. Her eyes closed as she gave a voice to the fear dwelling inside. "What if I can't bake anymore? What if my abilities are just...gone? How can my store name say anything about knowing or baking when I don't know any more myself if I even can?"

I knelt in front of her. She turned away as I took her hand. "Someone once told me, it's kind of an on the job training. You learn as you go." The corner of her lip twitched as I repeated the words she once said to me. Sure, this situation was a little different, and dealing with Oppressors wasn't the same as dealing with bakeries, but the advice would do. How could she deny her own guidance?

"Like you told me about when you're on an airplane. Remember?" I nodded with encouragement. "You have to take care of yourself before you can take care of anyone else. Just breathe, Ruthie."

Ruthie engulfed me in a hug. I closed my eyes, determined to hold back the tears threatening to fall. God, I missed her and her suffocating hugs.

"Ruthie?" I pressed against her shoulder. "Have you been staying away from the bar because of me? Was it a mistake for me to find my way...here?" I didn't mean the bakery. I meant the town, my home. This weird town was the closest thing I had to a real home, but I was still afraid that one day they'd ask me to leave. As much as I didn't want to hear her say it, I had to know. The guilt and pain of losing the woman who was the closest thing I had to a mother figure since I lost Aunt Tessa weighed on me.

Ruthie pulled back, lightly gripping my shoulders as she met my gaze. I averted my eyes as her scrutiny bored into me, probing for the feelings I could never successfully disguise from her.

"No, child." She stroked my hair, lifting a lock and smiling. She released the strand to smooth it in with the rest. "I did a good job on your hairstyle, didn't I? I knew what your hair needed after you tried to fix it once your brother did a number on it."

I nodded. Chance's gift of prompting one to take a chance not considered before worked, but often there were unexpected side effects. I was glad his gift didn't work well on me. I didn't like to think someone could influence my sub-conscience. Not that he did much of anything lately other than moping around and festering in grief, anger, or self-pity.

"I guess I did kinda let you think my avoiding the Last Call was because of you. I mean if I'm being honest, I must say that's part of the reason. You're a beautiful girl, and seeing how much you look like her, it does make me miss my other beautiful gal. I have the loveliest nieces, I must say. But one day that will be a good thing, because it will be like a part of her is still here with us. It gets a little easier every day." She pulled up her shoulders and smiled with mischief. "I must admit though, there was another reason."

I drug a chair over to sit facing her, feeling absurdly happy that a little of my old Ruthie was back. Even if it did mean enduring more comparisons to Destiny, who I'd never be as perfect as. "Really, and what would that be?"

She slapped her ample thighs and set them to jiggling. "I wanted you and Berta to become friends, of course."

"What?" I sank back in my chair. "Why?" Granted since Ruthie was gone we were forced to spend a lot of time together at the bar, and I could tolerate her more than in the past, but I still had no desire to be Berta's friend. I still didn't trust her, even more so after the necklace. "I don't need any more friends."

Ruthie laughed. "Sure, you do, everyone can use more friends. I mean, really, would you rather have more enemies?"

I twisted my lip to the side. "I don't think it's an either-or scenario."

Ruthie lifted her brows, causing them to rise above the ginormous frames of her glasses. "Really? With you I think it is."

I looked away. These short explanations of Ruthie's weren't what I was accustomed to. Generally, she rambled on long enough for me to gather my thoughts for my next retort. It made arguing with her much nicer than with someone else. I didn't walk away and suddenly think of what I should've said, because I usually waited so long to speak. This provided me with time to shape my response.

"Do it for Chance, if not for me. I mean, lands' sake, I don't recall the last time I saw him so happy. Not since before Destiny died. 'Cause we both know he was happier than a lark before that, always grinning those pearly whites of his. I'm not asking you to be best buddies with her, just try a little harder."

Ruthie patted my leg. "Think of it like that old song, or was it a saying? How does it go?" She scrunched up her face as she searched the recesses of her mind. "Okay, I got it. Something like make new friends, 'cause yours get old, or if one is too stupid, or starts to mold?"

A smile tugged at the corner of my lip until I couldn't hold it back. I laughed harder than I had in months. It felt good. My Ruthie was back. "That's a rhyme, but I don't think that's how it went."

I sighed. Even though I only gained my newfound family a short time ago, I would already do most anything for their happiness. I knew, more than any of them, how quickly joy—and hope—could be lost.

"Fine. I'll try a little harder, but I'm only doing it for you and Chance." Perhaps it wouldn't be so bad to follow the other old saying about keeping your friends close and your enemies closer. Berta might fall somewhere in the middle, but regardless, I needed to keep an eye on what she was up to with that reporter.

"So, you finally went ahead and did it. You got your bakery."

Ruthie and I both turned at what could only be the unmistakable sound of Aunt Tessa's voice laced with jealousy. The shop provided multiple reflective surfaces throughout it which would be convenient for my dead aunt's ghost to make her entrance. After a quick searching glance my gaze landed on the large gilded mirror near the counter housing Tessa's reflection. I walked over. How could Ruthie's deceased fraternal twin sister show up here when previously she only appeared in my apartment mirror?

I stood in front of the mirror. "What are you doing here? Or more like, how are you able to show up here?"

"What?" Tessa raised a thin brow. "You don't see

me for weeks and the first thing I hear when I arrive is what am I doing here? No 'how are you, Tessa,' or 'I missed you, Auntie'?" Tessa pushed her lip out into a pout, a look not commonly seen on a woman of her advanced age, but one she used as a core expression.

"I never called you Auntie."

She brushed me off with her hand. "Whatever, I've grown to like the endearment. Besides, it's boring at your place. Anytime I pop in the only one there is Tercet and all that darn feline does is hiss at me. No one comes over there anymore since you're always at the bar or gallivanting around town with that boyfriend of yours."

I furrowed my brow. "But how did you pop in? I thought *I* had to be standing in front of a mirror for it to work?" At least that's how Tessa explained it, although even dead she seemed to make up as many of her own rules as she did while she was alive.

"It's not always about you. I told you that requirement might change as your powers grow, and perhaps I did a little bargaining on my side to convince those that be that I would be of better use here." She spread her arms as far as they would go in the mirror as she encompassed the bakery.

"What use are you going to be here?" Ruthie waddled over closer. "It's not like I'm making those beans of yours. You never would give me the recipe," Ruthie complained, but the twinkle in her eye and the smile she couldn't restrain betrayed her happiness that her sister would be hanging out with her.

"Seriously? You're still only concerned about my recipe?" Tessa straightened her posture in whatever she sat on in the afterlife that she referred to as *the kitchen*, in preparation for the never ending verbal show down with her sister.

I held up my palms in surrender. "Okay, ladies, before you go at it I'm going to say goodbye for now. I have things I need to do." With Tessa and Ruthie's endless bickering resisting the confines of the mortal world, I'd better get started on mending fences with Chance unless I wanted to be arguing with him for all eternity.

Chapter Five

The day was unseasonably warm. After dropping my car off at the garage for repair, I decided to walk home. My piece of crap car barely functioned on its last legs, but I couldn't afford anything else right now. The colorful fall leaves helped distract me from my worries. I walked along the tree line of the woods to test my confidence while casting a glance into the thick shadows each time I heard what I hoped was a small animal scurrying. According to Griffith, the inflated gossip about my abilities continued to grow and distort among the Oppressors. I didn't dispute it because I hoped it would make them keep their distance.

My steps slowed as I approached my street. A familiar vehicle sat parked along the street. The pain-in-the-ass reporter who owned the expensive car stood beside it, taking pictures of my apartment. It seemed neither Griffith nor I were successful in scaring him off. Apparently Tom didn't hear, believe, or care about the rumors of what could happen to those who got on my bad side. "You've got to be kidding me."

I strode purposefully toward him, my anger building with the fall of each foot slapping against the pavement. The worries about my family and the threat the reporter represented molded together into one hot ball of anger in my stomach. My heart rate elevated until its rapid pace thudded so hard I feared it might explode from my chest. The internal anger I'd been hiding from my family rose up, and I directed all my rage at this annoying asshole. How dare he invade my home again? "What in the hell do you think you're doing? This is private property."

He'd crossed the line when he involved the people closest to me in his *witch-hunt*. As he snapped photographs of my apartment above Uncle George and Aunt Ruthie's garage, he captured their house in the shots. The last thing Aunt Ruthie needed was to see her photo in his shitty paper, just when she started to emerge from her depression and start her bakery. She didn't need this kind of publicity.

"I'm not on the property." Tom ran the toe of his shoe along the edge of the sidewalk bordering the land. He taunted me by touching the tip of his loafer in the yard, and then retracting his foot.

"You were taking pictures." My gaze ran over his lanky body, searching for a recording device. It wouldn't surprise me if he had a camera shoved up his ass. If not, I might be glad to put it there for him. His khaki pants and polo shirt hung on his bony frame, making me wonder if he sustained himself on rumors alone.

"So? There's no law against taking pictures of the clouds. Or is the sky your private property, too?" He smirked and cocked his head.

I folded my arms, tucking my fingers underneath my elbows. His expression dared me to act. He was trying to push me over the edge—and it was working. The tingling elevated to a burning sensation; I didn't have to look to validate that a dark fog snaked from my fingertips. "You weren't taking pictures of the clouds."

"How do you know?" He lowered the camera. It hung against his scrawny chest on the strap. "Is that your secret power? Can you read minds?"

"You just don't quit, do you? I can't read minds, you idiot." The black fog crept and trailed to the ground toward him. I ignored my body's betrayal by neither encouraging the impulse to steal the hope from this asshole, nor attempting to squelch the building desire to obliterate all his happiness either. If I didn't try to gain control over my anger, I might not be able to stop myself from using my ability to overpower his emotions. To feed upon his excitement and joy until he was only left with despair—and God help me—that didn't sound like a bad idea.

"What can you do then? *Hope*. I wonder how you ended up with a name like that?" He cocked his head and raised an eyebrow.

"Shut up." His words only fueled the fiery rage within me.

He smiled, igniting a gleam in his eye. "People around here seem to think you can do something. Something not quite ordinary—or is that all rumors? Are you just a bartender in a hole-in-the-wall town full of losers? Aren't you *hoping* to be a little more?" Tom held up the camera and aimed, the distinct click followed a whirring sound. He took a couple of pictures…of me. "Say cheese."

The last click silenced. He lowered the camera to his chest and winked slowly and deliberately. He was trying to provoke me. Despite knowing that one important fact, his efforts were working, and I could no longer control how I might react.

His probing gaze traveled over me, violating me in

its wake. I shuddered with revulsion. This guy wasn't the first person to taunt and ridicule the *different* that wasn't hidden well within me, and he wouldn't be the last—unless I stopped the cycle.

I rushed him and grabbed for the camera. He laughed and anticipated my move and swung the camera to the side so I ended up with a handful of his shirt instead. I yanked him toward me. The fog poured from me into him.

He smirked. "That's it girl, show me what you got."

His delight was short lived as I did something I had only done once before. I drew his essence into me. It was an accident with Chance, and only for a moment because that was the first time I realized I could do more than just dispense hope. I could suck the hope away just like any Oppressor. Hecate said she gave me this gift by accident, because this was her most powerful ability of all. When people lost all hope, it left little to live for.

Tom's eyes widened, and the smile faded from his face along with his confidence, optimism, and dreams. I silently agreed with what Griffith's creepy half-brother Drake told me, but until now I didn't truly know how or what I would feel…fear tasted delicious.

My anger and disgust emptied from me into him. My fury rankled because I was forced to hide what I was because of people like him. People who strove to exploit or humiliate me. They were almost worse than the monsters.

Tom's knees buckled and his eyelids grew heavy and he began to sink to the ground. The sensation of power and control strengthened my grip and boosted my confidence. His legs quivered and bowed as if I had deflated a balloon. I maintained my hold to lower him to the earth and feed from his depression more thoroughly. I knelt with him and stared into his face. "I don't like my picture taken without my permission. You didn't give me a chance to fix my hair."

His gaze became drowsy, and his mouth opened. I knew what he felt, and it wasn't good. The Oppressors fed from me more than once, and I had no desire to relive that feeling of helplessness and desperation. Right about now I'd guess he contemplated why it was worth continuing to live, rather than pondering what my special abilities were.

I couldn't fix Chance. I couldn't save Destiny. But I could correct *this* problem before he became one. I was tired of being the victim.

Thick arms wrapped around me and pulled. I lost my grip on Tom as I flailed at my attacker before falling on my ass. Griffith drew me away from the reporter. "Hope. What are you doing?"

The abrupt halt of absorbing Tom's essence left me slumped in a confused daze. The tendrils reverted to me in a rush. A dusky haze lingered and floated around my fingertips. My thoughts danced around my head. The prolonged feeding from Tom left me feeling like I woke with a hangover.

Tom lay unconscious in a heap. Drool trickled out of the side of his mouth. I looked to Griffith. His exasperated expression confirmed that he'd tried to get my attention for some time, and that he knew exactly what I was doing. Even if I wasn't sure I did. The haze cleared along with my thoughts, leaving me with feelings of shame and embarrassment. What was I doing?

Griffith knelt by Tom and checked his pulse. "You're lucky. He's alive. You do realize you could've killed him?"

Part of me did realize the risk, but I hadn't believed it. I wasn't a killer. I was the good guy trying to make things right. *Wasn't I?* The weight of Griffith's stare bore into me. I didn't like what I saw, and I suppose he didn't either. Despite being a Splice all his life, he rarely used his abilities to oppress anyone. He found that part of himself disgusting. The way he studied me now, it appeared I disgusted him more. "It's not my fault, I didn't know—"

"Save it." Griffith stood, brushing his jeans as if he could rid himself of the filth accompanying me. "You knew you held this power within you and what it could do. You chose to use it…for this." He pointed to where Tom lay on the road.

My heart raced as Griffith stood above me, looking at me with aversion. He was the only one who understood me. Surely he recognized that I didn't intend to overreact? That Tom gave me no choice? He had to.

My words tumbled out as I struggled to make things right. "He was taking pictures of Ruthie's house, of me. He said terrible things."

"He goaded you into using your ability." Griffith narrowed his eyes. His angry words were laced with frustration. "You gave him what he wanted."

When Griffith's voice rose, it boomed. Its resonance ensured he didn't usually require more than his words to make a point. I quivered under the weight of his disapproval.

"No." I shook my head. What he said rang true, but I didn't want to believe it. I'd fallen right into Tom's trap and freely provided the reporter with the evidence to prove I was a freak. That I wasn't normal. That maybe I was the devil's spawn as the nuns from the orphanage insisted when they tried to draw the evil out of me.

"Yes." Griffith let the word sink in.

Tom twitched. A few tremors racked his body. His limbs rose and fell several times as he struggled to regain physical control.

"We can't leave him here." Griffith reached down and lifted the flaccid reporter.

"What will we do with him?" The magnitude of what I did and had almost done sunk in. I hadn't considered the possible consequences. I never did. I paid the price of acting without thinking before, and I didn't want to pay it again.

"I'll take care of him." Griffith sighed, as if accustomed to cleaning up other people's messes.

"What do you mean?" I tensed, a terrible part of me hoping he would rid me of having to worry about the reporter at all.

Griffith must've read my secret desire in my eyes. "Not that, Hope." His voice sounded sad, defeated. His expression reflected his disappointment. "I don't do that anymore. I'll drop him off by B.B.'s and start spreading rumors about his drinking."

Since he managed the liquor store, he knew all the town drunks. No matter how discreet they chose to be, they always needed to replenish their supplies.

"What about me?" I dreaded his response. What if I had ruined everything with Griffith before we really had a chance to begin?

"Go take a shower and maybe a nap." He hesitated. "Think about what you did. Decide what kind of person you want to be. If it's the kind of person I think you can be, start acting like it."

He walked away to deal with Tom. He never even looked back at me. The heavy steps of his departure seared into my mind. I watched him go, hoping he would turn and give me some sign. Something to indicate that he still had faith in me, that I hadn't sealed the fate of our relationship.

****

I hadn't talked to Griffith since he carried Tom off yesterday. His brief lecture left me feeling like a chastised child. He appeared to be avoiding me, but unfortunately for him, I planned to make that difficult. If he had too much time to think about my actions by using the whole "out of sight, out of mind" tactic, I was doomed. By now he'd probably already determined I was more trouble than I was worth. I had to dispel that thought and quickly. He was working today. Direct confrontation was preferable rather than avoidance.

The bicycle was one of those old models with the brakes on the pedals and the basket on the front, but it worked. George found it at one of the flea markets he frequented. When I mentioned my car was out of commission, and that the cost to repair it was more than I could afford, he brought this home.

My purse landed in the basket, and I slid onto the long banana seat. The trip up and down the road a few times on the bicycle had me wobbling precariously, but I didn't crash. Apparently what they said about not losing the ability to ride a bike once you acquired the skill was true. Practice might improve my confidence in my ability to balance.

I arrived at the liquor store wearing a sappy smile, a layer of sweat, and my hair a frazzled mess. But the relief at making the trek without falling off made the disorderly hairdo worthwhile. My white knuckled death grip on the shaking bicycle didn't evoke the image I strived for. This one small step toward increasing my independence from trusting my unreliable car for transportation made me smile.

After dismounting, I panted and rested my hands on my quivering thighs. My muscles ached from the unfamiliar exertion. The unaccustomed burn of pressing my limits left a warm fuzzy feeling of satisfaction in my chest. Maybe a little exercise was what I needed to help dissipate my festering anger from erupting at inappropriate times.

After a few deep breaths, I straightened and leaned against the brick of the building. Before making my entrance, I wanted to compose myself and attempt to tame my unruly tresses.

A few people exiting the store cast disdainful glances as they departed with their liquor of choice. Apparently arriving at the liquor store on a bicycle formed an automatic assumption. A few gave me a smug look, as if mocking me they could still drive for their fix. I swallowed the temptation to shout that I didn't lose my license, that my car was a piece of shit. Because booze wasn't on my agenda today, Griffith was.

I strutted into the store, ignoring Andy's curious stare. He opened his mouth to deliver his programmed line directing me to the alcohol showcased in the front, but I cut him off. "I'm going to see Griffith."

His words evaporated, and his gaze strayed to my hair. My guess was that my attempt at controlling my curls failed. I didn't hesitate in my pace and stormed past. When Griffith's office door filled my vision, my confidence waivered. Perhaps he'd grown tired of dealing with my messes. My stomach rolled with nausea, and my throat tightened. What if Griffith didn't want to see me? Before I could lose my nerve, I rapped three times and then rubbed my damp palms on my jeans. Even if he was upset with me, perhaps he'd be too polite to turn me away.

He pulled the door open, his expression faltering when he met my eyes. "Hope?"

I pushed past him into the office and turned to confront him when he reached his desk. I folded my arms over my chest. "Why have you been avoiding me?"

"I'm not avoiding you." He walked past me to settle in his large burgundy chair, assuming the position of authority. It was unnecessary, since his confidence, size, and attitude made him reek of authority no matter where he sat.

"Oh, really?" I sat on the edge of his desk. His eyes strayed to where my ass perched on his precious papers. His shoulders relaxed while he stared at my behind. I took advantage of his distraction. "Yes, you are avoiding me."

He shoved away from the desk, dropping his nonchalant pretense. His feet hit the floor with a thump. "Fine, I am. But for god's sake can you blame me, Hope? You could've killed the man. That's not you. That's never been you."

"You were the one who told me I had a choice. I made it. I can't help what's inside of me." I spoke softly. "I think you were the one who told me the same thing about yourself, so how can you judge me?"

His eyes blazed with tempered rage, and the frustration that festered within him now and always. It had to continuously be a battle for him. To not want to spread desolation and oppress wasn't normal for his kind. It couldn't be easy to have an old soul with a young mind and centuries worth of responsibilities.

"Why do you think I worked so hard to change that?" Griffith grimaced and ran a hand through his hair, appearing uncertain as to whether he wanted to hold me or hit me. "Why I struggled to avoid doing anything to harm anyone else? I don't want to be like that. I *won't* be like that. I can't stand by while you do the very things I avoid. Especially when you show absolutely no regret about your actions."

"Who said I had no regret? I didn't say anything about regret. I did what needed to be done. He can't go tell his story about me, or anyone here. I won't have it." Those last words wavered as they fell from my lips. The four words came across as weak and begging, but I had to convince him to understand my impulsive actions. I was the good guy. Griffith should know that. He'd fought similar demons his whole life. He had to understand. He was my only hope to change who and what I was.

"You can't be the judge of what you feel needs to be done. Believe me, you don't want to have that responsibility." He ran his hand through his hair again and the errant strand in the front rushed to hang over his forehead as soon as he released it. "I think about what I did to Drake every day."

"He deserved it." The words came out harsher than I intended, but I wouldn't take them back. I felt bad about what happened to Griffith's half brother, but I didn't miss him or regret that he was gone. He killed my sister.

He cringed. "Justice may have been served, but why by me? Dammit, Hope, he was my brother. Could you do that to Chance if you thought he deserved it? Could you be the one to make that decision?" His eyes pleaded with me to recognize the pain housed there, but all I could think of was what Drake did to Destiny. What he stole from me.

I looked away but didn't answer his question. Chance wasn't anything like Drake, so his question wasn't even relevant.

Griffith instinctively verbalized my thoughts. "Drake wasn't always like that. People change." He slumped into the chair, deflating after his outburst.

"He wasn't a person." I shuddered, recalling how Drake could invade my mind and flash into a room and disappear effortlessly. I despised him on sight. It wouldn't matter what Griffith said, and who Drake might have been to him, he couldn't convince me otherwise.

"How can you say that? He was a person. He was my brother." Griffith's words were forced, and bore the pain he must harbor every day about what happened. What his feelings for me forced him to do.

"Half. Half-brother," I said, as if that would absolve him for what he did. Griffith looked at me with a new wariness. The intensity stripped me bare as if it were the first time he'd really seen me. "Okay then, he wasn't human."

"Then neither am I." His gaze locked on mine. "Neither are you."

****

"Just the person I wanted to see." Officer McCrory's deep voice always came as an unwelcome surprise. The throaty tone was better suited to a radio host than a meddlesome, disapproving policeman with a pale, thin physique. He strolled with a slow and deliberate pace. His gaze rested briefly on the bicycle and then at my wind-battered hair. He raised an unruly eyebrow.

I sighed. He wasn't someone I wanted to see…ever. The last time I went to him for help, he practically proposed I plan a long-term visit to the state mental hospital. Since then, I avoided him as best as I could in a town as small as this one boasting a three-man police force. The town could've used a lot more policemen, but I guess finding anyone with a backbone of steel willing to turn a blind eye to ongoing unusual happenings was a challenge.

Although not everything was overlooked where I was concerned.

"I had a conversation with that reporter fella this morning." Officer McCrory tucked his hands in his pockets and rocked back on his heels. He thrived on his lawman persona so much that most didn't even know his first name. He insisted everyone refer to him as Officer McCrory, even when off duty. Which was rare to never. "He had some interesting things to say about you."

"Really?" Tension gripped me. I averted my eyes, busying myself with unhooking the bicycle lock. "I doubt that. Making up interesting things is how he makes his living. That reporter probably doesn't have an honest bone in his body. He's greasier than a used car salesman." I stood, face-to-face with the lanky officer. He didn't budge against my assertive stare.

"He looked a bit messed up." He drew a toothpick from his pocket to chew on. I'd heard they were what replaced the cigarettes he gave up years ago. "Black and blue marks were on his cheek. He looked like he hit his face pretty hard on the pavement, or some other hard surface, I'd say. He's looking all around sickly and unwell."

"He's saying I beat him up? A girl?" I raised my brows and placed my hands on my hips to display my arms, which blatantly lacked adequate muscle tone to overpower an adult male. At least what he saw on the outside would make me an unlikely suspect. He didn't know what I housed on the inside. At least I didn't think the cop did.

"I didn't say anything about beating anybody up, and neither did he." We continued the staring showdown with his gaze locked with mine.

A depth of silence stretched between us. He waited for me to fill it with an explanation. That wasn't going to happen. Stan from the barbershop walked by. Officer McCrory tipped the cowboy hat he insisted upon wearing daily. The barbershop owner gave me a curious glance to store away tidbits of information. He'd recount them when patrons visited him today, or later at the Chamber of Commerce meeting, or tomorrow when he worked at the Homeless Center's soup kitchen. The man was everywhere—and he never stopped gossiping.

After determining that a silent standoff might not

be the best way to discourage McCrory's interest, I dropped my gaze. I turned to throw my purse in the basket on my bike, hoping that busying myself with the task would still my shaking hands. "Why are you talking to me about that reporter?"

"Because he told me other things, unusual things about you. Things you did to him." He twirled the toothpick around in his mouth.

My frustration rose, getting the better of me. I didn't like to play games. The way he drew the conversation out, lingering after every sentence to savor the toothpick, and my responses, had me ready to snap. Dark tendrils crept from my fingers and swirled around the tips. The wisps flickered between shades of dark fog and light glitter, portraying my uneasy mood.

"I doubt there's a person in this town you couldn't find something unusual about if you looked." I leaned toward him. "But are you sure you want to start looking for the unusual around here? Who knows what you'll find." I paused, letting him absorb my comment.

Officer McCrory didn't move an inch. The only thing moving on him was the damn toothpick he spun in his mouth as he waited and watched me for my next move—or to see how much I might babble under the pressure of his stare.

"Are you here to arrest me, or what? Then take me down to the station, but you better have a good reason why." I tempered my rising hysteria. This day was really starting to suck, just when I thought it couldn't get worse after Griffith's indifferent goodbye. I couldn't catch a break. It was as if the whole damn town was against me. "Rather than worrying about me perhaps you should be checking into the latest death."

"It was a suicide." He shook his head and reached to pull the toothpick from his mouth to study the damage inflicted with his teeth. The end of the wood lay splintered and raw. "He didn't press any charges against you. In fact, he seemed kind of excited about the whole ordeal."

I frowned, annoyed at how easily he dismissed the death. It might've been a vagrant, but it was still a mortal, and very concerning. Officer McCrory had to know these weren't all suicides, but I couldn't figure out why he wasn't looking into the death further. Was he that stupid or afraid? "Excited? What is he, some kind of pervert?"

"Whether he's a pervert or not, I can't likely say. But it wasn't that kind of excitement. It's because he said he thought he might have finally found the real deal. I thought you'd like to know. We don't like that kind of attention around here. Makes some of the natives restless if they think someone is drawing it in. One difficult girl is easier to deal with than a whole town of, well… Just know that I'll be watching you."

Chapter Six

"Maybe you should just talk to Tom. Then he might leave you alone." Berta rested her hand on her hip and turned her attention on me.

So now he was Tom to Berta. "Are you crazy? God knows what he'd print, especially after..."

"After what?" She tilted her head, narrowed her eyes, and looked at me like a parent willing their child to confess.

Evidently, Berta hadn't heard about what happened between Tom and me the other day, and if I had my way, she never would.

"Let's go for a bike ride." I threw the statement out like a challenge I didn't think Berta would accept. I knew that Uncle George got one for her. Part of me suspected it was Aunt Ruthie's idea to try to build a bond between me and Berta.

With the bicycle being my current state of transportation, I'd become a fairly seasoned rider pretty quickly. I smiled. It might be the one thing I could do better than her, and a way to work on developing just a tiny bit of that friendship I promised to Chance and Ruthie. With Griffith avoiding me, and Officer McCrory bothering me, a bike ride seemed like a perfect distraction. Perhaps it would help decrease the nervous energy that kept me looking over my shoulder.

"What? I don't have a bike." She resumed drying

the dishes.

"You do now." I smiled, but she didn't appear very happy about the surprise. "George picked up a bicycle for you at one of his yard sales." Chance was right. After being judged my entire life it was pretty hypocritical to do the same to Berta. "It's right out back. He dropped it off before you arrived today."

"Well, Tom did ask about doing another reading. I thought I could catch him before the shift started." Her brows drew down into an expression of unease. "Although I haven't seen him lately, have you?"

"Tom can wait." Forever, if I had my way. "You don't want to let George down, do you? At least let him know you tried it out." I pointed through the window at the bike leaning against the side of the building. It was just as old as mine, but a deep purple color. The basket attached to the front appeared a little rusty on the edges, and from the shades of discoloration, it looked as if it once displayed a large flower.

"George is a sweetie." Her compliment fell flat. "Although he wasted his money. I haven't ridden a bicycle in years."

I shrugged. "Neither had I, but it will come right back to you. It did for me. Look, he even got one a little smaller so your feet can reach the pedals." I meant it in a nice way, but Berta rolled her eyes, taking the comment as an insult.

"You said you wanted to hang out." I gave her my most endearing smile, because I did want to try to make things better between us, and not just for Chance and Ruthie. This would be a way to do something together. Something that might put us on an even playing ground without feeling like a bumbling idiot around her all the time. "The bar doesn't open for a few hours. Why not go out and enjoy the beautiful fall weather with the last of the leaves?"

"But I'm wearing—"

"You have sneakers in the back." I crossed my arms and leaned against the counter. For once I was happy that Berta stashed shoes for the annoying aerobic routines she performed in the back room during her breaks.

Berta sighed after I abolished her prepared excuse. "Fine, but I don't know how well I'll be able to do it."

I clapped my hands and tossed my apron on the counter. Before she could change her mind, I rushed out the door. A glance behind me confirmed Berta's reluctant participation. She trudged slowly to the back for her sneakers.

The gravel crunched under my feet while I paced the parking lot to loosen up my muscles. The crisp air promised a refreshing escape from the confines of the kitchen, and hopefully my worries. I swung my arms back and forth and smiled.

I may have tossed out the idea of the ride to change an uncomfortable subject as well as show off my newly acquired skill, but honestly, I felt that a bicycle ride was indeed a fabulous idea. A great way to relax before our shift, and maybe a way I could drop my instinctive defensive guard enough to let Berta in. Aunt Ruthie was right. I should give Berta a chance. I had enough enemies and needed more friends.

The thump of the door banging against its frame announced Berta's arrival. Her lower lip protruding in a pout conveyed her mood. I pushed my bike beside hers. "Hop on your bike. It's fun, you'll see." I straddled my seat with ease and pedaled around the parking lot. My hair lifted from my forehead to trail behind me. The breeze cooled the sweat beaded on my brow from the heat of the kitchen.

Berta tilted her bike from side to side, trying to determine the best way to mount it. "It's not very pretty." She frowned as she poked at the rust spots speckled over the frame.

"It was free. What do you expect? You can clean it up and paint it any color you want." I pedaled circles around her until she batted her hands at me and giggled.

With a grimace, she mounted the bike and gingerly settled on the seat. The bike wobbled as she pedaled at an excruciatingly slow pace. "Shouldn't we wear a helmet?"

"You'll mess up your hair." The one thing Berta would never argue about was her impressive coif. Her typical hairdo must take hours to perfect, but she claimed she just ran a brush through it. Like I was stupid enough to believe that. It takes a lot of work to be a natural beauty.

Berta scanned the area. "I don't want to go on the road. What if a car comes racing down and I fall over? Can we take the trail?"

My confidence waivered as I met her challenging gaze. She constantly harped about there being nothing to fear in the woods, but she knew I remained wary, and she knew why. Yet she still didn't believe me. The moisture in my mouth disappeared as I studied the thick trees flanking the trail. It was still daylight, so it didn't look nearly as menacing as it did at night. I didn't want to back out now. "Sure." I swallowed. "We'll just do a quick bike ride."

I angled toward the trail, pedaling slow enough for Berta to fall in behind me a few feet. She wore an expression of intense concentration as she alternated between studying the pedals and then the road in front of her. My hard heart softened a little with the realization that she was doing this for me. Maybe there was hope for us to become friends yet. "You're doing great, but if you don't speed up, your bike will fall over."

"This is kind of fun," Berta admitted with a small smile. "Makes you remember riding your bike as kid again. I used to go with a bunch of girls and we'd ride down to the corner store."

My smile faltered. If you were like me, it reminded me I was without a car and that I didn't have many friends while growing up. Bike riding was more for necessity and not pleasure, but I didn't point that out. I sped up a little as I turned on a narrow path, peeking over my shoulder to see if Berta would protest. My hair flew over my face when I did. I brushed the strands away with my fingers.

"Where are you going?" Berta yelled, drawing her brows down. "That path doesn't look as easy to ride on. There are sticks and rocks on that trail."

"It's fine, it's made for biking." I didn't know that, but Berta didn't need to realize my limited expertise on these trails. The way her voice rose to a whine spurred me deeper into the surrounding trees. This would be my first ride in the woods. I had ridden along the side but had yet to muster the courage to enter. Berta's company gave me the nerve to accept the challenge. Besides, she was the one who continually insisted we shouldn't fear the woods.

My confidence grew the deeper we went. I picked up my pace, pumping my legs on the pedals hard enough that my hair lifted behind me with the breeze. This was fun. Despite my irritation at being forced to rely on the bike for transportation, riding provided me with a wonderful sense of freedom. Traveling through nature on these two wheels was the closest feeling to flying, besides riding on the back of Griffith's motorcycle.

I glanced over my shoulder and met Berta's gaze.

"This isn't so bad." She forced her legs to keep pace with mine, lingering a few feet behind me. She smiled broadly, closing her eyes, and laughing with glee every few minutes.

My legs and lungs suffered from the exertion of pedaling at this pace, but Berta didn't even appear to be out of breath. I hadn't counted on her increased endurance from those aerobic routines. *Damn it.* She couldn't be better at bicycling, too. I couldn't let that happen. "Let's go," I shouted and pedaled faster.

"What?" Berta's response faded in the wind.

My thighs screamed in protest. The only thing I could do better than Berta was foretelling, but I couldn't control my gift and didn't even want the ability. Berta went around bragging about her palm reading despite everything she predicted being pretty much an educated guess. Sure, she took the pressure off me, but her flaunting was irritating as hell. Biking was my only hope at being better at something, and fitting in.

I leaned forward and lifted slightly from my seat to enable me to pedal in earnest. My breath came out in harsh pants as I pushed my body to my physical limit.

The trees parted and I rode across a bridge over the river, speeding down the other side to press into the thickening woods. The trees were closer together and almost intertwined. A few paths broke apart the foliage, leading deeper into the undergrowth of the woods. Despite the danger, it was absolutely beautiful.

Exhaustion overwhelmed me, and I slowed to a stop at an opening to yet another pathway to wait for Berta to catch up. I never realized how many trails snaked through the woods. We'd need to turn back soon. I bent to tie my loose shoelace before it accidently caught in the chains. The action presented as a perfect excuse to justify my reason for stopping. Not that I needed the break to catch my breath.

After shielding my hand over my eyes to block the hints of sunlight peeking through the trees hindering my vision, I spotted Berta's silhouette far behind. I smiled. I'd finally got ahead of her.

A rustling in the woods caught my attention. I tensed and scanned the thick foliage. Beautiful or not, I couldn't let myself forget where I was. The woods. The breeding ground of the Oppressors. The newly formed ones weren't nearly as polite as the ones who had been around for a time. They'd yet to learn any manners, and they had no fear of anything or anyone.

I gripped the handlebars, searching for anything resembling a low-level Oppressor or for mounting feelings of misery to confirm if one of the damn hope suckers lurked nearby. A chipmunk scampered out. I stifled a scream. The animal stopped on the path to peer at me. I chuckled at my overreaction.

I straddled the bike, preparing to continue a little further before Berta caught up. I'd never ventured this far into the woods before. My desire to prove the chipmunk hadn't destroyed my mounting confidence pushed me to ride deeper. I'd made it this far. Maybe Berta was right. I overreacted too much.

A twig snapped. My hands froze on the rubber bike handles, clutching them tight enough to notice every groove shape imprinting my palm. I stared straight ahead. No way a chipmunk made that noise.

I didn't have to turn to see the entity of misery for confirmation. It was an Oppressor. I could feel it. The feeling of desolation and hopelessness sought and surrounded me. The reaching tentacles of the Oppressor caressed me like an ocean wave seeking the shore. My breath caught. The chorus of the creatures living in the woods silenced as effectively as a flipped switch.

How could I let this happen?

Discovering a lower level Oppressor in the woods, where they preferred to hide until fully developed, didn't surprise me. My cockiness in thinking none would deter me did. The forest served as their womb as they gained strength to mature into a human form. Then they could walk the earth freely to feed off human anguish and despair. I raised my foot and placed it on the pedal, leaning forward over the handlebars—and froze.

Most of me wanted to flee. Part of me wanted to test myself and see if I could emotionally ward off the Oppressor. But all of me needed to see it. To stare down the creature pouring the oily residue over my brain and making me consider infinite methods of agony to end my existence.

As I struggled to maintain my wavering strength to resist the seductive offer of a tempting escape to a blissful death, I turned my head to the left. At the last second, crushing fear prompted me to shut my eyes. I gasped and slumped over the bike. The creature probed within the corners of my mind, seeking an entrance into my heart and soul.

I have to see it. With an effort equivalent to pushing against the weight of a thousand grains of sand resisting my desire to see what taunted me—I opened my eyes.

It wasn't quite formed. Presenting as more of a shadowy creature, it looked like a combination of the wooded area surrounding it with meager clues of the person it longed to form into. Though his figure was uncertain, his intent was not. Promises of agony and depression leaked from every orifice of the creature. The bordering foliage curled and died within its wake, too weak to resist the temptation of demise.

The Oppressor opened its mouth, struggling to form a word. The stench of brimstone and death poured out, fouler than any odor I'd ever encountered on this earth. "Ginge—"

I gasped at the term and gagged on the cloying familiar odor. The word prompted me to fumble with the pedals until my feet caught and gripped. Pushing down with desperate force, I skidded on the path in a wake of dirt and dust to escape the Oppressor's grasp. "Fuck you, death breath."

My heart thudded as fire shot through my weak legs, unaccustomed to intense spurts of exercise. *Ginger.* That thing couldn't have been about to say Ginger. Drake was gone. I glanced over my shoulder but didn't sense anything in pursuit. Double-checking was purely to calm my anxiety because the retraction of the feelings of desperation, washing away as thoroughly as a bath, confirmed I'd outpaced the creature.

As exhaustion overtook me, and the woods became denser, I slowed to a stop. Leaning forward, I hung over the handlebars and gasped to catch my breath. My throat ached. My wheezing had worn the flesh raw. The sound of trickling water prompted me to lift my head. A spring ran over the rocks a few feet ahead. I pushed my bike closer and propped it against a tree. I knelt to dip my hands in the flow.

After rinsing the sweat and dust off my skin, I cupped the water and brought it to my mouth. My trembling hands spilled most of the water on the first few tries until I began to gain control. Sporadic tendrils of fog leaked from my fingertips, confused by my overwhelming fight or flight reaction.

Finally, I maintained enough liquid in my palms to obtain a drink. The cool water refreshed me better than any beverage on a hot day. After getting my fill, I splashed my face and ran my hands over my frizzed hair to cool my body temperature.

I stood and peered down the road. The foliage lay so heavy that the trees hung over the path. The birds had returned to chirping with the retreat of the Oppressor. The usual sounds of the normal creatures residing in the woods resumed. Otherwise the only sounds were those of nature, giving me the feeling that I was the closest thing to human for miles.

"Shit. Berta."

I forgot all about her when I panicked. Surely, she turned around to head back to the bar before she bumped into the Oppressor, or else I would have passed her. Hopefully the thing retreated deeper into the woods, or wherever the hell it came from, to wait for another victim to feed from.

I squinted down the barren trail. If anyone could deter an Oppressor with too much optimism, it was Berta. She probably smothered the damn thing in compliments and false bravado until it withdrew of its own accord. At least I hoped so. Her clueless enthusiasm made her vulnerable—and a huge temptation to an Oppressor who fed off hope and happiness.

I pedaled back the way I came, taking deep focusing breaths to try to tap into my new, undeveloped abilities. The little control I'd gained over my foretelling ability continued to frustrate me.

"Berta?" I whispered, as if the Oppressor required sound to locate me and couldn't pinpoint me on the temptation of my essence. If silence was required to protect me from detection, the spinning of the bike tires over twigs, rocks, and dry leaves disintegrating as I passed would've thwarted my attempt at stealth.

"Berta?" I yelled louder this time. Dread settled in. She should've caught up with me, unless she turned around and returned to the bar. My irritation faded, and my thoughts flew into a panic. What if the Oppressor laid in wait for her, and she couldn't resist? Not many could ward off the lure of an Oppressor.

I cringed, recalling how I instigated the creature with an insult as I saved myself and totally forgot about Berta. She didn't have any abilities to identify the advance of an Oppressor in order to protect herself.

I slowed when I approached the area where I first encountered the Oppressor. The torn-up dirt on the path from the speed of my escape confirmed that it was the correct spot. The rutted dirt also deterred me from discovering whether there was another set of bike tracks from Berta.

"Berta?" I shouted over the chatter of the birds in the trees. Their chirping ensured me no Oppressor lurked nearby or they would've silenced and high tailed it out of there. I pedaled slowly, finding no sign of her in the woods, or on the path. My attempts to study the trail for signs of her tire tracks proved futile. Much of the path was uneven and looked as if it got little use. I sucked as a detective.

I stopped and steadied the bike, stirring up a cloud of dust with my feet. A claustrophobic feeling gripped me as I studied the thick foliage surrounding me. I tilted my back, cupped my hands around my mouth and shouted as loud as I could. "Berta!"

The trees soaked up the sound. The silence loomed overwhelming and absolute despite the sounds of the wildlife filling the forest with random noises of scurrying or chirping. I never would have thought I'd be grateful for the sound of Berta's voice. An ache formed in the pit of my stomach while I retraced my steps toward the bar as one thing became certain.

Berta wasn't here.

****

The ride back gave me time to gather my thoughts. I convinced myself Berta got irritated and rode back without me. She didn't want to go on the ride in the first place because she was worried she'd miss Tom before the shift started. Or maybe she thought I meant to turn back when I said 'let's go.' That must be it. It had to be. She'd be waiting to chastise me for being late for the start of the shift.

She would've wanted to return in time to fix her hair and primp. I scowled, finding comfort in the familiar irritation at Berta's antics returning. The pleasure at using the bike ride to prove there might be one thing I could do better than Berta was fleeting. She'd still emerge looking fabulous while I modeled sweaty attire and a bug splattered face.

I propped my bike on the side of the building and scanned the parking lot. My attention strayed to the sky. A hawk circled over the trees. As I studied the winged predator unease traveled over me, leaving a smattering of goose bumps on my forearms. I dropped my gaze to the ancient tombstones on the hill. The breeze prompted leaves not confined by markers to rush and scatter across the gravel parking lot. A few briefly caught and molded to my shoe before breaking free to scatter.

The lot was ominously empty of Berta or her bike. Chief's big old boat of a car and a few of the other regulars lined the front of the parking lot. I frowned. Although with Berta's meager biking skills, she might've left the bike and walked back to arrive sooner. I gathered my thoughts with a deep breath. Most likely Berta was already inside having a good laugh at how she ditched me in the woods.

The heavy metal door squawked in protest as I yanked it open to enter through the backdoor to the kitchen. I mentally prepared the rude comments I planned to hurl at Berta for leaving me behind. The noise from the bar drifted to me. The chatter lacked one distinct noise...Berta's distinctive sugary sweet voice. I would've welcomed the sound. She had to be here. I couldn't consider the alternative.

Chief ambled across the kitchen, winded from

crossing the short distance. "Where the hell were you, Red?" His gasping breaths made the longer hairs around his mustache float up and down.

Despite his small frame, and advanced age, his arms were roped with muscles straining from gripping packages of meat. He dropped the sealed packages on the counter with a clatter and then reached in the freezer for more. His feet lifted from the ground when he groped to the bottom, seeking the oldest meat to use first.

"Um..." I anticipated being chastised, but from Berta, not Chief.

Shit. Where was Berta? She was never late. She reminded me of her stellar attendance record every day if I was even one minute late. "I'm sorry."

Chief frowned when I apologized, most likely anticipating my usual excuse or defensive argument. Although he insisted women should be quiet and biddable, the women he hired proved challenging because none of us were anywhere near quiet or biddable. If he hired meek women to work the bar, they'd leave in tears. None would survive working here and tolerating Chief's ranting, and the obnoxious men who frequented the bar. To avoid making eye contact with Chief, I pulled my apron from the drawer. "Where's Berta?"

I tied the apron on and then moved to the sink to wash the dirt and sweat from my hands. Moistening a paper towel, I rubbed it over my face while being careful not to remove my eye makeup. I might not wear much, but I needed a little battle paint to boost my confidence. When working alongside Berta, I needed all the help I could get.

"I was going to ask you the same question." He rubbed his chin after parting his long white beard to find it. His bristly beard separated over his knobby knuckles. "Funny though, I'm usually asking Berta that question about you. I thought by hiring her I might have at least one partially responsible gal here. Now I'm not so sure about either of you."

I glanced out the window to the parking lot. A few motorcycles pulled in, but no bicycle. *No Berta.* My heart clenched with wisps of unease.

He scowled before continuing with his rant. "You got Ruthie gone baking her stuff. Stuff she hasn't been baking for the bar for a while, I might add, leaving me high and dry. Now her replacement, who's supposed to be cooking today, is nowhere to be found. So now all I've got to count on is, is…you." He regarded me in utter disappointment that I remained as his only option.

Chief's expression softened as he changed the subject. "You haven't seen that reporter guy, have you? I wanted to see if he'd autograph one of my magazines."

"No. Why is everyone so concerned about that reporter?" I scowled. The reporter. The vision. Maybe that was it. Berta might've gotten irritated with me and come back to meet Tom. She was probably getting back at me for racing ahead of her on the bike ride. It would be like her to want to teach me a lesson. Or perhaps she hurried home to shower again before coming to work.

Chief threw his hands in the air. "Whatever. Get busy, the bar is already filling up. Don't know how you're gonna manage all this by yourself."

"Thanks for the help." I called after him as he ambled down the hall to his office, most likely seeking a nip of his stash without considering the possibility that he might need to pitch in and help. Not that he'd be any good in the kitchen since his diet consisted of wheat and grains—all found in the bottom of a bottle. I shook my head in resignation as Chief yanked at his pants before disappearing into his office. The suspenders were the only things sparing us the sight of his bony behind.

I made a mental note to talk to Berta about Chief's diet, or lack of it, when I saw her. After I gave her a piece of my mind about ditching me, of course. Lately his oversized pants began to resemble something more suitable for a clown. I didn't consider the ill effects of not having Ruthie around to continuously remind Chief to eat.

I turned to face the empty kitchen. The small room appeared larger without Berta's overbearing presence. I glanced to the window and out to the parking lot. Still no Berta. No way would she trust me alone in the kitchen for long. She'd be along any minute.

I busied myself with routine tasks to keep my mind off Berta. The freezer-burnt slab of meat defrosted in the microwave, rotating around like my thoughts. The only recipe I could think of was disaster, for the food and for Berta.

It was past three o'clock. Grumblings filtering into the kitchen validated my observation. The regulars would be lining the bar by now and waiting for their drinks. If I left these guys too long without a drink, they'd be a bigger problem than Berta. I pushed through the swinging door to the bar. First hydrate the guys and then figure out what happened with Berta.

I lined a few glasses up at the tap, and while tilting

them to limit the foam, I mulled over my thoughts. Unable to avoid it any longer, I reflected upon my biggest fear.

It couldn't have been an Oppressor. Otherwise I would've found Berta, or what was left of her, on the way back. As much as she aggravated me, I didn't want anything to happen to her, and I certainly didn't want to find her body. I hadn't found my sister's body. Although viewing her death in a vision when I gained Destiny's gift of foretelling was bad enough. Oppressors didn't take people with them to whatever hell they returned to until they formed enough to pass as human. At least I didn't think so.

Just then, the man I could question about Oppressor behaviors entered the bar, even though he might not want to talk with me. I didn't want to discuss any of my concerns about Berta with my boyfriend, but I needed to find a way to probe for information without setting off his alarms. If one person could help me, he could. But he might not want to. The rippling muscles he presented when he splayed his arms out in a stretch distracted me from my worries. No low-level Oppressor drawn to the bar in the hope of a nip from my fountain of hope, or unsavory parking lot exchange of goods or services, stood a chance.

Griffith perched at the end of the bar, glancing from me to the customers. His worried gaze swept over my face, and his slight frown confirmed he detected my anxiety. Each time I had a moment to get near him, someone else demanded my attention, or Griffith found a reason to make his rounds in the parking lot. It sure seemed like he was avoiding me. After months of studying Griffith's gorgeous and mysterious face, I'd begun to successfully distinguish some of his moods.

I turned around and gasped. "Where did you come from?" Chance sat in front of me holding up a pink and black striped scarf. He waved it to and fro until he gained my drifting attention when Griffith reentered the bar once more.

Chance stepped off the stool, wavering a little as he did, and then glanced between Griffith and me. He leaned heavily on the counter for support. "Did you guys have a fight?"

He whispered the words, but I could tell Griffith caught them by the slight wrinkle to his forehead and the way his lip pulled down on the corner. Unlike me, he excelled at concealing his emotions. He used to insist he didn't have any, but I determined he was just good at disguising them.

"Yes…no…it doesn't matter." This wasn't the time, or the place, for the discussion. The relationship between Griffith and Chance remained tenuous. Either one latched on any opportunity to criticize the other. Although I thought in this instance, Chance would be inclined to agree with my boyfriend. Having the two men in my life finally reconcile, only to join forces and gang up on me, was the last thing I needed now.

"We're fine," I said, ignoring Griffith's piercing stare indicating the contrary. "You better go to work so you're not late."

"Can you give this to Berta when she comes in? She forgot it in my car. It's supposed to get cold tonight, and she might want it when she gets off work," Chance explained.

"Sure." I took the scarf. The roar of the television commercial during the period break of the game partially concealed my gasp. The noise was hidden from everyone—except Griffith. His eyes focused on me, watching me like a hawk.

It was the same vision I experienced before which depicted Berta and the reporter. That never happened before. The few visions I had were a once and done kind of deal. There was no opportunity for me to gather additional facts if I didn't pay attention the first time.

I needed to figure out what happened to Berta before anyone realized she might be missing. Chance's body flickered in and out of my view like a strobe light. "Chance?"

I recoiled as he waxed and waned in front of me, looking as if parts of him were melting. The warped image of my brother remained even after squeezing my eyes shut and opening them again. He didn't look well, kind of pasty and pale. "You're working yourself too hard, you look…tired." I couldn't think of a better way to describe it—other than transparent.

"I'm worried about Berta." His voice sounded distant and fading. Then he was gone.

I clutched the scarf and stared at the space where he'd stood a moment before.

Griffith walked over and rested his hip against the bar. "It was a clone, Hope. You know that. What's going on with you?"

"A clone?" Of course it was. *Why didn't I think of that?* When Chance's ability grew stronger, in addition to being able to influence a decision by visual hallucinations, he could clone himself to explore different choices…and apparently to deliver a scarf.

"He hasn't done that in months." I looked toward the door, only then realizing his delivery truck wasn't parked out front.

Griffith furrowed his brow. "Did he say anything before he left? I thought he only used the clone if it was absolutely necessary. Said that it wore him out too much."

I rolled the scarf through my hands, the soft texture binding me to reality. "He said he was worried about Berta."

Griffith surveyed the bar with the careful attention of a predator. The heightened senses of the Oppressor part of him shone through. "Should he be? I thought she was supposed to work today."

"I didn't think I'd see you today." I retrieved a bottle of vodka from under the counter with a shaky hand, stalling on my awkward explanation.

"I work here." Griffith held up his palm as I inclined the bottle toward him in question, glancing to where my hands shook. "Which is why I'll have cranberry juice."

Of course he would. Despite having the ability to be the epitome of evil, he was the healthiest guy I knew. It was irritating how he sucked down protein shakes with dark, green, leafy everything when the only shake I wanted to drink contained nothing green unless it was mint chocolate chip. My reservations about my vision were squelched with my concern about Berta.

"Where's Berta? Who's cooking the eats?" One of the men at the bar grumbled.

I avoided the hungry men's stares and pondered the same dilemma. My mind welcomed the brief reprieve of fretting about Berta as I refilled drinks. Although contemplating the crisis of who's going to do the cooking didn't provide any more of an easier answer than determining Berta's current location. The frozen slab of meat should be thawed by now. What in the heck was I going to do with it? Ruthie or Berta always did the cooking. "I better get something on the grill."

Griffith scanned the bar, and looked longingly toward the kitchen, as if Berta would emerge at any moment. "Isn't Berta supposed to be cooking tonight?"

"She is but..." What could I say? My anxiety mounted with each passing minute she didn't return. Berta was probably at home laughing to herself about how she left me on my own at the bar to make me deal with Chief. She'd later inform me how she did it for my own good, insisting I needed to learn a lesson. If I was actually enrolled in what I liked to call the *School of Berta*, I'd have failed miserably long ago.

"Out of the two of us, I'm our best bet at producing anything edible." He moved toward the door. "After I walk through the parking lot, I'll see what I can do for food. I had your hamburger surprise. It's not something we want to surprise anyone with."

There was no use worrying Chance yet, but Griffith would know what to do. No matter whether Berta was missing, an Oppressor was involved, or she was blabbing to the reporter, I had to admit I might be in over my head. This wasn't just about our relationship. I'd deal with that later. Right now, I needed his help.

Chapter Seven

Guys continued to pour into the bar, but there was no sign of the reporter. Only brawny men with short-attention spans and even shorter fuses. My time was limited, but taking care of these dudes was a priority. Sometimes the booze was all that held them together. By the time I caught up on drinks, Griffith was already returning from the kitchen. There was still no sign of Berta. I trailed him around the bar. "I need to talk to you."

"Not now. We talked earlier. The food will be ready shortly." He scanned the crowded area and headed toward the door, dismissing the conversation and me.

I grabbed his arm. "Not about us." I lowered my gaze so he wouldn't see my pain at his rebuff. "About Berta." I had to make sure she was okay before Chance showed up. I couldn't have him rushing to the woods in order to look for her. He would be totally reckless. I couldn't lose him too.

Griffith studied me for several moments, probably mulling over the past events between us. He took a sip of his drink and then sighed in resignation, probably expecting me to complain about her again. 'What about Berta?"

I leaned closer to him. "We went for a bike ride in the woods."

He nodded, the slight flicker in his eyes portraying his shock.

Either I stunned him by admitting I willingly did something with Berta outside of work, or my saying we went on a bike ride together, or suggesting I entered the woods—determining which fact surprised him more would be a challenge.

He tempered his disbelief with his usual placid expression while he waited for me to continue. "And?" His unwavering stare made it difficult to remain silent. Besides, I needed to unburden my concern to someone.

I swallowed my pride, and a large lump of guilt lodged in my throat. "I kind of lost her."

Griffith's calm expression dissolved. The way he dramatically choked on his cranberry juice might've been funny if he didn't look as if his head might explode. "You lost her? What the hell is that supposed to mean? Why would you take her in the woods?"

I should've realized my third comment would bother him the most…the woods.

"She didn't want to ride on the road. It was her idea. One minute she was right behind me and the next she was gone." I wrung my hands as the flimsy excuses I'd banked on to assure me of Berta's safety were revealed for what they were—excuses. "I know, it was stupid, but the woods have been fine lately. I went back to look for her and then thought she might've came back to the bar. The Oppressors are almost gone—"

Griffith laughed bitterly. "Are you serious? Gone? They'll never be gone. They aren't as confident without Hecate, but they're still here and will be back stronger than ever. I think…" He paused and tightened his jaw. "I think they're looking for a leader, but they're certainly not gone. Have you ever known a time when there was no hate, anger, or crime in the world?"

I opened and closed my mouth a few times like a fish out of water while I sought a retort, but found none. Griffith's observation morphed my worry into anger, and I tossed it at the closest target. Him.

"Then what the hell is the point of what we do? If Enchantlings can't get rid of the Oppressors, why do we bother?" My whisper came out harsher than I intended, and a few men looked my way. Although their interest could only be that they needed another beer. Most tended to look the other way at anything unusual. People didn't like to get involved around here, because you never knew *what* you were getting involved with.

Griffith narrowed his eyes at my childish outburst. No doubt regretting his personal vow to avoid using his Oppressor ability to influence and persuade me to bend to his bidding. Not that he could do it easily if he tried, I'd become savvy to that skill.

He settled on a stool with a look of resignation at his never-ending responsibility of reining in my stubbornness. He reiterated, "Because every life matters, doesn't it? I know you've heard that before. The last six months have provided people in this town with a much-deserved break. They can breathe a little easier when they're out at night. That's the gift you've given them."

My retort died on my lips. I didn't try to disguise the trembling of my lower lip, hoping my self-pity would soften Griffith's irritation. First the incident with the reporter and now this. I didn't want to consider what could get worse.

He leaned closer, his gaze holding the intent focus

of a seasoned predator. "Tell me what happened. Every detail and every step, exactly. She was right behind you and yet you lost her? Where were you at in the woods?"

"Well, I wouldn't say she was right behind me." Guilt made me squirm under his scrutiny. The time I'd spent reviewing every step of my time with Berta already made me realize that what I initially justified as a fun outing was just stupid and reckless. But admitting that to Griffith made me feel even worse. I studied the scratched countertop. "I got a little ahead of her since I'm more seasoned on the bike."

He cocked his head. The muscle along his jawline twitched. "You were showing off."

"I was not." Being so transparent to him was frustrating. Just like him to cut right to the heart of the matter where my guilt festered. "We were on the path."

"The path? Which path?"

"The one…" My mind drew a blank. The paths snaking through the woods all looked the same. They had little to no markings to indicate where I last saw Berta. If I could convince Griffith that there was a good chance Berta's absence might be intentional on her part, perhaps it would lessen my nagging guilt. "I had a vision about Berta, actually a couple of times. We have to consider that this might be something else entirely."

"Such as what?" He raised his eyebrows.

His expression told me he doubted my justification before I shared it. This irritated me more. He was supposed to be on my side. "Berta and the reporter. She was planning to meet him. She's always trying to flaunt her palm reading ability."

I made air quotes around the last three words, although I didn't need to emphasize my thoughts on

Berta's sideshow act to Griffith. The way I couldn't keep my voice from stating the words with a tinge of mockery, and the number of times I complained before solidified my opinion on the matter. "She probably snuck off to meet him before I could talk her out of it. Who knows what she'll tell him? Berta will do anything to get her name in the spotlight. That's what she's always wanted."

This was one of the times Berta being an airhead, and a disbeliever about most of the oddities around here, might prove beneficial. Although by wearing the necklace that had to have been Mrs. Shaw's, there was a possibility there was more to Berta than I realized. Perhaps she'd been playing us all.

"Really? You think *that's* what she's always wanted?" He stood and the chair smacked off the counter with his sudden departure.

Parroting what I said infuriated me. That might've been his intention, since obviously his anger about Berta, and probably Tom, simmered beneath his exasperatingly calm façade. I gripped the counter, turning my fingers under so Griffith wouldn't comment on the tendrils of black fog leaking out. "Don't you have someone to bounce out of the bar or something?"

When the muscle in Griffith's jaw twitched, I knew I'd worn him down. In addition to struggling to express his emotions, he didn't know how to deal with anyone else's. Especially mine. He closed his eyes and took a deep breath. The shimmering haze building around him decreased with his frustration. "Fine, tell me about the vision."

"Well, when you put it like that, maybe I won't." I turned to walk away, and would've continued with my immature impasse if Griffith hadn't touch my upper arm. The lightest bit of pressure of his fingers against my skin was all it took. Damn if he still couldn't send tingles along my flesh as if I'd never felt his touch before.

I leaned close, eager to share my suspicions with the only person who might believe me. Griffith knew the history of the Oppressors and the Enchantlings and how imperative it was to keep our skeletons in the closet. Airing our dirty laundry wasn't good for anyone, especially me. "In the vision, Berta is talking animatedly with Tom. He has a huge microphone pushed in her face and the cameras are rolling. You can tell she loves every minute of it, too. Spilling all our secrets. She probably ran off with that reporter to avoid facing the wrath of everyone who wants to keep the secrets."

Griffith sat back on the stool. His critical gaze followed me as I retrieved and filled the empty drink glasses lining the bar. He continued the conversation when I returned, as if we never left off. "Do you seriously think that in all the years this town existed no one has tried to *tell our secrets* to the outside? The outside doesn't want to know our secrets. That's why the town doesn't show up on a map. They'd rather we just disappear. The people who show up here aren't wanted anywhere else. Do you really think anyone outside of this town would believe what we told them?"

I opened my mouth to protest but stopped, remembering how when I arrived here, I thought the stories about this town, about me, were ridiculous. I grew up as a misfit, an oddity. Yet I still resisted believing the good and evil in the world could be manipulated. Some strange force had drawn me to this backwoods town. That irresistible lure turned out to be my brother, using his ability. I immediately assumed he was a *nutjob*, classified Aunt Ruthie as a crazy old lady, and Griffith…well he was something else altogether. What Griffith said rang true, seeing was the only way to believe.

That is if seeing didn't prompt a desire to admit yourself to the overflowing psychiatric hospital. Tom had experienced me in action, but who would believe him? People didn't want to accept there might be more to the world than the eye could see—more than the mind could rationalize.

"You have a point." I looked to him, pleading with my eyes. "But people will talk to you about things they won't tell anyone else." I had to stop avoiding the possibility that something more sinister might've happened. Even though he'd never admit it, Griffith still had unsavory connections. A few hoped he'd lead the Oppressors, but he had no desire to assume that responsibility. But people talked to him. They remembered who Griffith's father was, and the role Hecate planned for Griffith. That knowledge made many uneasy. To refuse to be the Goddess of the Underworld's right-hand man took someone special, someone to be reckoned with—or dreaded.

"I'll ask around." Griffith unfolded from the stool and towered over the bar. Whether it was his healthy habits, or something in his genetics, he could never contain his restlessness. "Call Chance, and ask him to look for Berta while he's doing his route. I'll ask around while I do my rounds for parking lot predators."

The phrase usually made me giggle, but not today.

Despite personally experiencing the unpleasant effects of leaving the parking lot unsupervised, I wanted to delay Griffith's departure. I dreaded my brother's furious reaction. Even though he suggested I befriend Berta, he never considered the potential consequences of my friendship. I frowned, hoping to stall the inevitable. "Don't you think we should wait to call Chance?"

Griffith momentarily failed at maintaining his expressionless face and genuine astonishment flashed over his features. "Did you ever consider there might be other possibilities? That she might've gotten lost on the path? Or had a flat tire? She might need help. You might not have come back the same way. Those paths are confusing and they can …change. Do you always have to assume the worst?"

"Yes." How could he question that? Long ago I learned to expect the worst, if nothing else.

****

Griffith's attempt to concoct something semi-healthy out of the plethora of questionable frozen lumps in the freezer resulted in an uproar. These men would drink moonshine festering in an unknown mountain man's still, consume meat of questionable origins, but drew the line at what Griffith tried to pass off as a garden burger.

I tried to tell him his whole turning over a new leaf thing didn't apply to everyone. The men at the bar weren't turning over anything—unless it was someone's car.

I hated to do it, but calling in Ruthie to help presented as the only alternative rather than facing hordes of hungry men with a patty of mashed beans, spinach, and spices. Most of our regulars were naturally cantankerous. But depriving them of our pathetic, greasy, bar food could demolish the last straw binding them to their civility.

Once Ruthie arrived, Griffith muttered something about beggars shouldn't be choosey and prepared to leave. He insisted he'd ask around about Berta at the liquor store. At my begging and insistence, he convinced Ruthie that Berta either got mad and stormed off, or needed assistance—as he seemed to think most females did. Being a six foot-three hulk of a man with the ability to gain his way through physical force or mental oppression made him view most women as delicate creatures. Except for me. Although technically I didn't count, I wasn't a normal woman.

I barely got accustomed to the absence of one overbearing man when Chance barged in, banging the door off the wall.

"Is Berta in the back?" Chance leaned against the bar, waiting for me to finish serving drinks.

Damn it. As I served the drinks, I searched my mind for something—anything—I could do to avoid my brother. He moved in front of me, blocking my potential escape and feeble excuses as I wondered how to explain that I managed to lose his girlfriend in the woods. Chance would never forgive me, and I didn't want to involve him yet if we didn't need to. He was far too reckless. If he went running in the woods, there was a risk that he might not come back out.

He craned his head to peer down the hall, knowing better than to go check. When he walked to the back a few weeks ago, Chief chased him out. Despite Chief being a tiny man, there was something to be said about being small and mighty. I never realized Chief could move that quickly. He'd muttered something about setting precedence and that if he let one guy go back, then all the guys would plow back and help themselves to his stuff. If nothing else, Chief maintained little tolerance for anyone breaking his rules—and a lot of unfounded paranoia.

"No, she's not here yet. I'm sure she'll be here soon." I busied myself with filling napkin dispensers and tossing paper coasters to the guys, even though Chief giving up liquor was more probable than these guys using them. The coasters were Berta's new thing. She insisted all the bars used coasters. I pointed out how other bars might have counters worth protecting, but she wouldn't relent on using the pointless paper countertop protectors.

"Do you want something to drink?" The more I talked with Chance, the more likely I might blurt something out of guilt. My skill at lying ranked up there with my cooking. Berta would be here soon. She had to be. There was no use worrying Chance. I was the big sister. It was my job to protect him.

I turned with the weight of Chance's questioning, furious stare. *Too late.* I sighed. He already knew. Someone told him and it should've been me.

"How could you leave her out there?" Each word he spoke fell heavy with blame.

His accusation drew my shoulder blades down to meet in the middle of my back and ignited my defenses. "I didn't realize it was my turn to watch her," I muttered.

Chance frowned. "What did you say?"

"Nothing." I released my tightened grip on the

knife and laid the small blade by the lime slices. "Lower your voice, or Chief will throw you out."

Chance rolled his eyes. "Let him. I'm not afraid of him."

"You should be. He has more connections in this town than anyone. People that make him mad end up in trouble in more ways than one." The guy who complained about being shortchanged last week later found himself without a job and evicted from his apartment without warning. For whatever reason, no one messed with Chief.

I put my hands on my hips and narrowed my eyes. This town brimmed with hooligans, entities morphing into human form from the Underworld, and a host of other misfits, yet my family blamed me for anything amiss. "And for your information, I didn't leave her out there."

Chance's angry expression dissolved to reveal the underlying fear it masked. My irritation wavered. "Your delivery shift is over, isn't it? Sit down and have a drink."

He slumped into the stool and accepted his customary drink from me, a root beer. "Where the hell could she have gone? You're the one who kept insisting she'd give me trouble when I tried to help her. Yet you weren't even there when she needed help."

I ignored his accusation and concentrated on drying a glass. "She might not need help."

He lifted the frosty mug and sipped his root beer. A foamy mustache appeared on his upper lip for a few seconds and then disappeared as effortlessly as Berta.

I dipped another glass into the soapy water, grateful for a productive outlet to alleviate my anxiety over the topic of Berta. "She might be mad at me and proving a point." Like the one I unsuccessfully attempted to make with the bike ride. My desired result of coming out on top, for once, was foiled by her disappearance. Instead I appeared selfish. "Griffith thinks so." He didn't, but it sounded better than if it was just one of my theories.

"I bet he does. That would sure make it easier on him wouldn't it?" Chance shook his head. The longer pieces of hair flopped around on his forehead, completely ruining his ability to look furious or intimidating. "He's wrong. Berta wouldn't do that."

"What's that supposed to mean? Make it *easier* on Griffith? He doesn't have anything to do with Berta." I knew what he implied. My brother and my boyfriend's constant digs at each other were getting old. Chance frequently verbalized his belief that Griffith would eventually return to his origins and allow his Oppressive nature to consume him.

Griffith, on the other hand, insisted Chance's insufferable happy nature was a façade to cover his true self, which could be part Oppressor. Instinctively I defended one to the other, but being caught in the middle of their unmerited dislike for each other made my life a constant dispute.

Chance slammed his mug down hard enough to send foam over the top. He slid it toward me with a frown and a smear of the sticky beverage on the counter. "Get me a real beer."

I steadied the wobbling glass and raised my brows. A declaration of his undying love for Mrs. Dwight over Berta would've been less surprising than his request for alcohol. "You don't drink beer."

He straightened and raked me with a challenging stare. "I do now."

The firm line to Chance's mouth confirmed he wasn't going to relent, and I preferred to avoid another argument. Regardless, if Ruthie got caught up in the kitchen and came out and spotted him drinking, she'd give him an earful. Not because of what he was drinking, but *where* he was drinking. In her opinion, drinking anywhere outside of our house and losing one's inhibitions with alcohol provided an open door for manipulation or intimidation. *Especially at this bar.*

I extricated myself from her theory. A nip of tequila now and then kept me sane, and besides, unlike Chance, I could hold my liquor.

With a sigh, I turned to the tap, letting my back convey my displeasure at his decision. I didn't know what kind of beer he would prefer, and neither did he, so I chose the lightest beer we offered, hoping he could handle his liquor. Most likely a couple of swallows would be enough to convince him to return to non-alcoholic beverages and quit acting like a child. He was the youngest, but his immature behavior was really testing my six minutes of seniority.

He took a sip, grimaced, and then swallowed.

I hid my amusement at his obvious dislike of his chosen beverage and decided to resume our conversation about Berta. Of the three potential topics of discussion, musing about Berta's whereabouts was preferable over rehashing Chance's dislike of Griffith, or his decision to join the boozers at the bar.

"Then what? Where do you think Berta is?" I was eager to hear his opinion. No one seemed to coincide with me that she might've went off on her own accord.

Either amusing herself by intentionally abandoning me to deal with Chief's wrath, or by risking us all by blabbing to that reporter.

"She was taken by an Oppressor to get to us." Chance spoke with calm certainty and loud enough for the men nearby to overhear.

Several large, perpetually angry men turned our way. One or two displayed the telltale signs only I could see which indicated they were Oppressors—and none were too happy about Chance's accusation. I tensed. No matter how frustrating Chance could be when it came to Berta, he was my brother. Protecting him was ingrained in me.

I met the Oppressors glare with one of my own until they turned away. Whether they backed off because of their desire not to upset Griffith, Chief, or me didn't matter, as long as they backed off.

My brother had broken an unspoken rule. No one discussed Oppressors, or other potential Underworld happenings, at Last Call. Let alone openly state one of their kind abducted one of the bar's employees. Mortals weren't the only ones a little leery of getting on Chief's bad side. Chief declared Last Call neutral ground, or at least it was supposed to be. If not for Griffith's rounds of the parking lot, there would be a lot more rules broken.

If I let Chance continue to flap his gums, he'd soon get his ass kicked. More likely than not, he couldn't hold his liquor either, so the gum flapping was bound to get worse. I tossed my bar rag on the counter.

"Let's go outside. I'm due for my break anyway." Actually, I never got a scheduled break, but Ruthie would cover for me for a few minutes. Chief already initiated his afternoon booze fest with several drinks long under his belt, so he was unlikely to notice my absence.

After the door swung closed behind us, Chance turned on me, shaking his mug in my direction. Beer sloshed over the top and ran down the sides of the glass. "You're the one who said having Berta around was a risk. You insisted someone would use her to get to us."

I furrowed my brow, deciding since Griffith wasn't nearby to chastise Chance, I wouldn't point out that taking alcoholic beverages outside wasn't permitted.

"I did?" I said a lot of things, mostly because I didn't like Berta…at first. The last few days I thought we'd started to establish a common ground in which we didn't irritate each other *every* minute of the day.

"Yes, you did, and obviously, I still don't agree with avoiding having a relationship with her because of *your* fear. Aren't you the one who told Ruthie Destiny's death wasn't her fault, since no one should live life as a self-imposed prisoner? That Ruthie was right to encourage Destiny to explore the world?" He chugged the rest of his beer and twisted his face as if he'd bitten into a lemon.

"I said that?" I crossed my arms. I didn't realize he ever listened to me, or that I talked so much. I needed to choose my words more carefully if they were going to be served back to me.

He nodded and studied the mug. Moisture glistened in his eyes, but no tears fell. A muscle along his cheek twitched as he clenched his jaw. "I'm going back to the woods to see if I can find anything. She must be out there somewhere. Nothing could've happened to her, because you would've known. If it did, you would have had a vision like you did when Destiny…"

The words caught in his throat and he looked away. "When Destiny died. Right? You would've known if something happened to Berta."

He studied my face, desperate for me to agree. I couldn't remind him about my total lack of control over the visions and reiterate how the visions were unpredictable and appeared without rhyme or reason.

"Sure." The way his face sagged in relief made the lie worth it. I couldn't break his heart—again.

His hug, and the thump of the heavy beer mug against my back, was unexpected. I relaxed into him and my tension lifted. The mere minutes dubbing me as the big sister meant nothing compared to the approval and acceptance from my brother. I couldn't let him down again.

"How come everyone I love dies? I can't let something happen to her too." His words were muffled.

"She's not dead." I mustered as much conviction as I could into the words. He buried his face in my neck, so I patted his back. "We'll find her, Chance. Berta's fine, don't worry. Please don't go looking for her in the woods. It's too dangerous. Let's try every other option first."

The door creaked and Chance moved away. He shoved the sticky beer mug at me and then turned to wipe his arm across his face in embarrassment as a man exited the bar. My brother endured a lot in his lifetime. In the short time I'd known him I only saw him break down one other time, when Destiny died.

Ruthie stuck her head out the door and glanced between Chance and me. Her brow furrowed in concern as she took him in and then looked at me in question.

Her eyes bulged behind her thick glasses. When her mouth opened slightly, I feared what I suspected she was considering.

I held up my hand and shook my head with vehemence, hoping she accepted my unspoken indication that he'd be okay without one of her homemade interventions. That she didn't need to rush to make one of the terrible concoctions she insisted would make you feel better. Even if you felt like death, it would be preferable over drinking the foul-smelling, terrible-tasting beverage.

Ruthie met my eyes, accepting my unspoken plea. "Hope, you're wanted at the police station. Officer McCrory called. Well, it was Mrs. Dwight. She's the one that does all his secretarial things. I don't know how she does it. With how hard of hearing she is, how can she make a call? Or take a call? Plus, the woman is nearly blind."

Ruthie leaned against the open door. The smell of grease and the noise of the bar leaked out as she settled into the conversation. She tipped her huge glasses, amplifying her eyes to enormous proportions. "Sure, I need these things, but then again, I can see. Now Mrs. Dwight, her face is practically on the counter trying to read or write on any piece of paper. She needs one of those big magnifying glass things—"

"Ruthie." Chance pushed his hand through his hair, making it stand on end like a deranged rooster. Despite my concerns about visiting the police station, I didn't interrupt Ruthie, because I was grateful to talk about anything besides Berta. "What do they want Hope for? Is it about Berta?"

"Why would it be about Berta?" I snapped. Why

did my brother continue to imply that I had something to do with her disappearance? Apparently, our *moment* together hadn't dissuaded his preference for his girlfriend. "It's probably about that stupid reporter again. Officer McCrory cornered me once already about that jerk, probing for details. He doesn't like me."

"Who doesn't like you?" Ruthie cocked her hip and rested her hand on the fleshy shelf provided, ready to commence battle against whomever dissed her niece. "The reporter guy or Officer McCrory?"

"Both." Unfortunately, in the last few months, I'd accumulated more than my share of enemies. My sarcastic wit, teamed with a coveted ability to control the flow of hope and happiness, didn't endear me to many.

Ruthie waved me off and made a chuffing sound. "I doubt that. What's not to like?" She beamed, displaying her unusually white teeth.

"Anyway, Mrs. Dwight wasn't clear about why Hope needed to go to the station. Wouldn't even give me her recipe for blueberry pie." She shook the dishtowel decorated with roosters replicating Chance's current hairstyle. "Darn women and their possessiveness of their recipes. She's as bad as Tessa."

Chance and I were accustomed to Ruthie's verbal tirades and waited impatiently for her ranting to cease. Lucky for us, nothing irked Ruthie more than a woman taunting her with a coveted recipe. It might be the only thing that saved us from her perpetual chatter. Or it might be the increasing verbal annoyance from the men at the bar waiting for food and drink.

Ruthie turned toward the kitchen, muttering as she departed, "The recipe-hoarding secretary woman only insisted Hope needed to go down to the station. Now."

Chapter Eight

The door swished closed behind me as I walked into the station. My heart thudded against my ribcage. How was it that in a town full of potential suspects for all sorts of wrongdoing, I was always the first one questioned for anything? What did they want me for now?

My attention strayed to the large bulletin board plastered with a multitude of faces all labeled *Missing* at the top. Several covered flyers beneath them were yellow with age. Their corners lay deteriorating and curling at the edges. Either the old ones weren't routinely removed, or more likely, they were never found.

I pulled my attention away, resolving that Berta's face wouldn't join the others on the forgotten board. Mrs. Dwight was bent with her nose inches away from a form. I steeled myself to commence the near impossible task of gaining her attention. Unlike the attentiveness she lavished upon Chance, she found me practically invisible. "Mrs. Dwight?"

No response. After enduring the limited faith of my boyfriend and family today, I abandoned my tenuous grip on appropriate manners. I gripped my hips and leaned in to shout, "Mrs. Dwight!"

The rise and fall of her head a few inches above the counter height provided the only indication that her vertically challenged body jumped. Her startled expression might be humorous if I didn't fear my impatience might send her to an early grave.

"What are you yelling about?" She scrunched her face and reached to fiddle with her hearing aid. The tip of her tongue slipped out as she concentrated on adjusting the aid with her thick fingers. "There. I got the volume set pretty good now." She squinted toward me.

"Oh, it's you, Hope." She hurried around the counter with her arms spread. Her rapid pace caused her to waddle like a charging gorilla and appear just as frightening.

I stumbled back from her unexpected response and braced myself for whatever she had in store. At my last visit, the elderly woman didn't give me the time of day, let alone the hug she appeared intent on delivering.

I tensed, unaccustomed to touching anyone but my family, or Griffith, since they were the only ones unaffected by my gift. My abilities of giving and receiving hope stirred as she embraced me. I held my breath and squeezed my eyes shut, blocking my thoughts to prevent from inciting my ability with her physical contact.

She pulled back from where she buried her cheek on my chest. "It's so good to see you."

"Really?" She'd never been happy to see me before. Ever. She usually didn't acknowledge me. I snuck a peek at my hands and sighed with relief. No escaping tendrils of fog seeking to feed on her emotions. "Well, you called to say I needed to come down here."

"What? Oh, yes, Officer McCrory did want to talk

to you. How is Chance, by the way?" She snagged a metal tin from the corner of the counter and shoved it at me. "I made peanut butter cookies for him. Could you please deliver them?"

"He's fine. I guess." I clutched the cookie tin like a shield and moved further away in case she considered another awkward hug. Although she had little chance of winning my brother's affection, since she was well over seventy years old, she clung to the possibility. She went through varying degrees of what I thought of as *courtship by baking* by either overwhelming Chance with baked goods or withholding the treats. The police station was on his route, so she ordered and returned stuff constantly to see Chance. That was, until Berta showed up and dashed her hopes.

She rocked on her heels and beamed. "He's better off without that Bertha girl anyway."

"Her name is Berta." I lifted my brows. The root of Mrs. Dwight's bizarre affectionate behavior toward me now revealed. It was part of her quest to eliminate competition for my brother's affection.

"What's the difference? She's gone, isn't she?" Mrs. Dwight acted as if I were an ally. Her behavior might've been amusing before, but now with Berta missing—and the unwanted accosting of hugs—her possessive comments were disturbing.

"I don't think she's gone," I said. Mrs. Dwight's eagerness to be rid of Berta made me uncomfortable. Until now, I'd never considered her capable of anything more violent than overfeeding Chance. Her grateful grin made me fear she believed I had something to do with Berta's departure. "Where did you hear she was missing? It's only been since this morning."

She shrugged. "You don't need to be missing for long around here to be gone."

Once I inserted enough personal space between us, I determined what else was different about the cookie cajoling cougar. "You changed your hair." The bun was gone. The chic cut was better suited for a woman half her age. Though a poor style choice for her, the hairdo knocked a decade off her age.

The day was getting stranger and stranger. If I thought I lived in the twilight zone before, this confirmed it. I self-consciously touched my kinky curls, regretting that I barely took the time to douse them with product as I eyed her smooth locks. Even this gregarious grandma had better hair than me. "Did you use a flat iron?"

"Is that what that thing is called?" She patted the hair resting at a sharp angle against her puffy cheek. "The lady at the salon insisted I needed the contraption to complete the style. I darn near burned my fingerprints off trying to figure out how to use it."

"I never used a flat iron." One glance at my hair on any given day validated my confession.

She squinted to study me. "You should try it. It could help with your hairstyle. That," her glasses rose when she scrunched her nose, "or something. You really should do something if you want to get a man."

"I have a man." At least I think I did, despite Griffith appearing none too pleased with me lately. I crossed my arms, deciding I'd had enough chitchat. It was time to get to the point of my reluctant visit. Besides, receiving beauty tips from Mrs. Dwight was almost worse than Berta's unyielding advice. "Can I see Officer McCrory now?"

I wanted to get this over with and get the hell out of here before having to endure further beauty advice...or hugs.

Mrs. Dwight flinched away from my icy stare and opened the internal door to the office. As I passed through her voice trailed me. "Before you leave I have more cookies in my car for you to take to your brother. Chocolate chip, I know how much he likes chocolate."

The door closed behind me, yet her chattering drifted through the barrier about the things Chance liked to eat. My brother rivaled a beanpole. Lucky for him his metabolism could withstand the likes of Mrs. Dwight.

Officer McCrory's feet were crossed at the ankles and propped on the desk. He didn't move an inch when I entered, but his gaze never left me. He sighed and linked his hands over his large belt buckle, one that had gone out of style with the mustache sprouting beneath his long, thin nose. I fidgeted beside his desk until he gestured to the chair facing him. "Take a seat."

I would've preferred to stand, but without knowing why I was summoned here yet, I didn't want to risk aggravating him more than necessary. The wooden, hard-backed chair with the spindly bars trailing the back pushed my spine to assume an unnatural, uncomfortable posture. The small couch against the wall looked more comfortable, but most likely housed a multitude of germs. And I didn't want him to think this was a social visit.

I perched on the edge of the chair, lacing my fingers to tuck them under the hem of the fabric of my jacket. He wouldn't be able to see the fog if it leaked from me, but I would, and it would rattle my taut nerves. The struggle to maintain a firm grip on my emotions was real, and significantly more challenging when sitting in a police station for unspecified reasons. "You wanted to talk to me?"

"Yes." He drew the word out.

Despite my desire to remain annoyed at the inconvenience of making the trip downtown and abandoning Aunt Ruthie at the bar, his deep throaty voice tempted me to relinquish my guard—which is exactly what he wanted. But I was more than aware that this wasn't a friendly visit. With Officer McCrory, it never was. We waited, as if challenging the other to blink, until I tired of staring at his pasty white face, which conflicted with his sexy deep voice. "What did you want to see me for?"

"What do you think?" He inclined his head to the side.

I recognized this game. He was waiting to see what I might admit. If I'd cave under the uncomfortable pressuring silence before he revealed what information he'd acquired—if any. This intimidation tactic probably gained more than one spilled secret. As tempting as his voice was, I wouldn't fall for his lame attempt at psychological intimidation. "I have no idea."

I had an idea, but I wouldn't share it with him. That damn reporter had caused me enough trouble.

The officer dropped his feet to the floor and leaned over the desk, closing the space separating us. "When did you last see Berta?"

The unexpected question made me lose my perch on the chair. I slid back to catch myself before I slipped over the edge. My floundering body made me lose my grasp on the calm, cool, façade I struggled to maintain, and I blurted out the first thing springing to mind. "What? This isn't about the reporter?"

I winced at my novice mistake and slipped my fog leaking fingertips under my thighs. *Damn it.*

"Why? Do you have something else to share about the reporter?" His brows rose in a failed attempt to meet the edge of his sandy-haired crew cut. He dipped his head to scribble on the tablet. When he snapped his head up, his gaze locked on mine while he hovered his pen over the page, waiting for me to elaborate.

"What? No. I mean there's nothing else to share. Nothing of significance." Once I lost my calm and cool pretense, reclaiming it proved to be a challenge.

His eyes narrowed as my words tumbled out in a nervous babble. I craned forward to attempt to get a glimpse of what he'd written. Most likely it contained something unrelated, like a grocery list, just to rattle my nerves.

I took a deep breath and shifted against the wooden spindles. The bumpy wood grounded my racing thoughts. Surely his notes were additions of bread, milk, and toilet paper. He probably utilized the note-taking tactic to attempt to make me crack under the pressure and confess to…who knows what?

I leveled my gaze with his. Hopefully my expression portrayed confidence. Too many times I'm assumed guilty until proven innocent. This was not going to be one of those times. Disliking Berta wasn't a crime and neither was going on a bike ride. It figured, the first time I try to be nice it stirs up more trouble than all the times I was rude. "The last time I saw Berta was when we went on a bike ride. I've done nothing that would require me to visit the police station. I'm starting to think you have something against me personally."

He scowled, as if sensing the shift in control and being none too happy about losing the upper hand. "I told you before, we stick together in this town. Since you arrived things have changed. People are disappearing. Not just vagrants or others passing through, but *townies*."

I lifted my chin. No matter how long I lived here, or how many of my family members did, I'd never be considered a townie. Not in this town. I didn't need his disdain. Not when I judged myself all the time, and so far, I'd not been happy with the verdict.

McCrory tapped his pen on the pad. "First Mrs. Shaw and now Berta? People claim there's something different about you, something they can't quite describe. People around here realize when they've got something uncommon about themselves they best keep it private and not go flaunting their…differences."

The town overflowed with weirdoes and misfits. My only blunder was arriving on the scene and propelling Hecate to act. I wondered who reported me to put me back in McCrory's radar, and for what? Had he followed me around or checked on my past? Neither made me comfortable. "From what I've heard, lots of unusual things have always happened here, long before I showed up."

"Not like this," he shook his head, "and not with them all having one common factor—you."

"Listen, I want to find Berta as much as anyone else. But she's only been missing for a day—"

"Around here, a day is a long time. Too long. Especially for a sweet, pretty, young girl like Berta."

He let his inferences hang heavier than the mustache drooping to his chin.

He didn't need to verbalize my fears about Oppressor involvement. "I don't know how your attempt to scare me by throwing out these ridiculous questions and accusations will help find Berta."

I gripped my knees as the anger built. It churned within me like an animal vying for release. The cold tendrils of black fog leaked from my fingers and chilled me to the core. They curled around my calves and rose to press in McCrory's direction, longing to suck the smug smile from his face. I'd grown far too accustomed to the familiar condescending look over my lifetime. "*You* should be out there looking for her. Do your job."

McCrory maintained his position over the desk, unaware of the ribbons of despair desperately seeking his essence. "Where would you suggest I start?"

I cocked my head, ending my role as a damsel in distress. Everyone wanted to save Berta, but only I could save myself. "Ask the reporter, he seemed to know everything about everyone. He was very interested in Berta." I didn't add how Berta verbalized an interest in talking to him as well.

"Seemed? That would be convenient, wouldn't it? The two people giving you trouble in town happen to be in cahoots to cause you distress. Now you're totally innocent and the victim." He tapped his pen on his chin. "Seems I recall you coming in here before, playing the victim. That turned out to be a ruse by you too, didn't it?"

"You called me down here, remember?" As the black tendrils crept across his desk I stood, hoping to rein them in but instead inadvertently released more in their wake. I gritted my teeth, concentrating on controlling them, until one touched the tip of his finger.

His mouth gaped. He felt it. The look on his face confirmed it. First confusion, then fear, and then he focused on me with eyes wide with terror. "What are you?" He whispered.

"Not someone you need to worry about."

****

The bar was packed shoulder to shoulder when I returned. It was almost like old times, seeing Ruthie at the bar serving drinks and straightening every drink stirrer and napkin within her reach. *Almost.*

I stopped in my tracks, stumbled over my feet, and ran into a man waiting to be served. I braced myself on his leather jacket, grateful the fabric shielded my touch. "I'm sorry, I tripped." The man gave me a once over, and then returned his attention to the bar.

The scene would've looked familiar except for Chance. He was doing two things I'd never seen him do before. He sat at the bar with not only a beer, but also an empty shot glass. Remnants of the whiskey he always refused—claiming the potent alcohol would prompt him to make bad decisions and accumulate regrets—lined the glass. He leaned close in a hushed conversation with a huge, tattooed, perpetually angry-looking man.

It appeared Chance had already begun making bad decisions.

Chance couldn't see the Oppressor for what he was like the way I could, but surely he detected the filth encompassing him. The black cloud of oppression swimming around the man couldn't be more clearly revealed to me. The cloud recoiled to swarm around the man when it got too close to Chance. The extraordinary effort to keep his oppressive nature reined in was obvious by the strained expression on the Oppressor's face. A black film briefly coated the whites of his eyes. The Oppressor grimaced, squeezed his eyes shut, and then the black film cleared.

While dodging an elbow from one of the men crowding the bar, I noted the bill folded under Chance's hand. He slid the money toward the man.

Apparently, Chance had purchased his temporary shield from oppression and despair, but for what purpose? It was the equivalent of making a deal with the devil. The sight of the money, and the words Chance shared but I couldn't hear, appeared to excite the creature that constructed his human form from death and desolation. My brother's current state of despair over Berta would be hard to resist for the beasts that fed off hopelessness and misery. The fog of oppression expanded and rose until it mingled in the air with the cloud of cigarette smoke.

Chance raised his beer and took another drink. I gasped and covered my mouth when a slight black residue filmed over my brother's eyes before he closed them with the swallow. Tiny tendrils of fog leaked from his hand before dissipating. "No."

I shoved through the throng of men with renewed vigor. Despite being five-foot-nine, my head only reached the armpit of most men in the bar. I dropped my hand on Chance's shoulder. He startled and then turned.

"Can I talk to you a minute?" I raised my brow with the clipped words, implying it was more of a command than a question.

Chance looked to the man. "I'll be right back." He slid off the stool to follow me.

"I'll be here." The tip of the man's tongue peeked from his lips, tasting the essence of those nearby—especially me. His mouth gaped when he took me in. No doubt he could sense my overabundance of hope, ripe for the taking. My intense glare prompted him to turn away.

"Outside." I tugged on Chance's shirt and marched ahead. The crowd parted as I went. They couldn't see my face but must've detected the anger shimmering from within me. I spun toward Chance as soon as we reached the parking lot. "What the hell do you think you're doing? Do you have a death wish?" My gaze drank in every part of him but didn't detect any more Oppressor fog. "Show me your birthmark."

"What?" He gaped in confusion.

"Show me your birthmark, now." I grabbed for his belt and fumbled with the buckle before he shoved me away.

"Keep your voice down. Have you lost your mind?" Chance gripped my elbow, and we moved further from the door as a motorcycle pulled up and parked at the side. The man looked at us with interest and then went inside. Luckily most people in this town excelled at evasion.

I jerked away from him. "Just do it."

"Whatever, if it makes you happy." He unbuckled his pants and lowered the right side on his hip to display the arrow shaped birthmark identical to mine.

A sigh escaped my lips. "I thought you might've been a clone." He wasn't. The clones didn't have the birthmark. It was a sure way to tell them apart from the real thing. Unfortunately, demanding my brother drop his pants to confirm his identity wasn't always convenient—and was perpetually awkward.

"Why, because I was talking to that guy?" He studied me with defiance.

"Yes, that and…" I didn't know if I wanted to tell him about the Oppressor residue I saw in him. *Did I imagine it? Could he handle it?* He had worried so much when he discovered he might be part Oppressor. Revealing this latest observation could propel him further into his rage and recklessness. "I think you're the one who's losing your mind. You do know that guy is an Oppressor, don't you?"

He ran his hand through his hair. The longer pieces flopped down, but a few short ones remained upright. This habit resulted in him always looking like he just rolled out of bed. "I suspected as much. That's why I was talking with him. I sought out the creepiest guy in the bar."

"Why? Besides, I don't know if he's the creepiest, it would be tough to narrow that down." Drake had been worse than all of them put together, but that could've been because he was the only one so far who could invade my mind. He might've been Griffith's half-brother, but he was one hundred percent Oppressor. A shiver ran through me at the memory of the words the one tried to speak in the woods. That couldn't be Drake. He was gone.

"If something happened to Berta in those woods. Something that involved an Oppressor. They'd be bound to know." Chance pushed his hands in his pockets to still their shaking. "Did Griffith say if any of them mentioned anything unusual? Or about where to look for Berta?"

I grimaced, rethinking my initial angry retort. Here we go again. Somehow Chance always reverted the conversation, and the blame, back to Griffith. "Griffith doesn't talk to the Oppressors anymore. Not like that at least. I don't think they trust him after what happened to Drake."

Banishing your own brother did make you kind of a badass, even if he did do it for me. Chance conveniently forgot time after time that Griffith attacked Drake to save him. "He's trying to be a normal guy. But despite that, he's going to ask around."

"A normal guy?" Chance's expression bordered on incredulity. This wasn't hard to achieve, since his normal pleased expression fringed on surprised. "I can't imagine that happening. Don't you think he could make an exception with his whole supposed reform into a good guy to determine if something happened with Berta? Use his influence." His expression hardened. "Whatever means necessary."

This conversation was taking an annoying detour back to Chance's *I don't trust your boyfriend* lecture, and besides, I had to ask. "Has anyone talked to that reporter?"

Chance scowled and raised his voice over the roar of an incoming motorcycle. "Drop it with the damn reporter. Your paranoia is making you blind. She didn't go running to that reporter. She wouldn't do that, and besides, she would've contacted me."

So, that was the problem. Chance had to believe Berta was being held somewhere against her will so he didn't contemplate the other painful possibility. That she might've left him.

My heart clenched at the anguish in his eyes. If Berta was alive, and broke my brother's heart, I might have to kill her myself. My irritation deflated. "Did that guy tell you anything useful?"

He shrugged and studied the ground. "He mentioned a couple places in the woods I could check. Places where he thought lower level Oppressors might fester and breed."

"What? I bet he did. You can't go there and expect to return unscathed. Besides, what if it's a trap? You can't trust that guy. He's telling you to go into the middle of no man's land so he can eradicate you himself."

"I have to. What else do I have to go on?" He tilted his head to study the sky and took a few shaky breaths. He returned his gaze to me. "What did they want with you at the police station?"

Might as well tell him, he would find out eventually. "McCrory wanted to ask me about Berta. Oh, and Mrs. Dwight has more cookies for you. Perhaps you should look at *her* a little more closely. She was awful excited about having Berta out of the picture."

His eyes lit up, but his excitement wasn't about the cookies, or the geriatric jezebel. "Do they know anything? Does Officer McCrory have any suspects?"

I threw my hands up. "Suspects for what? I don't think they've even officially listed her as missing yet. Besides, the only suspect McCrory has is me."

Disappointment clouded Chance's eyes, and his animated expression dissolved. "You? Why would they suspect you?"

"Thank you. At least one person doesn't

automatically blame me for everything that goes wrong around here." I shrugged and then averted my gaze. "He claims because I'm the last one to see her and…apparently, there's been *talk* about me." I made air quotes around the word *talk* and scowled. "I'm too weird to fit in with a whole town of weirdoes."

"We're not weirdoes." Chance straightened. His mouth took on a hard line, displaying his willingness to defend our inherited talents.

"Right. Because everyone has clones and can dispense emotions, that's just as normal as can be." Even though many in this town knew and accepted everything about Oppressors and Enchantlings, and dubbed the Crossroads as the place where the heavens, the earth, and the Underworld met—most weren't comfortable living amongst us.

That could be because we were the only Enchantlings that survived past our twenty-first birthday. This enduring feat resulted in the influx of our abilities when I banished Hecate. Or the locals' discomfort could be because my personality wasn't all that enchanting.

The door banged off the building as Ruthie stepped into the opening. She stood with her hand braced on her thick hips, and her gray braid was coming loose. Her hair frazzled around her scalp like a warped halo. "Would you two stop bickering like a bunch of rug rats and get in here and help me before I pull out the few hairs I got left?"

We silenced when the door slammed behind her and studied each other like a couple of chastised children. I never experienced sibling spats growing up, but Chance had with Destiny. He recovered first and burst out laughing. "I don't think she has to worry about not having enough hair. Have you ever seen her hair out of the braid?"

I smothered my suppressed laughter with my palm. "Nope."

"You don't want to. I stopped at her house one morning after she washed it. Before she took the time to wrestle her hair into the braid. She looked like one of those dandelions exploded on her head. No wonder she braids it." Chance smiled and patted my arm, fulfilling his expected role as referee. I was grateful to glimpse some of his old cheerful self resurfacing and a hint of his sappy smile.

I pulled him into a quick hug. "She'll turn up. You'll see. It's probably all a misunderstanding."

The wind rustled the nearby trees and set them swaying. My smile faltered. Now if only I could find Berta.

Chapter Nine

I deeply regretted suggesting riding bicycles to search the woods for Berta. Initially, I thought the bikes were a good idea, assuming they'd provide a faster escape route, if necessary. Although with how far I lagged, if we were forced to flee, I'd be the first one picked off.

Keeping pace with Chance proved impossible, even after his beer and whiskey overindulgence last night. No hangover for this dude to slow him down. Sweat trickled down my back. I determined my brother should from now on be referred to as *Mr. Superfit*. Now I understood how Berta must've felt trying to keep up with me. I mulled over the apology I owed her while desperately hoping to find her before I collapsed.

With no word from Berta all evening, and no leads from Griffith, Chance grew increasingly distressed and downed beer after beer to calm his fears. Against my better judgment, but desperate to get him to stop his drinking binge, I volunteered to go back in the woods with him to look for her. My fears of what might happen to Chance, vulnerable and distressed on the Oppressor's home turf, outweighed my fear of what we might find. At least he had the sense to agree to wait until morning to venture into the woods. No one was foolish enough to brave these paths in the dark. We'd be no good to Berta dead.

We retraced the route Berta and I took, at least to the best of my recollection. The deeper we went, the more evidence of magic seeping into the soil was confirmed. Like a bizarre, foliage kaleidoscope, the woods shifted and changed with the shedding of the leaves, making it difficult to procure an adequate marker to ensure we were going the right way. The paths crisscrossed and divided like a maze. Unfamiliar paths cropped up, stealthily changing like a hologram, making me question my memory—and my mind.

I realized we'd taken a wrong turn when we arrived at a swampy area. I clamped my hand over my mouth and nose, but the odor still penetrated. My eyes watered. The desolate area, and the unbearable stench, would've been hard to forget.

"This is one of the places that guy, the Oppressor, recommended checking." Chance straddled his bike. He wrinkled his nose from the reek and peered over the still, stagnant water.

"We were nowhere near here." My feet sank in the mud surrounding the area. I knew without a doubt I hadn't been here on the previous ride and could only hope Berta hadn't either. Drowning in the muck of brackish water, crusted with moldy pond scum, would be a horrible way to die.

"Let's keep moving. We can check if any of the places the guy alluded to are nearby." He hopped on his bike and took off before I protested.

I struggled to gain traction in the mud, spewing dirt behind me and up my legs. Once I returned to the stable ground of the trail, I had to hurry to catch up with Chance and not be left in this godforsaken area.

He pedaled with increasing speed, as if his haste

would reduce the minutes from passing. He stopped at a narrow, overgrown path to the left of the trail and yelled, "Did you turn here?"

I swallowed to moisten the dirt and desert-like quality of my mouth but was unable to respond. The exertion and my efforts to keep pace had me winded. Perhaps Chance secretly desired to lose me in the woods in payback for my carelessness with Berta.

I slowed my bike and dismounted when I reached him. The long pull from my water bottle couldn't have been more delicious. Sweat trickled down my face and arms and pooled in every crevice of my body. My muscles quivered with the unaccustomed exercise two days in a row, and my ass ached from the hard, unforgiving seat.

"No, we stayed on the path. I told you I didn't want to risk getting lost. We didn't go that far." I wiped my brow with the back of my arm. My orange windbreaker glowed like a beacon, just as I intended. The hunters in these woods weren't of the human variety and wouldn't be deterred by camouflage. Their senses peaked on emotions. My choice of the bright obnoxious color would assist Griffith in locating me if I got lost, collapsed from exercise overdose—or worse.

At least I assumed Griffith would look for me if I didn't return by the time I designated. I didn't ask him if he thought this was a good idea or let him know about my plan. His response was bound to be incredulous and angry. So, I left him a note after he went to work at the liquor store.

No doubt he'd be furious that I went this deep into the woods without him. I'd deal with his fury later. I couldn't let Chance go alone, and calming the savage beast that was my boyfriend was preferable to enduring Chance and Griffith's bickering the entire time. There was only so much male ego I could stand. I was liable to sacrifice myself to the first Oppressor we came upon to escape their quarrelling.

Chance knelt in the dirt and pointed at faint tire tracks, pushing aside the heavy leaves that concealed most of the rutted dirt. "It looks like you stopped here. Are you sure you didn't turn?" He stood and peered up the path. The thick woods allowed very little visibility to determine where the path led. The heavy branches hung low and swallowed up the narrow trail.

I scoured my memory. "I did stop once for my shoelace." I peered around. The woods all looked the same once you were in them. They presented with rows after rows of thick, menacing trees and impenetrable underbrush. "Maybe it was here. But I didn't turn, I kept going."

Chance's eyes narrowed, and his mouth formed an unnatural hard line. "You kept going without her?"

"At that time, she was still behind me." At least I thought I could see her then, and that this was where I might've tied my shoe. My defense sounded weak against his accusation, but I was tired of being the scapegoat. I pressed my lips together to prevent from blurting out how this wasn't my fault, and that I didn't realize I needed to babysit Berta on a bicycle ride. Somehow, I didn't think whining would gain me any sympathy.

Chance stared up the narrow path in indecision. A crease of worry lined his forehead. "Maybe she went up the path and got lost. Why don't you put your hands on the ground to try to get a vision?"

"What?" Put my hands on the ground? He knew me better than that. "I don't know how I get my visions." I backed away. His hopeful expression deterred me from insisting that he consider the possibility that Berta might've left town on her own accord.

The longer strands of his hair clung to his cheeks among the smears of dirt and dust. His exhaustion was barely concealed by his sheer determination. "Just try, it can't hurt, and you might see something about Berta that could help us."

That's what I was afraid of more than seeing nothing—seeing something. A vision could hurt in more ways than one. In these woods, there were probably a lot of horrific things that remained unseen. Especially if I received a vision like the first one I experienced when Destiny died…

After meeting my brother's optimistic expression, I dropped my attention to the ground. The swirls of dirt and leaves appeared innocent enough. I knelt, resting my hands on my knees. I took a few deep breaths and ignored Chance's puzzled expression. I'd never told him all the details of what I see in the visions. No reason for us both to be tormented.

My hands trembled as I laid them on the hard, cool dirt. A rustling in the foliage had my eyes opening wide, and my lingering boldness fading. A chipmunk peered back.

"What?" Chance laid a hand on my shoulder.

"Nothing." Infecting him with my fears wouldn't be good for either of us. I drew courage from his close presence in order to close my eyes. The sounds of the animals of the forest assured me there were no

Oppressors nearby. Thus providing me with an earlier indication before I came face to face with a hope-sucking, desperation-inducing asshole. The animals would become silent if an Oppressor approached, as if their stillness could shield them. They didn't realize their sound didn't give them away. The scent of their fear did.

My thoughts raced. I sought a pleasant memory to still my anxiety. The dry, earthy scent of the leaves reminded me of the time Aunt Tessa and I rented the small house with a smaller back yard. We raked a big leaf pile in the back yard. I even convinced her to jump in once. The leaves embedded in Tessa's hair had given her the appearance of a deranged scarecrow. The image made me smile.

"Do you see something?" Chance's voice quivered with excitement.

My smile dissolved with the guilt of dwelling in a happier time when I should be thinking about Berta. "No. Nothing."

I stood and brushed dirt from my knees. A thick millipede raced across the path. "I don't think I can call for a vision."

"You said it happened when you got the business card, and when you touched the scarf." Chance grabbed his bike, booting the kickstand with frustration.

I shrugged, understanding his desire to cling to any hope when faced with being powerless. If only I could provide him with a little hopefulness, as I could others, even if it was false. His desperation broke my heart. "I guess it did, but that's the first time that happened."

Chance mounted his bike and pushed off with renewed vigor. "Fine. Let's go further up the path."

"Chance, wait." He ignored my plea and sped away. Without Chance, I didn't know if I could muster the courage to explore that path. It didn't just look ominous…it felt like it.

"Wouldn't this be a good time to send a clone?" I yelled at his back. Even if the process exhausted him, it would be worth avoiding an off-road excursion into the depths of this foliage funhouse. Going into the woods was never a good idea, but veering off the trail into this beaten bush, well this was just stupid. Chance was desperate to find Berta, and desperate people did crazy, unreasonable things. I only hoped his foolishness didn't kill us both.

"Wait for me." I mounted my bike and picked up my pace to keep Chance in sight. There was no way Berta would've followed this path. It was too damn creepy and dark. Even with the sun out, the trees blocked the sky from view and cast the path into permanent twilight. It was like being swallowed up by a branch entwined, leafy coffin, and it was all uphill. *Damn it.*

Eventually I succumbed to the burning in my thighs and dismounted to push to the top of the hill. Chance, of course, was already there. His silhouette reflected where he waited. The trees spanned open with a break in the uppermost part of the leafy canopy. The sunlight shone on him, making him appear luminous. He stared off into the trees, lowered the kickstand, and disappeared into the woods.

"Chance? Wait." I struggled to pick up my pace on the steep hill. My ears popped with the elevation, and my leg muscles screamed. By the time I reached the top, I hung over the handlebars for support. I wiped sweat from my forehead with the back of my arm. My hand trembled on the bottle as I took a swig of water. There was no sign of my brother.

My heart rate elevated as I scanned the vacant space and slowed my bicycle. "Chance?"

"Over here."

His voice came from the left, muted by trees and thick woods. My feet connected with the path, and my terror abated. My heart raced from pedaling, and my mouth had long gone dry, but my unease increased at the thought of leaving the path. I considered waiting here. Then I contemplated how I'd feel if I ended up responsible for the loss of Berta and my brother.

I straightened in my unforgiving bicycle seat and dismounted. I was an Enchantling, damn it. I'd wrestled with the Queen of the Underworld and won. Time to prove I wouldn't be scared off by extra foliage. Plus, I was hungry, dirty, and more than a little sick of these woods today.

I pushed my bike across the path and parked it beside Chance's. It leaned to the side in the soft earth, risking tumbling. Although it wasn't like there were going to be any other bikers coming this deep in the woods or up this mountain to worry about my bike being in their way.

I stormed across the dirt and stones and parted the shrubbery like a curtain. The branches of the trees swung back as fast as I pushed them away, swatting at my face and slowing my pace. I cursed under my breath and then yelled to Chance, "Keep talking so I can find you."

"Okay."

I rolled my eyes. "Yeah, that one word helped.

Now I can easily find that needle in the haystack."

I strained to hear the birds and animals scurrying through the underbrush and caught a glimpse of what resembled a cabin through the trees. While stepping over a log, my toe snagged on the rough bark. A tree trunk provided a brace to catch myself to avoid falling face-first to the ground. The rough bark cutting into my hand and the moss tickling my fingertips grounded me. Haste wouldn't help in the woods. It would only increase my probability of doing something reckless. A few deep breaths slowed my racing heart and enabled me to focus.

The heavy foliage thinned, then ended. I stumbled into a small clearing surrounding the cabin. The trees shied away from the front. Swarms of cicadas gathered in the trees closest to the cabin. Their loud ominous song vibrated through the air and made my skin crawl. The poor excuse for a structure had foliage pressing against the wrecked building from behind. Moss climbed the sides and vines snaked across the roof as if attempting to swallow the building. My gut clenched and raised all my alarms. Everything about the place just felt wrong.

Chance stood in front, peering at the structure with his hands on his hips. He stepped on the sagging wood serving as a flimsy excuse for a porch.

The confidence I mustered waivered. The dilapidated structure looked like something built for one of the horror movies I snuck in as a kid. Tessa hated them. She forbade me to watch the flicks promoting monstrous people, which made them even more tempting. Little did I know she despised the shows so much because many of the creatures in the movies—the monsters—were more real than I realized.

"Chance? Maybe I should wait by the bikes. We don't want anyone to steal them." The feeble excuse sounded legitimate enough. That is, if we were in an area boasting any people other than Chance and I, and if our old, used bikes combined weren't less valuable than the cheapest new one you could buy.

The only thing we might run into out here was a low-level Oppressor. An unformed Oppressor would be as likely to successfully hop on a bike and steal it as I was to cook Thanksgiving dinner.

I shuddered. The ominous path I braved to get here felt like a walk in the park compared to this creepy-ass monstrosity of a shack. My breath caught when Chance opened the makeshift door and disappeared inside.

"Shit." The isolation of the woods weighed heavy without my bike and my brother. I shoved my hands in my pockets and hunched my shoulders, trying to make myself as small as possible. Despite my desire to stay as far from this shit hole as possible, Chance was in that creepy cabin, and maybe Berta was too. *Damn it.*

I had to go in.

I stamped through the long weeds in front of the cabin. The dry stalks caught on my pants and clung like skeletal fingers. No one in their right mind would willingly enter a house resembling a prop on a horror set. But my brother wasn't currently in his right mind. Love had that unfortunate side effect.

Hodgepodge décor decorated the outside, as if the clutter of the owner's mind spilled out to the porch. An oar from a paddleboat hung across the side, tangled within a bunch of fisherman netting and a few oversized bobbers. A plethora of odds and ends littered the netting, creating a creepy display of discarded junk.

My step slowed as I approached. Thanks to Chance barging in, I couldn't leave him now, but it took all my willpower to approach this monstrosity.

My heartbeat raced as if it might burst from my chest. My palms became sweatier than they already were, and I repeatedly wiped them on my pants. Any possibility of drawing out my hope-stealing tendrils to use as a weapon dried up as fast as my saliva.

Apparently, I'd discovered my kryptonite. A creepy abandoned cabin in the woods.

Dirt crept over an engraved stone that lay partially buried, as if trying to reclaim the rock to the earth. I leaned over and squinted at the faded, worn date. The inscription might as well say *shit, this place is old*.

The cabin's ability to remain upright amazed me. It validated the expression of how things weren't made like they used to be...or that evil never dies.

I shuddered with an unexpected chill when I tentatively placed my foot on the bottom porch step. The wood groaned as I released my full weight to test its strength and didn't give me confidence that it would hold. The trek back to town would be exhausting enough without a sprained ankle or a broken leg if I fell through the floor.

After gathering my limited courage, I sprung up the remaining two steps. I stood on the porch, as if I were just popping in for a visit with friends. Although if any friend of mine took to decorating their stoop with a mixture of garbage and empty bottles, I'd push them for an intervention of their hoarder ways.

I walked slowly across the narrow porch, rotating my gaze and anticipating an attack from something at any moment. Since Chance went inside, the silence loomed. The window situated to overlook the porch was completely occluded with wine bottles. They lay vertical, stacked upon each other, replacing the glass that once occupied the window. Whether it was to prevent anyone from looking in or out of this window, or an alternate odd decorative use for the empty bottles of someone with an obvious affinity for booze, the reason was unknown.

Alcohol also happened to be the Oppressors' drug of choice. Liquor helped to crush and forget the overwhelming desire to feed upon others' misery. Otherwise Oppressors would never be able to seamlessly blend into society. Great. Why not just barge up to their house? Although I supposed if you lived in the middle of nowhere and were required to tackle that massive hill every day, you might be more inclined to drink at home to avoid the trip to the bar.

A chair leaned toward the right with an uneven leg. It sat beside a small makeshift table outside the door. A dirty mug was abandoned on the table with a muddy inch of stagnant liquid in the bottom. I grimaced at the large bug crawling along the inside of the glass after it partook in a drink of the brew.

The seat provided a perch to observe anyone climbing the hill long before they were aware of the discreet observation. It provided a lookout of sorts. A perfect place to sit and study the path, ensuring there were no unexpected visitors. Perfect for someone, or something, that didn't like surprises. *Had whatever dwelt here seen us coming? Was it waiting inside?*

I stood in front of the wooden door with paint chipped and peeling in long layers. "Chance?"

My voice came out much lower than I anticipated as fear gripped my vocal chords. The knob felt cool under my hand. I wiggled my fingers to stimulate the ability I usually forced to lie dormant…nothing. I took a step away. I wasn't ready.

I never called upon my gift like this, but I couldn't walk in unprepared. Up to this point, only anger awakened my ability to oppress. Apparently fear and repulsion didn't provide enough stimulus. My severe unease even crushed my natural irritability.

I clenched my fists and focused on rousing my emotions. Each time I sought to elicit hostility at the reporter, my concern for Berta—and now for Chance—doused the fiery burn in a smoldering pit of worry. A glance at my fingertips confirmed my attempts at inducing my oppressing abilities were failing.

Too much time had passed since I heard anything from Chance. I couldn't delay any longer. My brother might need me.

After twisting the knob, I shoved the door hard and stepped to the side. I tensed, raised ineffective fists, in case someone or something anticipated my entrance. The door shimmied in a few inches and then stopped. The wood of the door was swollen and distorted from years of exposure to the elements.

Using my hands, and scarce upper body strength, I leaned against the wood and pushed with all my might. The door groaned with resistance and scraped loudly against the floor. When the door gave, I grunted with the release of the dead weight and stumbled through the dark entrance. My sprint stopped unexpectedly when I bumped into something. Once again, I bent into what I hoped was an intimidating fighter's stance.

My ears pounded with the echo of my racing heart and my shallow breathing. A few rays of sunlight permeated the cracks in the walls and windows. I turned as my eyes adjusted to the dim lighting. My stomach plummeted with fleeting relief as I confronted the accosting furniture. Mounds of clutter filled the cabin.

A metal bunkbed rested against the back wall. The stench of the filthy mattress reeking of mold and mildew had me wrinkling my nose. A stone fireplace flanked the other wall. Its dilapidated state made its functionality questionable. Sections of wood leaned against the side of the hearth. It wasn't clear whether the tinder pieces were to mend the ill repair of the place or for burning. This house of horrors would require much more attention than a few sections of lumber.

A chair with a pink and green flowered décor looked awkward and out of place. The outdated, once stylish furniture appeared as if it belonged in someone's grandmother's house. The middle of the cushion was sunk in from either years of wear, or an internal nesting space for all manner of rodents.

I shuddered and clutched my arms. Despite not encountering Chance, any Oppressors, or even one rodent, once I entered the house, I became convinced I wasn't alone. Something alive dwelled inside. I suspected the abnormal awareness emanated from the cabin itself. The certainty that a malignant sensation seeped from the dwelling and penetrated my tense shell making me extremely uncomfortable.

The cabin noted my presence. It knew I was here, and I wasn't sure if I was welcome. Pinpricks tracked my skin as if an animal tested my scent. The hairs rose on my arms and neck. I drew my shoulders up in response.

I should run. I should leave. I stood frozen to the spot.

My muscles tensed again and contracted in preparation to flee, but I froze. I was too frightened to initiate the movement. The paralyzing feeling, the hypnotic effect, was reminiscent of the time Griffith called upon his Oppressor skills to convince me to follow his bidding. Except the cabin's lure to obey was ten thousand times stronger. Tentacles of longing craned toward me, demanding I relinquish the hope I stored within.

I had to find Chance and get out—before I couldn't.

I clenched my teeth and called upon all my willpower to break free of the invisible clutch. With a gasp, I lurched forward, my feet stuck to gummy spots on the filthy floor. No other footprints joined my own in the dust I tracked through, but it did reveal substantial amounts of mouse droppings amongst the cobwebs and crud. At this point I would welcome vermin. At least I wouldn't be completely alone in here.

"Hope?"

I spun to locate the source of the voice. My ricocheting heart slowed when I recognized the owner. "Chance?"

Heavy silence greeted me. I frowned. *I know I heard his voice.* With an effort, I peeled my feet from the sticky floor and turned to study the surrounding walls. The crackling of my now crusty shoes echoed throughout the cabin. I strained my ears, and racked my brain, to recollect which direction the call originated from.

After suffering the constant invasion of my dead relatives chattering in my head, I became more attuned in determining the source of a voice to avoid appearing unstable by seeking out unseen dead people. The call had been faint compared to the amplification of each sound surrounding me. It couldn't have come from inside.

"Don't go."

I froze. Oh, hell no. That was from inside the cabin. The otherworldly whisper from the wood prompted me to rush for the door. Somehow the heavy, swollen door had soundlessly closed behind me.

I fumbled with the knob, rattling it with enough force to knock one of the screws free. It bounced off my shoe and rolled to join the discarded rubbish piled in the corner. The knob thumped back and forth against the door with my struggle. As another screw shook loose to dangle from its perch, a moment of terror embraced me. I considered the possibility of unintentionally tearing off the knob and being stuck within the cabin, leaving me with no method of escape.

I lunged for a discarded piece of wood and swung it against the door like a makeshift bat. "Let!" The wood struck against the door with a thud. "Me!" Splinters flew from the log. "Out!"

As I recognized the fruitlessness of my behavior, I stopped. I couldn't even hold the upper hand with a nonliving structure. I bent over my knees, huffing. The additional exertion had exhausted me, and the action did little to contribute to my escape. Although it did help to alleviate my building frustration.

Tendrils of black fog rushed from my fingertips to surround me. The power seeped into me, soothing and channeling my anger. I dropped the wood with a clatter and placed my hand on the knob. "I'm leaving *now*."

The subtle shift in the air surrounding me had to be my imagination. Because believing I upset the cabin by announcing my imminent departure opened my mind to a whole new level of insanity.

A slight twist to the knob prompted the door to open smoothly, without the prior resistance. I stepped on the porch and greedily gulped the stagnant air. The sounds of the forest came back in a rush, as if someone turned the muted volume up full blast.

I blinked a few times to allow my vision to adjust to the overwhelming brightness after my abrupt departure from the twilight zone. The hazy fog emanating from my fingertips dissipated. My initial concern about my brother rushed to consume my thoughts until I spotted him a few feet from the cabin.

He cupped his palm over his eyes to shield them from the ray of sunshine peeking through the thick canopy of trees. I smiled. I was never so happy to see his face. His forehead was lined with concern, and his mouth pulled in a tight line. My smile faltered. He appeared worried about me. *Just how long was I in that cabin?*

I wouldn't think about that now. I sighed with relief when Chance performed his customary nervous gesture of running his hand through his hair. A light breeze fluttered through the trees. Until that moment, I hadn't permitted myself to consider what could've happened to my brother. The mystery of what did happen to me remained.

"How did you get out here?" I would've seen him if he passed me to exit the cabin. "Did you come out another way?"

"I never went in. Why would you go in there by yourself? I've been looking all over the place for you." He sagged with relief and leaned against a tree. He reached behind to brace his hands against the bark for support.

I put my hands on my hips, eager to defend what remained of my sanity after exiting the creepy cabin. I would never have gone in if it weren't with the intent to save him. "Yes, you did go in, I saw you. Then the house, I thought I heard it…"

"That was a clone. Do you think I'd actually physically go in *that* house?" His eyes widened. "The thing looks like it's about to collapse at any minute. Are you crazy?"

"Thanks a lot." I stormed down the steps, hoping none of the weak lumber would snap from my weight. My worries about the resounding echoing noise dispelled, since the cabin frightened me more than any Oppressor ever had.

"Wait, you thought you heard what? The house?" He furrowed his brow. "That's not possible."

I raised a brow. "Oh, we have been way past possible for a while, brother." Despite realizing my irritation prickled more because his comment about my sanity landed too close to home after my odd experience, I vented anyway. "I went into the house because you did. How in the hell am I supposed to know when you're sending a clone to do your dirty deeds? Do I have to ask you to drop your drawers every time to make sure it's the real you?" I poked my finger in his chest, leaving a smear of grease and dirt on his shirt.

"Did you see anything?" Chance rubbed the spot where I jabbed him.

"Didn't you? Or should I say your clone?" I tilted my head back and forth with exasperation. My poor attempt at intimidation floated away with dust, splinters of wood, and my lingering unease.

He shrugged and then reached to free a chunk of spider web ensnared in my curls. "Not much, I couldn't maintain the clone long after exerting so much energy bike riding. I was too exhausted. I only got a glimpse while I was inside. It looks deserted, though."

I opened my mouth and closed it, stopping myself from blurting, *at least from human habitation*. Saying that would arouse Chance's curiosity, and he'd question what I experienced. How could I describe the weird phenomenon? Plus, I was trying to present as more normal than not. Telling him that the cabin spoke to me, and that I upset the dilapidated shack when I left, would only confirm his casual concern about my sanity, or he'd want to go back in to investigate.

The dark rings under his eyes confirmed how much the cloning exhausted him. He'd be no match against a wet noodle, let alone whatever entity claimed that cabin. Besides, I…was afraid to return. "You're right. I think it's deserted." The prickling of the skin along my spine challenged my declaration.

Chapter Ten

"What are you doing here?" Griffith stepped away from the door to permit me to enter.

"Not quite the welcome I expected. I'm here because you're avoiding me—again." I crossed my arms to appear irritated. This was a challenge, since Griffith's scent alone always soothed my frazzled nerves. "So, I came to you instead."

I couldn't believe I found his house on my own, but after trekking through the woods seeking Berta, I shouldn't be surprised. When I asked him for directions a few weeks ago, he provided cryptic rhyming instructions about closing my eyes, and following the skies, and a bunch of other *mumbo jumbo*.

After I complained his whimsical directions wouldn't get me anywhere but lost, he explained the route in a logical way with odd landmarks. There were no real road signs, and the trees shifted with a mind of their own, so I doubted any method of explanation would ensure I arrived at my destination.

In retrospect, I suspected he performed some kind of hypnotizing spell so I could find his place. The ability to alter my memory like that would've come in handy for high school algebra. He'd swayed my thoughts before without my knowledge. Now that I was keen to his manner of influencing, he tended to avoid doing that because he realized I didn't like it. In this instance, I'm sure he justified his action as safeguarding me from becoming lost in the depths of the woods, which was much more dangerous than my wrath.

"Was it worth it?" Griffith remarked cryptically and stalked away, leaving me frowning at his retreating sexy behind clad in tight jeans.

He was worried about me? That must mean he still cared for me. For the love of tequila, his exasperation made me desire him more. I shook my head to dispel his delicious scent filling my nostrils and thoughts of his stare-worthy ass.

I doubt he referred to the courage I mustered to mount the steps to his porch, which freaked me out more than the woods. The house looked like an entity of its own, and felt oppressive and evil with the dark, gloomy exterior and ancient structure. Although if I compared it to the cabin, Griffith's house felt as welcome as a bed and breakfast and just as cozy.

I shrugged out of my jacket and hung it on the old wrought iron coat rack flanking the door. My steps echoed through the large foyer. A shiver ran through me. How could he stand to live in this huge old house alone in the middle of nowhere? He claimed he was accustomed to his solitary existence and preferred his privacy. Not that he had anything to compare it to since he lived here most of his life. "Was what worth it? Coming here or seeing you?"

He spun to face me. His underlying anger erupted through his standard composed expression. "No. I'm referring to your gallivanting around in the woods. You left me a note. Really? A note?" He shook the offending paper. The wrinkled, torn document appeared to have taken the brunt of his anger. "I swear you have a death wish. Are you looking for any excuse to use your abilities again?"

The ferocity in his remark drew my back up in defense. He was supposed to be my ally, but I should've anticipated his reaction. "I had no choice."

"Only because you chose to take her in the woods in the first place." The tiny haze of lights ignited around him as his frustration built.

I pushed my hands in my pockets to keep from reaching for him for my own selfish comfort. *He had to understand.* Griffith was the only one who truly understood me better than myself. He was my rock in this ever-changing town. "I had to help look for Berta. There isn't a choice in everything. I couldn't let Chance go on his own. Yes, I went because it was my idea in the first place, but also because he's my brother. It's not safe for him."

His gaze locked with mine. "You didn't worry about yourself? Or consider how much worry you've caused me? Damn it, Hope, you, of all people, should realize what lurks undercover in the daylight has little fear at night and outside of town."

Griffith always saw right through me and my petty motives. The trait was what I loved and hated about him. I dropped my gaze, wishing I'd never suggested the ride to Berta. That I'd continued with avoiding and aggravating her rather than trying to make an effort. Things were just starting to get better. "I wanted to ride my bike."

My excuse came out like a childish whine, and the tone even irritated me. I didn't want to argue. We hadn't been alone together in days. I missed him. I thought he'd be happy if I surprised him here, since he probably thought I'd never ride all the way to his house. He surely considered his house safe from a pop-in visit from me due to multiple factors such as exhaustion, my terrible lack of direction, and my fear of the things lurking in the underbrush.

"Why won't you just let me buy you a car?" Griffith asked with an air of exasperation.

"No. We talked about this. I'll save up for a car." Griffith already supported me emotionally and protected me physically, I'd be damned if he had to financially support me as well. Although ever since the garage declared my car a worthless piece of junk, I was left trying to figure out how I could afford another vehicle. It was as if the old car gave up after it deposited me in this town.

The twitch in Griffith's jaw revealed how desperately he wanted to continue this argument, but there were more pressing disagreements to pursue. "Regardless, there are paths you could've ridden your bike on in town."

The calm, matter of fact way he spoke validated the depth of his displeasure. The shifting color in his eyes revealed the inner turmoil he struggled with. His stoic strength was displayed, and suppressing his anger validated why he would've made a wonderful leader. "There are plenty of sidewalks and other appropriate places for riding a bike. Especially for someone inexperienced like Berta."

The way he said it, he meant Berta was more than inexperienced on a bicycle. He was referring to her being naïve about the Oppressors as well. "I admit the woods might not have been the best place to ride, but if you're asking in a warped, roundabout manner if we found out anything about her, we didn't."

This further validated my theory about her and the reporter, but I wouldn't press that subject while Griffith was angry. His silence spoke louder than any words. "If you're trying to make me feel worse about Berta, it's working. Besides, there's nothing you can say that I haven't considered, but dwelling in my mistakes and regrets doesn't help."

He turned from me and braced against the wall. He leaned into it, resting his head against his forearm. He clenched and unclenched his hand as the haze waxed and waned around him while he struggled to gain control of his temper. His words were soft and heavy with emotion. "I'm sorry."

I slowly approached. My gut twisted with discomfort at his disapproval. I longed to comfort him, and touch the warmth of his skin, but I wasn't sure how he would respond. I rested my hand on his back. When his shoulders drew together stiffly at my caress, I dropped my hand. "What's wrong? Why are you so angry with me lately? Is it something I said?"

He turned and cupped my face in his hands. I pressed my cheek into his palm, craving his touch. He focused on me with breathtaking intensity. "It's nothing you said."

"Something I did?" I put my hand over his, relishing the familiar tingle running from him into me.

He closed his eyes and lowered his voice to a harsh whisper. "You can't help it. It's who you are."

My stomach dropped. If there was something about me he didn't like, or that upset him, I couldn't fix that. All my life I'd tried to change myself. I finally accepted that I couldn't alter what was inside of me any more than I could change my fingerprint. Good or bad, I was stuck with it. It was what made me who I was. "Who I am?"

He leaned his head back to draw a ragged breath. He dropped his hands, and I immediately noted the absence of his touch. "I've had the dreams again," he said.

His statement chilled me to the core. "What?" Surely I misunderstood him. "You can't. I mean that's impossible. She's gone. Hecate gave us the dreams…right?" Our identical dreams brought me to him. My eyes sought his for an answer, but his expression wasn't the reassuring one I needed. He appeared distraught.

He shook his head. "I don't know. I thought so, but maybe…maybe the dreams have always been our own."

Some of my tension eased, considering the possibility that the connection was ours alone and had nothing to do with Hecate or the Underworld. "Well that wouldn't be so bad, would it? We've always felt connected, like we belonged together." I curled my fingers in the hair at the base of his skull, and then stilled. "Which dream are you having?"

Once I found Griffith I no longer experienced the odd, recurrent dreams. When he told me we shared the dreams, he said he had two very different dreams. In one we ended up together, and the other—he killed me.

He stared at the window over my shoulder, as if either recalling the dream or memorizing the pattern of the heavy drawn curtain. "The dream isn't the same as the one before. We're physically fighting. You're aware of your abilities, as you are now, and you're fighting back."

"Are you...are you hurting me?" I couldn't ask if he killed me in the dream. I didn't want to hear him say it. The problem with his immunity to my ability to give hope or take it away was that I'd never experienced a vision about him yet, either. Perhaps he was immune to that ability of mine as well.

"I'd never hurt you. But your anger, your gift, it excites me—in the dream." He hurried to add and then averted his gaze.

"Just in the dream?" I didn't have to ask. I saw the answer in his eyes. The reason he avoided me. The tables were turned. Just as he'd tried to tempt me with the darkness inside him before, I tempted him now to unleash the part of himself he despised without realizing it.

He returned his attention to me and touched my face, running his thumb over my cheek to settle on my mouth. His breath caught when he pulled my lip down on the corner. "You are so much temptation for me to go dark. For you I could abandon my attempts at shunning my nature and forget the evil that exists inside me. The ecstasy in your eyes as you fed from the reporter, as you absorbed his hopeful essence, was a rush."

He sighed. "I almost didn't stop you because part of me wanted you to finish him. To allow me to enjoy the satisfaction on your face. You're like a drug, tempting me. The problem is that you're an addiction I can't break." He closed his eyes. "I'm not sure I can resist."

"I don't want you to resist me." I captured his thumb in my mouth and lazily circled it with my tongue.

His eyes darkened with desire, and his mouth found mine as he pulled me against him. I molded to his lean muscles and hungrily devoured his lips. His hand rested against the small of my back. The warmth of his touch and the slight pressure burned through the thin fabric of my shirt where my skin begged to be touched. My head fell back, and he trailed kisses along my neck. The damp moisture was rapidly stolen by the heat of our attraction.

"Hope, you will be my undoing." He breathed into my skin, pressing my hair against his face to inhale. "You smell of the woods, of dark and forbidden. Of desires locked away and secrets long buried. How can I resist all that promises? How can I live with myself if I don't?"

With a groan he pushed away to hold me at arm's length. His pupils were expanded huge and dark with desire, practically obliterating the gray of his eyes. His lips were red from our kisses, trying to hold back the words yearning for release. Words I didn't want him to say.

"Is it me you want? Or is it what I can do that you crave?" I trembled from fear, and the overwhelming urge to hear the response I needed. It pained me to ask, but I had to, even though his answer may not make a difference. I couldn't walk away from him if I wanted to. The dreams had brought me to him. I'd endured a nightmare to claim him. I wouldn't lose Griffith now.

He shook his head slowly, keeping his eyes locked on mine. "I'm not sure. The only way to find out is to stay away from you."

"Stay away?" An icy fear chilled my heart. "I don't want you to stay away. I need you."

The whine creeping into my voice should have embarrassed me, but it didn't. The pain burned too raw to conceal. He knew all my secrets anyway. There was no reason to hide how much his words hurt.

Griffith stroked my hair. My curls sprang back with more determination and resistance than I could muster. I ducked my head, but he tipped my chin to face him. "I need you too much. I can't function without you. I must learn how to do that, if I'm to be true to myself."

"It's because of Drake, isn't it? You blame me for what happened, don't you?" My despair morphed into anger, into blaming something, someone else besides me. His feelings had changed after he banished his brother. He may never forgive himself for saving my brother and me over his own. Evil or not, family was family.

"No." He averted his gaze to land on my hand resting on his shoulder. His eyes widened when he noted the telltale tendrils of fog leaking from my fingertips. He looked away.

I persisted, unwilling to drop the subject. "Did you do it because of me? Would you have banished him otherwise?" If he resented me for that, he may never be able to move past that.

"Yes."

He hesitated long enough for me to realize he wasn't sure, and that he didn't clarify which question he answered.

I shoved away from him and turned to grab my coat off the hanger. The rack teetered with the forceful action despite the heavy weight of the wrought iron supporting the jacket. My arm caught in the fabric when

I roughly forced the jacket on. I struggled until I slid my arm through and stomped away to grab the doorknob.

"Please, Hope. Don't leave angry," he pleaded. "I'll still look for Berta, and I'll see you at the bar when I'm working. Chief needs the help. I don't want to let him down."

"But you have no problem letting me down." I didn't turn. I wouldn't allow him to watch me blink away the moisture dampening my eyes. I wanted his love and acceptance, not his pity.

I rushed through the door before he could reply and slammed it behind me. My vision blurred with tears as I fled down the steps. The sound of the masks rattling against the porch in the wind sounded as if the house was laughing at me.

****

Andy looked me over like a starving coyote. I narrowed my eyes. I didn't trust him, but I didn't have much choice. I was almost broke and I wouldn't borrow anything else from my family, and I would never ask Griffith. Especially now. I didn't need a handout when I could take care of myself.

After making my hasty exit from Griffith's on the bicycle and pedaling through the woods, I realized the bike might not be the best choice as my only method of transportation. My desolation drew all likes of Oppressors looking for something to feed on. Leaving Griffith's in a distraught and exhausted state made me an easy target. Luckily my anger overtook my despair. The Oppressor scum searching for a method to take advantage of me hung back, uncertain how to approach.

I was lucky that time, but I wasn't banking on the

bicycle the next time I was alone in the woods. Right then I decided I needed a better mode of transportation, and I couldn't afford a car. "Is it a deal?"

"Sure is." Andy reached to shake my hand, but I drew mine away before he touched me. The eagerness in his eyes betrayed his true intentions.

"On my terms. Always on my terms, not yours." I laid my hand on his arm. Andy and I gasped simultaneously. His from the pleasure I infused into him, mine from the pain in doing so. I gritted my teeth, struggling to maintain control as Andy strained to take more than I intended to give.

"Yes, that's the stuff." He closed his eyes, and his mouth gaped with gratification.

"That's all you're getting for now." I ripped my hand away as he groped for me. "Touch me and I'll knock your teeth out." His teeth weren't in the best repair, so that might be considered a favor. The threat must've made an impression, because he stumbled back a step.

"W—when?" He twisted his trembling hands together. "When can I have a little more? Please, I need it."

"Next week, and then one more time the week after. That's it." I had to space them out. For one, it depleted me if I gave too much, and because Andy was becoming increasingly dependent on the rush. The first time I thought I was helping him when he had a rough day. Unfortunately, I accidently made him an addict—of which I was the only supplier.

"I can't wait—"

"Shut it." I held up my palm. "Not one word to Griffith about this either." Andy worked for Griffith at the liquor store, but he'd more than lose his job if Griffith found out he was begging hope from me. More likely Andy would end up losing more of his remaining teeth. Besides, Griffith discovering Andy begged me to use the ability that drove him away, and my obvious compliance, wouldn't bring him back to me anytime soon. But I was desperate, and my hope dispensing ability was the only thing I had to bargain with.

Andy recoiled. "Seriously? Do you think I'm crazy? I would never tell Griffith *that*. He'd kill me. Heck, he'll kill me if he finds out I gave you the motorcycle."

"If he finds out, just tell him I bought it, fair and square." I winked. That wasn't a lie. I bartered for it by offering him something money couldn't buy in exchange for something he didn't want. At least Andy didn't want the motorcycle as much as he wanted what I offered.

"He'll still be pissed." Andy pouted, appearing to rethink the consequences of his decision.

Too late now. A deal is a deal. Why I took pity on Andy remained a mystery to me. He'd devoted his pathetic life to worshiping Hecate and spent more than one night in the local jail for petty crimes. But he was always nice to me, and he didn't treat me like a freak. Except for his desire to suck the life out of me with his addictive need for hope.

"Just tell him I made you sell it to me if he finds out." There was a strong possibility Griffith would find out. Despite the number of secrets contained within this small, backwoods town, most people seemed to be aware of everything going on with everyone else.

Griffith would believe I intimidated Andy into

selling the motorcycle to me, because Andy realized what I was capable of. Andy knew Hecate hoped I would've chosen to become her protégée on earth. Then she wouldn't have to worry about her underlings wreaking havoc until she walked the earth during the ebony moon. She didn't realize the blood ties with my family were thicker than the watery promises she'd offered.

I lifted the helmet off the back of the motorcycle. Andy always made excuses about having such a small bike, saying it was an old girlfriend's he never got rid of, but that was a lie. He was a little guy. The motorcycle was his. He hadn't ridden it after pulling into the parking lot on his *chick bike* and getting ridiculed by the other guys who rode the big metal beasts.

After I overcame my initial fear of falling off, I discovered I loved to ride on the back of Griffith's motorcycle. The freedom it provided, the thrill of the ride, and the rush from tempting fate were wonderful. I enjoyed it so much I convinced Griffith to let me ride on my own a couple of times.

Even though *on my own* meant sitting in front of Griffith with him pretty much doing everything, either from his fear of my killing us both, or potentially wrecking his precious bike. Regardless, I got the hang of riding. His motorcycle was three times the size of this bike. The laps I'd already completed around the block made this bike feel like it would be a piece of cake compared to Griffith's beast.

My thick curls protested the confinement when I crammed the helmet on my head. I started off slow, coasting down Andy's driveway, wobbling a little as I turned on the road. I barely suppressed a chuckle at Andy's anxious expression. He ran his hands through his thinning hair, probably envisioning the potential consequences as he watched me leave. If I wrecked before making it to the road, my body sprawled on his driveway would be all the evidence Griffith needed to prove Andy was responsible. Griffith's wrath would be undeniable.

The road was empty. I jerked back as I gunned the engine. My long hair was tugged in all directions by the wind. I regretted not braiding it or tucking my hair up under my helmet before I got on. I would have a tangled mess to deal with once I arrived at work.

Unfortunately, with bikes being the norm for the bar, and mine emitting a measly grunt compared to the roar of the beasts the regulars rode, no one noticed my tame entrance. This was a good thing. Despite my comfort in riding, I was still learning how to slow down enough to stop quickly. I narrowly missed the pole for the light in the parking lot before bringing the motorcycle to a stop.

I strutted in the bar through the front entrance with my helmet tucked under my arm. I could've left the helmet on the bike. No one would steal it. For one, most of their heads wouldn't fit in it, and secondly most of them didn't wear a helmet. Let alone one plastered with stickers I'd spent years hoarding just waiting to find something to stick them on.

My eyes locked on Griffith. He hadn't spotted me yet. Griffith was one of the few bikers that wore a helmet when he rode, but only because I insisted. I often wondered if he wore the helmet when he wasn't going to see me.

The look on Griffith's face when he spotted me, and his astonished gaze dropping to my helmet, made all the dead bugs plastered on my neck and the rat's-nest hairdo worth the ride. He stopped polishing the glass and hustled around the bar, knocking his leg off the side of the counter in his haste.

He approached me, rubbing the spot on his thigh and scowling. "What the hell do you think you're doing?"

I pushed past him, enjoying riling him up, but trying to maintain my cool façade. Just being near him elevated my heart rate and initiated a warm pooling in my belly. *Damn, he smelled good.* "What's it to you?"

I bent to shove my helmet under the counter, taking the opportunity to give him the full view of my backside. I'd intentionally worn my favorite jeans today to remind him of all he was missing. Granted, I didn't have much to work with in the rear, but a girl had to use whatever meager assets she had. At this moment, I was the hottest girl in the bar. Only because the engine almost overheated during the ride. Plus, I was the only girl here.

"You don't know how to ride a motorcycle," he grumbled the words. His irritation prompted an iridescent haze to swirl around him as he trailed me behind the bar.

"I just did." I shrugged, leaning against the wall to cross my arms. "I know enough. I did just fine."

I didn't mention the near miss with the pole in the parking lot…or the pothole that almost made me airborne…or the fawn that crossed my path. What he didn't know, he couldn't use to prove his point about my insufficient motorcycle experience.

"There's more to riding than getting on and going. The gravel in the parking lot could cause you to skid." He held up his hand and ticked off a finger. "You could knock the bike over and be unable to pick it up. It could land on your leg and pin you to the ground. A deer could jump out in front or you...or worse."

I raised my brows as I poured a glass of water to soothe my desert dry throat from the road dust. My intention hadn't been to antagonize Griffith further. I wanted the motorcycle as a cheaper, faster method of transportation. But I had to admit, the bike got Griffith's attention. From the moment he deprived me of that, I sought a way to regain it, craving his overprotective, hovering, sexy self. "You forget, I'm an Enchantling. I deal with much worse than that."

"That doesn't mean you're invincible. You could get hurt." I thought his eyes told me he cared if I did get injured, but his recent actions and aloof behavior said differently.

"Like I said, what do you care?" I narrowed my eyes, my irritation building as I recalled his words about me being who I was, what I was. Things I had no control over. Inherited traits I thought he understood, since he was also born with an unwelcome burden of who and what he was.

When my hands tingled, I concluded it was only a matter of time before I started leaking and ticked him off further...or turned him on.

He sighed in frustration and then leaned closer to me. "You know I care about you. It's not you, it's me—"

My laugh came out harsh. "Are you really going to use that line?"

His cheeks reddened. He ignored my comment and changed the subject. "Where did you get the motorcycle? You don't have money for that."

He averted his eyes after he spoke, as if experiencing a twinge of guilt about pointing out my lack of finances. He wouldn't understand being destitute or having nothing to call your own. Something I was all too familiar with. Griffith was born into money. He never went without anything. What he couldn't buy, he took.

"They may not be worth anything to you, but I have *things* that are valuable to some people." My anger made me speak before considering how Griffith always read right through me. There were no secrets. Sometimes that wasn't a good thing.

I knew the exact moment when he figured it out.

He glanced at my hands. His eyes widened, and his mouth formed a hard line. The haze around him deepened, and black strings of rage threaded through the fog surrounding him. "You wouldn't. My God, Hope, *selling your ability*? That's wrong on so many levels. That's like…like prostitution."

I stormed away, cringing internally with his word choice. "You better go mind the door." I gestured at a group of four bikers striding in. They scanned the bar for a seat, their boots clacking across the wooden floor as they peeled off their leather gloves.

"She's right." Chief popped his head out of the kitchen, blatantly admitting his eavesdropping. "People are coming in. You need to get to your post."

Griffith stood his ground, festering, while waiting for me to respond to his accusation. By not responding, I pretty much admitted my guilt. "No one underage would even think about sneaking in here. They know better." Griffith never took his eyes from me.

"It's not just ID's you're checking." Chief looked pointedly between Griffith and me.

His unspoken words hung heavy between us. Berta was still missing, and Griffith needed to gain information, or gossip, from the Oppressors.

Chief dropped his gaze, eager to fill the uncomfortable silence. "I don't want your lover's tiff scaring off the customers, and Red needs to start pouring drinks. The natives are getting restless, and they don't like to wait."

Two of the men who settled on a stool emitted an Oppressor residue. The black vapor lingered about them. The other two sported deep scars on their faces and forearms, looking like they didn't need to be Oppressors to get what they wanted.

Griffith scowled and walked over to the stool by the door, giving me his back while he suppressed his simmering anger.

Chief was right. Glowers tracked me from every seat at the bar. Once I stopped concentrating on Griffith, I realized many of the men were yelling to be served. The noise was what drew Chief from his office. I'd grown so accustomed to tuning out the plethora of curse words that I didn't catch the words *beer* and *drink* sprinkled amongst the expletives.

I grabbed a few glasses and started pouring beers. I might not be the best bartender, but I'd memorized the preferred drinks of the regulars to make up for my inadequacies. Anticipating what they wanted before they asked scored me some points and bought me time.

Chief lined up shot glasses. Not because he wanted

an excuse to have one for himself, as many people assumed. He didn't need a reason to drink. He sought to keep the tempers under control. The room was filling up. Better to achieve appeasement by booze than by preying on another. I wrongfully assumed that with Hecate gone the Oppressors would dwindle and disappear. Despite my gallivanting around the woods—as Griffith crossly accused—I hadn't been aware how much they'd multiplied. With Griffith stepping as far away from his role as possible, they had no leader. That didn't appear to be a good thing.

Many Oppressors apparently didn't hear, or care, about the news that I chose not to follow in Hecate's footsteps. They were drawn to me like bees to honey. Chief usually didn't mind, because that meant more business for him, except sometimes they got rowdy. We'd already lost more than one bar stool—and worse—to fights.

I pushed into the kitchen and nearly collided with Ruthie. As I struggled to remain upright, the scribbled list of tickets fluttered from my hand. Ruthie was busy preparing several orders at once. That's why we needed my aunt here. Everyone needed a Ruthie.

The guilt I struggled to suppress about pulling her away from her own desires reared its ugly head from where I buried it in my subconscious. Ruthie wouldn't ask about Berta. She'd told me the worry would eat her alive if she had to dwell on it every time she saw me. More likely, I figured she didn't want to grow to resent me more, especially when Chief needed her. Instead, she told me to update her anytime anything changed. Unfortunately, there was very little to update her on. "I heard you opened the bakery yesterday. Who's minding it while you're here?"

"Yep. George said it was now or never. No use waiting to open. Tessa is helping to get things ready." Ruthie didn't pause in her prep. She lined hotdog buns the whole way up her arm. She tossed in the hot dogs with her other hand and then added what she called the fixin's. I grimaced as she reached the hotdog nearest to her armpit. Everyone was aware of her method of preparing the dogs. Many requested to observe her doing it. Instead of being repulsed by the close proximity of the last hotdog to her armpit, it was the most requested one. I found the process disgusting.

"How can Tessa hold down the shop? She's in the mirror or another dimension or wherever. As much as she'd like to, I don't think she can cook from there. At least not anything we can eat." It wasn't like I needed to remind Ruthie that her sister was dead. The idea of Tessa running the shop was the most ludicrous thing I ever heard. Perhaps Ruthie secretly wanted it to fail?

"Oh no, she's not actually in the bakery. George is doing that. Tessa oversees everything from her place in the mirror." She cackled. "When I called him, he said with Tessa ordering him around to do this and do that it's almost like I never left."

Ruthie ladled chili over the hot dogs, placed them on the plates, and then tossed chopped onions on top.

"When people come into the bakery, aren't they going to see Tessa?" This town was known for eccentrics, but ghosts talking to them in a mirror might top even the most unusual things they'd seen.

Ruthie shook her head. "Nah, Tessa will leave before the customers come in. George will wait on them. He loves puttering around there. Except for missing out on some of his flea markets, but for goodness' sake, that man has got so much crap he's picked up over the years he's not even sorted through half of it. Filling in at the bakery will give me a chance to keep our house from filling to the brim. We hardly have room for my dolls with all his stuff."

"So, George is going to serve the customers?" George hobbled around on his best days. I couldn't imagine him working on his feet for hours. "How will he manage that?"

"Yepper. Sure, he'll spend a lot of time perched on that stool situated behind the counter. He wanted me to put a recliner in the front there. Can you imagine? A recliner? When I refused, he snuck in an old rocking chair he snagged at an auction, but the first time he sat on it, the thing broke into kindling."

Ruthie grabbed her belly and shook with laughter. "I mean, thank goodness he wasn't hurt or anything, but I would've loved seeing that heap of junk collapse. I told him that's what that rocker was when he bought it. But does he listen to me? Nope."

Sensing Ruthie's imminent launch into one of her endless stories, I blurted another question. "How's business?" I feared people might shun the place to avoid George talking their ear off and I didn't want to come right out and ask how the baking was going.

"It's booming. I've made a couple of batches of cookies, and they came out pretty good if I say so myself. Plus this town doesn't have much, let alone any new businesses to check out, so people have been stopping in since the day we got the key to the place." Ruthie noted my skeptical look and pressed on to alleviate my concern. "I know, I know, my George loves to talk, but people love their baked goods more than he loves to chat. I'm thinking that they'll end up buying more stuff, thinking they won't have to come back as soon."

She winked. "But they will come back, all right. Once they have some of my cookies and pies, they ain't gonna stay away. I know that. There are just some things no one can resist."

I thought of Berta's naïve optimism, of how an Oppressor might view her clueless good nature ripe for the taking like candy from a baby. "That's what I'm afraid of." I mumbled under my breath.

Chapter Eleven

"Let's get this over with." I didn't need to tell Andy twice. He salivated, impatiently waiting to take his hit. I wished I'd only agreed to this transaction once, but the quantity I could give him without totally depleting myself, or worse, remained uncertain. Intentional hope dispensing was new territory for me.

I had no idea of what might happen to Andy if he overdid it by taking a heaping amount of hope all at once. I hesitated. *Could he overdose on me?* After years of hiding my ability, offering to share my essence in this manner was weird, and probably a bad idea. But I was tapped out of other methods to make money to get a new ride.

"Sure, whenever you're ready." Andy rubbed his palms together in anticipation. A strange glint reflected in his eyes when he looked at my hands.

I glanced at the back door of the liquor store. "When did you say Griffith was due to come in?"

Andy licked his lips. "Not for at least a half hour."

The parking lot of the liquor store was a better place to meet than the woods, where he initially suggested. With Berta missing, and the Oppressors gaining ground, I lost the little confidence I'd grown where the woods were concerned. I'd underestimated how rapidly hate could multiply and grow.

Andy had to return to work soon. This assured me

that he wouldn't try to detain me here longer than necessary and risk Griffith's wrath. I might not always be able to intimidate Andy, but Griffith could. I'd never considered Andy a threat before, but lately he made me uneasy. The greediness and need surrounding him when he begged for a hit might eventually override his common sense.

The hope addict rolled up his sleeve and stuck his quivering arm toward me. I reached for him, and then stopped. "Why do you want this so badly? Is it for the feeling you get?" I realized, more than most, that feelings were fleeting and not long lasting. But they sure made a hell of a difference about how your day was going.

"What? What does that matter?" Andy's face fell in disappointment when I didn't start immediately pumping him with hope. Once he realized I wouldn't give him his fix until he answered, he relented. "That's part of it. It isn't the only reason. It's because I'm getting a piece of her."

"A piece of me?" That part didn't surprise me. People had been vying for a piece of me my whole life.

"No not you, her. Hecate." He worried his lower lip in anticipation.

"Why in the hell would you think that? I'm not Hecate." She was the last thing I wanted to be compared to. I might thrive on irritability and sarcasm, but I'd yet to prey on the desperation of others or rule the Underworld. I could barely keep order at the bar.

"You have her power. There must be something of her in you," he argued.

He grabbed for me, and I stumbled back. Anxiety shone in Andy's eyes as if he considered the possibility that I might deny what he desired. His ghastly smile prompted the tiny hairs on my skin to rise. He took a step toward me, closing the gap I'd inserted between us. "Griffith will be coming soon. Are you going back on your word? It wouldn't surprise me if you tried, Hecate did that too."

I narrowed my eyes at the scrawny, sleazy checker. Despite recognizing that he spoke the words with a hint of manipulation, I couldn't stand the comparison to that bitch any further. *Was this the reason Griffith avoided me?* Was I becoming like Hecate, or was I already more like her than I realized? "My terms, remember?"

I braced myself with a wide stance and then lightly touched his arm. Andy shuddered and gasped as I willed hopefulness into him. I clenched my teeth as pins and needles of pain crept in my hands and up my arms, intensifying as it rose. The throbbing sensation reached my shoulder, and the agony amplified. I staggered. I'd given Andy enough.

Before I could release him, he clamped my hand and held it tight against his skin. The contact with his flesh prevented me from stopping the infusion. "More. I need more," he panted. His eyes rolled back in his head.

"No, you're done." I tugged weakly, unable to release myself from his grip. Fear seeped into my consciousness. I was losing control of the situation.

He restrained my arm and narrowed his eyes. "No. I'm not. Now it's my terms." He smiled with satisfaction.

My legs wobbled, and my vision blurred. Terror gripped my heart, and my eyes widened. *What had I done?* I couldn't break his grasp.

My legs shook, and I slumped to my knees, my

hand still pressed against Andy's arm. My hopeful essence depleted into him like a faucet, rushing out at a pace I'd never experienced before. Desolation and exhaustion took its place. Andy stood over me, appearing to expand as I shrunk.

The dirty parking lot rose to meet me when I collapsed. Granules of dirt adhered to my mouth. My breath disturbed the surrounding dust. My brain registered awareness of the gravel poking through my shirt, but I didn't care. Most of my cares dissipated with my remaining will. As my body crumbled, clarity flickered unexpectedly in my thoughts. I willingly gave what the Oppressors lived to take away and feed from. *What was I thinking?*

My sight grew hazy as I felt myself almost succumb to the impending darkness. I hoped Andy wouldn't leave me in the parking lot for Griffith to find. He'd be sure to irrationally blame himself for my death. I'd put him through enough. I should've never come to this town. Never should've stayed. I didn't belong here. I didn't belong anywhere.

Through cracked lids I viewed Andy's broken, stained, gleeful smile as a rush of joy and hope flooded through him. All the time I wasted worrying about dying at Hecate's hand. Instead my demise would be from my own doing by a checker at the liquor store who was intimidated by every man at the bar. No wonder none of the Enchantlings survived past age twenty-one.

My tenuous grasp on reality faded with the thoughts of the family I came to know and love in the last six months. I thought I'd have more time to get to know them. I hoped to create newer, better memories together, at least the chance to enjoy one of Ruthie's legendary Thanksgiving dinners.

What were my sister's last thoughts when she faded away? Unless Drake sliced her wrists as an afterthought to make it appear like suicide, Destiny's death would've been more painful than my quiet fading. Not that there was a point to staging her death other than for show.

What would Andy do with my body once he finished emptying me of my desire to live? He didn't seem smart enough to do anything creative, so I could only assume my suicide would present like the standard variety. Most people in this town didn't believe all the suicides the Oppressors racked up at face value, but not many questioned them either.

Andy's grip was broken when someone jerked me off the ground. I then smacked back down to the gravel to stare at my freed hand. It didn't look any different after its draining betrayal. I was literally killed by my own hand. A hysterical giggle rose up in my brain and throat.

My head lolled to the side, drowning in a fog of confusion. The strength left my body. An ant walked about an inch from my nose, appearing oblivious to me—while Griffith repeatedly smacked his fist into Andy's face. Maybe I was dreaming.

Would Griffith be one of the last images reflected in my mind? I hoped so. The haze of tiny lights surrounding him made him look like an angel. He was nothing of the sort, but to me he always had been. Too bad he never believed that.

****

The sunlight pressed against my eyelids. Would I

wake up in The Kitchen of the afterlife and see Aunt Tessa? I sure felt like I had unfinished business left in this world. Maybe I could still find a way to help Chance and Berta, to make up for all I didn't do while focusing on myself.

Tessa claimed they usually didn't see the others who resided in that weird afterlife purgatory they called The Kitchen. Hopefully I would see her one last time, if only to apologize for failing her and leaving her alone to die that day. Chalk it up to another one of my selfish actions.

I opened my eyes. The room didn't resemble any kind of afterlife. It looked like a woman's bedroom. White, lacey curtains were tied back at a set of large double doors leading out to a small, railed deck surrounded by immense, autumn colored trees. A dressing table pressed against the far wall. A delicate chair flanked it. The design looked old, but it appeared as if the table was finished later, giving it a newer appearance while still preserving the cherished antique qualities. A polished, silver tray rested on top with two bottles of perfume vaporizers, a gilded hairbrush, comb, and a handheld mirror.

The stone fireplace crackled with a wood fire. I pushed to my elbows, and the thick down comforter slid to reveal the pink satin nightgown I wore. Something warm and wet dropped to the mattress. I picked up the damp washcloth that fell from its place on my forehead. *Where the hell was I?*

The door opened.

Griffith backed into the room, holding the door with his shoulder as he carefully balanced a tray with a pitcher of water. When he noticed me studying him, he stopped abruptly. The water sloshed over the rim, dampening the doily underneath. "You're up."

"I guess so. I'm not dead?" Perhaps I was. Since when did a man like Griffith use doilies? Or even know what they were?

"You should be." He set the tray on the dresser. After pouring a glass of water, he carried it over to place it on the nightstand beside me.

What he probably meant was I would be, if he hadn't intervened. I sighed and studied the delicate eyelet design on the duvet. "Thank you."

He lowered himself on the edge of the bed. The mattress shifted under his weight. Making me acutely aware that I was alone, with Griffith, in a nightgown, in a strange bed. If I wasn't concerned about being dead, I might've considered the spiciness of my current situation sooner.

"For what?" He ran his gaze over me, as if checking for additional injuries.

"Saving me—again." At least this time he wasn't left with visual scars to remind him, just on the inside. Once again, I'd made him act outside of his comfort zone. "Everything."

"What was I going to do, let you die?" He said the harsh words with tenderness.

I searched his face for the meaning behind them. "So why did you save me, then?"

"I couldn't not—"

"No, that's not a reason, and don't tell me you had no choice. There's always a choice. We both know that." I slid my hand across the bed but stopped a few inches from his. After what he witnessed in the parking lot with Andy, I was uncertain how he might respond.

"You could've looked the other way. People do it all the time."

He curled his fingers over mine, his touch warmer and more comforting than the amenities of the room. "No. I couldn't."

He leaned over to place a gentle kiss on my forehead. I closed my eyes to savor his lips on my skin, painfully aware of how much I missed him. The ache he left in my heart was more distressing than any other physical pain endured. His warm breath caressed me as he tilted my chin enough to graze a feather light kiss over my lips. Inches separated us. There was so much more I wanted to do. We were alone in a bedroom. "I don't know what this is."

"What?" Worry furrowed his brow.

"Us," I whispered against his lips.

He ran a soothing hand over my head. "What do you want it to be?"

"I don't know," my voice cracked with emotion. Griffith insisted we take our relationship slow. With the tragic events that always accompanied me, he had good reason. My heart ached to mend his doubts, even though he might be better off without me in his life. I pulled away, respecting his prior request. More pressing questions needed answers anyway. "Where am I?"

"My house." He gazed at me with a new tenderness.

The overly feminine room didn't resemble anything else in his house. The decor was the exact opposite of everything I'd seen in the few rooms I'd visited in the ancient huge house that was ten times bigger than anything I'd ever lived in. It had been in his family for over a century and most of the décor looked as if it hadn't been changed for almost as long—except for this room. A twinge of jealousy churned in the pit of my stomach. *Just whose room was this?* I thought we quit keeping secrets from each other. Or was it just me that kept no real secrets from him? Perhaps there was a reason he wanted me to stay away. I steeled my heart for his answer. "Whose room is this?"

His expression faltered, and he turned away. He stood and pressed his hands in the pockets of his jeans, tightening the fabric as he did and drawing my gaze. "My mother's."

"Your mother's?" I couldn't have been more surprised by his response than if he said he'd opened his cold, manly mansion as a bed and breakfast. I was touched he permitted me to wear anything of his mother's. She couldn't have worn the gown for at least two decades. "But she's been gone for…"

He cringed as I did the mental calculation in my head. He'd told me his mother left him years ago, and then was confined shortly after that to the state psychiatric hospital. The last thing he needed was for me to point out what must be blatantly obvious. I'd seen Lucille myself, so I knew it was the truth. I also knew that it was more likely that Uncle George would stop wearing those god-awful shorts before Griffith's mother would return home.

The sharp prick of her absence in the pristine room was overwhelming. He'd kept her room in impeccable condition all these years. She could walk in today and sit at her dressing table as if she'd never left. I fingered the satin nightgown I wore. The heat of a blush warmed my cheeks. *How did he get the sexy, satin nightgown on me?* The relief that I still wore undergarments was fleeting when I considered the ones I chose. My shabby bra and panties contrasted terribly under the fine fabric. I'd be lucky if the elastic did justice and kept my underwear from drooping to one side. I studied the gown and stroked the satin. "Is this hers?"

"Yes, I kept everything. Except for some of her cosmetics. I threw them out when they dried up. I didn't want to remind her of the time…of how long she's been gone." He let out a sigh and studied the ceiling.

After running his hands over his face, he met my gaze. "I know, it's stupid. She's not ever going to come back, and if by some miracle she ever did, we can't just pick up where we left off."

"It's not stupid." It was heartbreaking and sweet and displayed a layer of vulnerability he kept buried beneath his tough exterior. He claimed he didn't have many feelings. That was a lie. He hid his hopeful emotions deep under years of hurt. "Isn't it painful for you to maintain this room for all these years?"

He shook his head and walked to the glass double doors. He pulled the curtain to the side to peer out and then released it. "I don't come in here often. Just enough to keep everything neat and clean, like I think she would like it. This is all I have of her, and besides, it's my penance."

"For what?" I shifted on the bed to view him better. His tense muscular back hinted at his repressed feelings and obvious discomfort at being in this room.

"For being what I am," he whispered almost as if he feared his mother would overhear.

"You can't help that. You're not required to pay a price just for being alive." I spoke the words to convince myself, as well as him. I had to believe that or spend my life suffering with self-loathing as he did.

He turned to face me. The light from the window surrounded him, highlighting his striking cheekbones. "Sometimes you must pay a price for things out of your control, just for being who you are...or being the one that lived."

I turned away from his penetrating stare, wondering if he realized how his comment reverberated within me. Despite the passing months since my sister's death, the guilt over Destiny was still painfully fresh. His statement revealed that it was more than the price of his mother's sanity he paid. It was for Drake and the others, who crossed him during the height of his Oppressor reign.

My guess would be that he wore his father's crimes around his neck like a noose as well. All this time I thought I was the guilt-driven one. We had something else in common.

I started to pull my legs around with the intention of getting up, but a wave of dizziness washed over me. The room spun. I gripped the mattress and squeezed my eyes to shut out the canopy above my head, which circled like the top of a merry-go-round in flight.

He rushed to the bedside and laid his hand on my arm with a gentle pressure. "Don't try to move yet."

I reclined on the pillow, comforted by its cushiony softness and Griffith's tender touch. "How long have I been here?"

"Two days."

"Two days?" I tried to sit up again, but he anticipated my reaction and held my arms gently, but firmly. I sighed as reality and responsibility crowded out my fantasy of playing house with Griffith. "I appreciate everything you've done, but I have to go. I missed work, and I have to feed Tercet and—"

"It's all taken care of." He shook his head.

"How?" I frowned.

He released me and sat on the edge of the bed. The mattress shifted under his weight, drawing me closer to him. "I talked to everyone."

"Did you tell them…" I ducked my head. Shame flooded me, and heat warmed my face as I considered what my family would think if they found out I sold my gift. Intentionally using it for everything we've worked against. I snuck a glance at Griffith. His expression surprised me.

His lips pulled ever so slightly into a sympathetic smile and then returned to their natural unreadable position. Empathy shone in his eyes. "No, I didn't tell them exactly what happened. I told them we were looking for Berta, together."

"What?" My family didn't trust Griffith. Ruthie tolerated him because I cared for him. She didn't understand my feelings for him, but neither did I. Chance sought every opportunity to prove Griffith masterfully hid his true motivation to destroy us all in a belated revenge for his father's death. Surely Griffith lied to ease my worries.

I winced as I imagined the reaction he would've received if he announced our intention to lead a novice search party through the woods without my presence. Then, they didn't hear a word from me for the last two days? Chance would assume Griffith already buried me in the graveyard on the hill. "They'd never be okay with that."

"They had to be." Griffith's shoulders rose, and his

jaw tightened in defense. "Chance is desperate to find Berta. He'll take any help he can get. It took an effort to talk him out of coming along. He was happy you were finally beginning to believe him that Berta didn't run off to expose you to the reporter, so he didn't ask many questions."

All this time had passed and still no sign of Berta. As much as she drove me crazy, I didn't want anything to happen to her. "What do you think happened to her?"

"None of the Oppressors I talked to have heard or seen anything about Berta. I think you might be right. She took off." He sighed. "But I'll keep looking for her until we decide it's pointless, just like I told your family we were. Your brother may never believe it, but I'm a man of my word."

The problem was that I was a terrible liar. To ensure I didn't ruin Griffith's efforts to protect my family from finding out what really happened, we needed to follow through with what he said we were doing and look for Berta. Long ago I learned the best way to quell a lie is to do something to make it at least partially true. A half-truth is better than a full lie in my book. "Okay, before we go looking, I better check on Tercet and the bar."

Griffith folded his arms. "Ruthie is holding down the bar, and George is feeding Tercet. Just be quiet and let someone take care of you for once."

No one had taken care of me since Tessa. Even in that relationship I often felt like the adult. "I don't know how."

"Learn."

Griffith made it clear the topic wasn't up for discussion. My mind wandered back to what he'd said.

"George is taking care of Tercet?"

For some reason, that amazed me more than anything else. Tercet hated most men. It drove George crazy that he had yet to succeed in befriending her. He'd gained more than one scratch in his futile attempts.

"You have more family and friends that love you than you realize. I think George won't have any trouble dealing with a cantankerous cat. Oddly enough, he seemed like he was looking forward to it. He made some comment about not biting the hand that feeds you." He walked over to a weathered oak wardrobe and opened the double doors. After a moment's hesitation, he reached inside the cabinet. He returned, cradling something in his arms. He bent and laid a leather jacket on the bed as lovingly as a newborn babe.

I studied the jacket and wondered if this was his subtle way of indicating I had overstayed my welcome in his home. "What is that for?"

He sighed in resignation. "Well, if you insist on riding that motorcycle, then I'm going to have to go with you so you can practice, and try to keep you from breaking your neck. Although your actions indicate otherwise, you don't have nine lives. You're the one who's always harping about safety. You're the reason I'm the only guy at the bar who wears a helmet. Luckily, none of the guys are thoughtless enough to comment on that." He raised a brow. "You need to dress accordingly. You can start with this jacket."

The size and cut of the coat identified it as a woman's, and it wasn't new. I considered the room with renewed interest. "Who's—"

"It was my mother's jacket." The twitching along his jaw betrayed his discomfort with the subject.

"Your mother's?" I sagged with relief and squelched my twinges of unfounded jealousy. If I would've considered that he removed the jacket from his mother's wardrobe, I might've surmised that. But I had a hard time envisioning Lucille riding the back of a motorcycle, and I excelled at jumping to conclusions. The woman I met at the state psychiatric hospital appeared too refined to ride motorcycles.

I stroked the fabric. The soft supple leather had thick, protective armor on the elbows, the back, and other spots to provide partial protection in an accident. Griffith's generosity in offering his mother's jacket touched me. If by some miracle, Lucille returned to her home, I couldn't imagine she would be happy to let me borrow it, or anything of hers.

She didn't hold me in the highest regard, since when I visited her at the hospital, I had unintentionally pushed her into hysterics. After years of being fooled by the Oppressor she married, and then birthing a half-human, half-Oppressor son, Lucille saw right through my charade. She knew I wasn't normal. "Don't you want to keep this with her things?"

He kept his attention on the jacket, avoiding my gaze. "If she ever did come back, I don't imagine she'll want to ride a motorcycle anymore. She used to ride with my father, or so I've been told. That was a long time ago. Before I was born. Before she realized what he was, and what he wasn't, before she changed her name to Lucille."

I heard many stories about Griffith's father. Until now, I never had a chance to validate any of them with him. His family was always a taboo subject. "What wasn't he?"

"Human."

Nearly dying had its advantages. Such as prying more information out of my boyfriend in the last few minutes than I'd been able to in the months since I'd met him. Determined to obtain as much knowledge as possible before Griffith's internal wall resurfaced, I considered some of the other unsolved mysteries making up his past. At the psychiatric hospital, they addressed his mother as Stella, but when I talked to her she insisted I refer to her as Lucille. "Why did she change her name?"

Pain and sadness flitted across his face. "She put everything behind her that reminded her of my father—including me. From what the doctors told me, she chose to go by the name Lucille because of a television program she watched at the hospital. She claims everyone was always happy in the show, and they made her laugh."

He frowned. His fingers curled as he tightened his grip on his forearms, puckering the surrounding skin. "I don't believe that. No one is always happy. People hide behind fake smiles like a mask to the world. Besides, I never saw my mother laugh."

His cheeks reddened and he looked away, abruptly dropping the subject. Once he composed himself, his closed expression deterred further questions. "Enough about me. I came upstairs to check on you. How do you feel?"

He'd already shared way more than I expected, and I didn't want to press him. I performed a quick internal assessment. It wasn't just the physical aspect, emotionally I felt better than I had in a long time. Despite my foolishness, my rash actions certainly revealed one thing. I have a family who cares about me. Unfortunately, it took almost killing myself to figure out that everything wasn't always about my problems. After determining there were no unusual aches or pains, I shrugged. "A lot better than I expected after almost dying."

"Stop being so dramatic." The tight line to his jaw and the way his gaze dropped to ensure I remained in one piece betrayed his concern.

My body disclosed my happiness by leaking out a little sparkly glitter from my fingertips. I smiled. I hadn't seen that for a while. It was a refreshing change after the endless black tendrils of anger and despair. I sat up again, slower this time, and the room cooperated by staying in one place as I dangled my feet over the edge of the bed. "Where are my clothes?"

"In my bedroom. I didn't think you'd want to sleep there. It's quieter here." His eyes lingered on the fabric of the thin nightgown, and his voice grew husky. "I'll get them."

His inspection also didn't cause me discomfort. Perhaps my attire would serve to remind him of what he shunned when he chose to determine if he was better off without me. "Can I come with you? I mean, I could see how well I'm walking and you could support me so I don't fall."

I was fine, but I didn't want to let him out of my sight, now that I had him back sort of. Besides, I hadn't seized this opportunity to play up the whole damsel in distress. This was a first for me, and I might not have this chance again. Might as well make the most of it.

"Oh, of course." He rushed over and bent to offer me his elbow. I took it and stood beside him, leaning heavily on his arm. A furrow of concern lined his brow. "Do you feel okay? Any dizziness? Do you want to sit back down?"

I bowed my head to hide my smile when he fussed over me. "I'm fine. Just walk slowly, please. I might need to lean on you a little." I didn't need to, I wanted to.

Chapter Twelve

The house resumed its familiar appearance and atmosphere of dark and foreboding once we exited his mother's room. I wondered why he didn't change any of the other décor. His office at work confirmed his style and taste didn't match this place. His father or other ancestors had apparently chosen the depressing colors and furnishings of his ancient house. Lucille must've decorated her room in a failed attempt to insert a woman's touch and add light to the living space.

We moved slowly down the long hall. Griffith opened the door to his bedroom, careful not to relinquish his grip on me in case I might collapse. I leaned into him, inhaling his scent. I love musk. The trace aroma of leather lingered around him, even without his jacket.

"Here you are," I said as we entered. The neat, clutter free, modernly furnished room was the Griffith I knew. Deep maroons and mahogany woods evoked a masculine sense in the space. The curtains were drawn to allow sunlight to enter and wash over the dark furnishings. The style provided an atmosphere of a bright and airy area, without reducing the relaxed ambiance.

"What do you mean? I didn't go anywhere." He furrowed his brow and placed a palm on my forehead, as if the action would confirm or deny the possibility of a head injury to explain my unusual comment.

"No, I mean the room. This looks like you. So far, it's the only place that reminds me of your style. Why didn't you change anything else in the house to make it your own, to make it your home? From what I saw, my guess is you've left everything the same since…"

I didn't finish the sentence to say since his father lived here. I never asked about other family members, or if he had any other family besides his half-brother Drake. The darkening of Griffith's face prompted me to save that conversation for another time.

He shrugged. "I'm not here much. There was no need to change things, and there is only so much alteration the house will allow."

"The house? What's that supposed to mean?" My laugh faded. His solemn expression was sterner than Berta's when she repeatedly explained the difference between tank tops and camisoles. "Wait a minute. Are you serious?"

He opened his mouth, and then closed it, reconsidering what he was about to say. "It's a long story for another time. Nothing you need to worry about. I told you before, sometimes there are things you're better off not knowing. We're here to take care of you."

I dropped the conversation for the time being because it obviously made him uncomfortable. Plus, if I kept harping on about the house and how it was decorated, he was likely to think I was planning on moving in soon. Which wouldn't be considered baby steps, like we agreed on for the progress of our relationship.

He led me to an ottoman at the foot of the bed

while keeping a firm grip on my elbow. I lowered to sit on the plush cushion. He handled me like a china doll threatening to break at any moment. Any other day and I would hate this type of hovering, but after the disaster with Andy, and Griffith's recent aloofness, I welcomed his fussing. I missed him more than I realized.

He straightened and ran his gaze over me. "Was the walk too much?"

"Really, it was only the length of the hall. I'm fine." I brushed him away with a laugh. "I'm enjoying the extra attention, but you don't have to hover so much."

He walked to the dresser. The surface lay bare except for a pile of neatly folded clothes. After a moment's hesitation, he scooped them up and handed them to me.

I examined my belongings, noting the crisp lines, fresh scent, and the lack of parking lot residue. "You washed them?"

My mind conjured up many images of Griffith, but none of them surprised me as much as the thought of him doing laundry. I ran my hand over the soft fabric. I suppose even big, brawny men needed to do the wash sometimes.

He ducked his head, but not before I noted his cheeks coloring. "I would've asked Cronin to do it, but he would ask too many questions, or make his own assumptions. Besides, I wanted to do it. Dust and dirt covered them from the…"

He grimaced and clenched his jaw. "I didn't want you to have to deal with that memory as soon as you woke. Your jacket is the only piece I didn't wash. The pockets are full of odds and ends. I didn't want you to assume I seized the opportunity to dig through your personal things."

I raised my brows. Just when I thought he'd made progress on the whole boundaries thing, he takes it to the other extreme. I shouldn't be surprised. A man like Griffith struggled with an all or nothing mindset. He could undress me and clothe me in his mother's nightgown, intimidate any man within a ten-mile radius of me, yet he worried I'd be upset about him rummaging through my belongings if he emptied my jacket pockets. Even I had no idea what kind of junk was crammed in my green surplus jacket. I wore the tattered coat almost every day. Its worn, soft material was a comfort I remained unwilling to give up.

"Who's Cronin?"

Griffith hooked his thumbs through his belt loops, appearing uncertain what to do with them now that he'd relinquished me and the laundry. "He's been our butler for generations." He straightened. "He's more of a caretaker for the grounds now, because I refuse to allow him to act like a servant for me. I don't need that."

"I've never seen him." This revelation made me realize how much craftier Griffith was at deterring personal conversation to me and my life than his own. I'd never heard him mention the name before. But I'd only visited his house a few times, and just assumed he lived alone. For the size of the structure, he could house a plethora of Oppressors, or half the town downstairs, and I'd never realize it.

"He keeps a low profile, mostly at my insistence. He'd have his nose in everything if I permitted him. He's not here, yet. I don't think he'll come around anyway because he can't tolerate being too close to you because of your smell. That's another reason I laundered the clothes and kept you in Mother's old room. I take care of that, as well." He stopped talking, as if realizing he'd said more than he intended. He turned to leave.

"Wait. What do you mean by my smell?" My cheeks warmed as I restrained myself from bending to take a whiff of my skin. I might not be as put together and coordinated as Berta, but I certainly didn't stink. At least I didn't think so.

"The human part of you and the...extra." His gesture encompassed me. His cheeks reddened, striving to match mine.

Previously Drake commented about noting my scent on Griffith. I never thought to question what he meant, but why would I? I would never understand many things about Drake, nor would I want to. Conversation hadn't been our thing since he'd preferred to chat by invading my thoughts like snake oil.

Griffith also verbalized his desire to avoid me, but I assumed he did so because of my abilities, and the temptation accompanying that, but perhaps there was more. This was the first time I'd heard about my unusual *odor*. Not something most girls want to hear. Whatever his reasons for evading me, I was done with that. If there was something about me he feared he couldn't resist, then he needed to face his fears.

I almost died. I didn't plan on leaving this earth without at least running my hands over Griffith's bare chest—or more.

"Go ahead and get dressed. I'll be back in a few minutes." He hurried to the door.

I stood and slipped the nightgown over my head,

belatedly reminded of my mismatched undergarments. Hopefully he would overlook my elastically challenged granny panties. It could've been worse. I could've worn my day-of-the-week underwear, which after two days here would clearly identify their lack of daily replacement. "Oh, before you go, I have something for you."

He turned from the door. When he saw me, his grip tightened on the doorknob. The knob rattled under his hold.

I dangled the nightgown toward him. He glanced toward the silky fabric. It swayed in front of me like a flag of surrender, or a cape waved to guide a charging bull. "In case you wanted to put this in the wash."

I gave him my best come hither glance. My inexperience at such acts of seduction must've been obvious, because it fell flat. He returned his focus to the nightgown, either masking his amusement, or resisting succumbing despite my lackluster efforts.

"Oh, thank you." His art of maintaining a neutral expression faltered at my unsophisticated strip tease. Confusion dominated the emotions shifting on his face.

He reached for the nightgown, trying to avoid looking at me. I touched his arm. He froze. Electricity tingled between us. Tiny sparks dropped from my fingertips. His gaze rose to mine and stayed, a question in his eyes.

Warmth pooled in my belly, and my mouth grew dry. My concern about my undergarments dimmed as my awareness focused on him completely. The gorgeous, tortured man I dreamt about. The man who saved me more than once, perhaps it was my turn to save him. "I might require your assistance getting dressed...or undressed."

Maybe awaking in his bedroom had ignited my wantonness. The intimacy he'd shared with me, coupled with a piece of his soul, by permitting me to stay in his mother's cherished room spoke for his heart better than any words. My decision to take our relationship to the next level could've stemmed from my fatigue, or my near death. I was tired of waiting until everything in our lives was perfect, because it never would be. We only had the here and now. I already missed out on enough in life because of doubt, fear, or uncertainty. I planned to seize the moment. This moment.

Griffith's tortured expression barely concealed the internal battle ensuing with his personal demons. Whether to follow his desires, or do what he believed was right for me. "This might not be the best time. You, well, you almost died."

"I didn't, and I want to feel alive." For far too long, he'd ignored the human side of him and presented a shell of the man I knew lay dormant inside. I ran my hands up his arms. He closed his eyes and groaned. "You make me feel alive, and you make me believe that I'm a good person."

"You are a good person, Hope. You're too good for the likes of me." He turned away, providing me his profile. "I'm not all good."

"No. I'm not too good for you. I'm not *all* good, either." My fingers trailed up his arm to my favorite spot, to curl in the hair at the base of his skull. I lightly scratched my nails against his skin, and ran my thumb along his jaw to caress his ear lobe. I laid my cheek against his and whispered, "Together we're perfect."

After inhaling his intoxicating scent of woods, musk, and forbidden temptation, I drew away, allowing the stubble along his jawline to scratch against my face. His eyes darkened with tempered desire. A hazy fog grew around him as I intentionally provoked the beast he kept buried within. With a growl, he unleashed his restraint and wrapped his arms around me. He pulled me roughly against him to find my mouth, all gentlemanly pretenses abandoned. I gasped as his tongue darted in to dance with mine.

He pressed against me. His broad shoulders dwarfed my own, making me appear small and vulnerable in comparison. His muscular arms surrounded me, making me acutely aware of his size and strength. The dark Oppressor part caged within him stirred. Yet I felt safe.

He drew back with an effort and touched his forehead to mine. His breath came in ragged pants. "My god Hope, how you continue to tempt me."

I closed my eyes, relishing his closeness and the comfort he provided. Heat raged through my veins as my need for more than he offered consumed me. My body trembled with unfulfilled desires. I couldn't demand his attention if I didn't first clarify their true origins. I had to know, despite how much I wanted to ravage him with no questions asked. "Do I tempt you for what my abilities can do?"

"Yes."

My heart clenched when he responded with the answer I didn't want to hear.

He cupped my chin to gaze into my eyes. "You didn't ask how I define your abilities. You tempt me with more than how you can give hope or take it away.

I also can't resist your ability to make light of the direst situation. How you make me want to smile when I don't want to, and how you can wear whatever the hell you want and it's the sexiest damn thing I've ever seen."

A smile quivered on my lips. This was why Chance, and none of the rest of my family, would never understand why I cared for Griffith. They never saw the gentle, loving side of him. This was mine.

I placed my hand against his face and ran it along the light stubble, igniting the glitter of emotion leaking from my hand, and stoking the yearning constricting every muscle of my body. He turned his head to kiss my palm, and then my wrist, and stepped toward me. I stumbled back and bumped into the bed. He guided my descent to the mattress and lowered himself over me.

A memory resurfaced. The dreams had filled my nights for years and then finally brought me to this town. Six months ago, I lost Tessa, the only family I knew, only to find another family, and then more. For too long I focused on the dream depicting Griffith trying to kill me, but I'd forgotten about the other. I touched his face, and he pressed his cheek against my hand. "I dreamt about this."

He balanced on his elbows above me, the muscles in his biceps bulging with the effort. "Then I'm about to make your dreams come true."

****

"Now I can face reality again." I didn't want to. I snuggled deeper in the crook of Griffith's arm. His scent surrounded me and coated my skin.

Pretending Griffith and I were the only two people in the world was a strong temptation, but there were others who needed me, and promises to keep. The lingering guilt about Berta, and my obligations to Chance and the bar kept resurfacing despite my efforts. Granted, Griffith made me successfully forget everything else for hours, but reality couldn't be denied. I could never forgive myself if I disappointed my family—again. I rolled on my back with a sigh.

"Yes, I suppose we must." He sat up and turned to settle on the edge of the bed. The sheet slid away and provided me my first full view of his naked back. I gasped.

"My goodness. How didn't I notice that?" Since I spent most of my time focusing on other delicious parts of him, it wasn't that surprising that I missed this. His entire back was painted with an intricate design of tattoos. The ink started on each bicep with tribal-like swirls and then spread to his back. The ink curled around his waist.

He scowled and reached for his shirt. "Because I keep it covered."

I put my hand on his arm, longing to explore the ink. "Why? It's beautiful."

He tilted his head back and sighed. "It stands for the part of my life that I'm not anymore. The tattoo is a reminder of what I don't want to be."

"All those years made you who you are. You had to go through those uncertain times to become the person you are today." He tensed as I ran my fingers along the tattoos. The ebb and flow of the pattern mesmerized me. "The design is almost like a maze."

He grimaced. Determination lined his jaw as it tightened. "It is. The ink is her mark—but I'm not *hers* to have."

He didn't have to elaborate for me to know whom he referred to. It seemed Hecate would never be completely gone. She wouldn't allow us to forget her. It pained me to think that somehow, she'd branded Griffith as one of hers—against his will. "All the tattoo is her mark?"

"No, it's within the design. I tried my best to conceal it because there's no way to be rid of it. It's part of me. I have to accept that."

He walked away, obviously uncomfortable with the conversation. He picked up the rest of his clothes to dress. I watched him, reveling in this intimate moment. Not too long ago I thought this man might kill me. Now I didn't want to live without him.

I gathered my clothes. The subject of Hecate and Griffith's tattoo could wait for another time. No need to let that hateful hellion steal this moment. She'd tormented me enough throughout my life and Griffith's as well. "You told everyone we were looking for Berta. I'd feel better if we did go look around a little. Even if she did leave town, poor Chance has been destitute. It's the least I can do."

Griffith slipped his shirt over his head. The fabric draped over his back and concealed the tattoos from my view. "I have been. I planned to continue to look. You can stay here and rest."

"I'm coming." He might've rescued me before Andy tapped me dry, but I'd be damned if I would sit here and do nothing. I was a woman of my word, even if it wasn't my word I honored, but Griffith's. "Did you bring my motorcycle?"

"No." Griffith presented his back to me, ending the conversation.

Nope. I wasn't going to let him end the discussion that easily. I scowled and braced my hands on my hips. "I thought this would be the perfect time to practice on the motorcycle."

"You can ride with me. It's safer that way." He turned to face me, a determined glint flashed in his eyes.

"But I—"

"You're still weak. You can't expect me to be comfortable with you operating a motorcycle in your condition." His voice rose with his distress. "Besides, I know the woods much better than you, and I can protect you from the worst parts on the path and...other things."

I met his glare with my own. Usually I could outstare the best of them, but I dropped my gaze and the issue first. Griffith's resistance had nothing to do with my condition. I knew it, and he knew it. This flimsy excuse was his way of keeping me off the motorcycle.

His inference to the low-level, unstable Oppressors lurking in the woods did cause me to waiver in my resistance. I felt fine, but the incident with Andy was still fresh in my mind. I never wanted to experience that again. Besides, it was hard to turn down a motorcycle ride with Griffith. Wrapping my arms around him and curling against his back brought me more solace than most things. I could benefit from drawing a little extra comfort from him now.

I picked up the motorcycle jacket Griffith provided and slid it on. It was a little big for me but fit well enough to enable me to leave my favorite jacket on underneath. The tank top beneath the jacket wasn't warm enough alone. I ran my hands down the front of the smooth leather and gasped. The vision came on hard and strong.

The scenery whizzed by at an awkward angle in my mind's eye as if I were looking at it upside down. Trees and woods surrounded me. The crunch of slow, heavy footsteps breaking through twigs and crushing leaves filled my ears—and terror cut me to the bone.

The angle provided me with the view of a large shoe. A man's foot moved below where he carried me. My arm dangled, and my fingertips touched the ground occasionally with the laborious gait necessary to carry me. My hand twisted to the side as it bumped a jagged rock on the ground, revealing long, coral colored fingernails.

The fuzz enveloping my mind cleared enough for me to realize that wasn't my hand. It wasn't me he carried.

A boarded-up sign hung on a tree. It depicted child-like handwriting in stilted capital script. I could make out the words GO AWAY.

My breath caught. I opened my eyes to meet Griffith's concerned gaze. He knelt in front of me. I glanced around, unsure how I ended up sitting on the edge of his bed, gripping my arms so hard my unpolished nails left half-moon imprints on my skin. My energy dispersed with the remnants of the vision as it cleared from my thoughts. I slumped forward and closed my eyes, grounding myself. Though unpredictable, and few and far between, the visions were exhausting.

Griffith's hands were on my thighs. He clenched and unclenched his grip. Although his impatience was obvious, he permitted me time to recover. "Hope. What is it?"

I locked my gaze with his. "I think I know where Berta is."

****

I clung to Griffith, feeling like a knight riding in to rescue a damsel in distress. Except we were on a motorcycle instead of a horse, and out of the two of us, Griffith probably considered himself the knight. Regardless, I was confident I knew were Berta was at…or had been …or would be soon.

That was the problem with the visions. I didn't know if they were past, present, or future. Plus, I couldn't tell if she was dead or alive, but I recognized the nail polish from her fingertips dangling to drag through the grass. Whoever took her didn't seem to be very strong, and had to be of average height or shorter, since carrying her seemed to be challenging.

I held to the image of finding Berta and bringing her back to Chance. Otherwise if I dwelled too long I would then recall I hadn't believed she was in any real danger, except from the Neb Knows reporter. Although I didn't know whose shoe I saw in the vision. For all I knew, it was the reporter dragging her up to the run-down cabin in the woods.

I tucked my head against Griffith's back, pressing away the thought of the beautiful tattoo he despised hidden beneath the leather. He had so many scars that he couldn't even contain them all on the inside. They seeped through to his flesh to mark him.

Though I put on a show of protest, secretly I was glad I didn't have my motorcycle. There was no way I could've ridden it safely going this fast. The cool temperature dropped close to frigid at this speed and chilled my exposed skin.

The path was much rougher on the motorcycle than I remembered from the bicycle. Going with Griffith also gave me more confidence than Chance and I poking around on our own. My previous victories stemmed from trial and error. That was one of the perks of having a boyfriend who could intimidate on sight and who had experience in dealing with unsavory situations. I didn't want to say anything to Chance yet, in case my vision was wrong, or came too late. He didn't need to see her like that, especially after he found Destiny.

The hodgepodge items in my jacket jammed in my side uncomfortably as I molded myself against Griffith. I shifted so my cell phone would quit trying to impact itself permanently between my ribs. It was useless right now anyway. I had no service the last time we stopped. I could only hope I might have something here if it was needed.

Griffith counted on me to direct him in successfully finding the cabin. I wasn't as confident that I could locate it again, nor was I eager to return. I'd neglected to mention about my unease during my last visit, or how I distinctly felt as if the dilapidated shack experienced disappointment at my departure. That would sound crazy. Plus, verbalizing such a bizarre admission to Griffith would convince him that I shouldn't go—or that I'd moved one step closer to losing my mind. Most didn't question the unusual in these parts, but explaining how the cabin whispered to me, and appeared upset, would be harder to sell than most of the strange occurrences accepted as the norm.

After dwelling on the experience, I realized I had a

similar, although less intense reaction to Griffith's house before. The only reasonable explanation I could produce, which wasn't reasonable in any sense of the word, was that both structures were made with wood from this area. Any trees from this part of the forest used in a structure were bound to leave an imprint on the emotional state of the construction.

The deeper we went, the more everything looked the same. My confidence in locating the origin of the vision wavered. Dense, ominous foliage surrounded us and hung heavy over the path. Even though many trees abandoned their leaves for the season long ago, the sheer number of them crowded together obliterated the view into the forest. The thick, dead, and shriveled underbrush made it difficult to see more than a few feet off the road. The roped roots which lay curled and arching as if reaching for our tires made me not want to.

Griffith said he didn't recall ever seeing the creepy cabin Chance and I stumbled across, but his mother must have, or else I wouldn't have had the vision. At least I thought that was how it worked.

I poked Griffith's side to gain his attention and then pointed to the right. I thought I glimpsed the sign as we whizzed by. Griffith slowed the bike. We pulled to the side of the road. He shut off the engine. It sputtered and silenced. The contrasting stillness of the woods made me cringe. There was no way we could arrive unannounced on this motorcycle. This beast announced its imminent arrival from miles away. Although there were a lot of motorcycles around here, so perhaps they'd think someone passed through if we didn't drive right up to the door.

After tugging off my helmet and placing it on the seat, I walked back to where we passed the sign. It was weird seeing it nailed to a tree here, just like it presented in my mind. I suppressed a shiver. This was the first time I viewed something in person after only seeing it in a vision. I bent closer to study it. The scrawled letters were comparable to a five-year-old writing them, painted on a broken piece of wood splintered and ragged at the edges. It hung crooked and drooped to one side. The words *GO AWAY* appeared more ominous up close. I touched the letters.

A vision came on with enough force to make me recoil and almost knock me off my feet. I stumbled to maintain my balance.

"What is it?" Griffith rushed to my side. He cupped my elbows to support me as my knees shook.

I closed my eyes and then blinked a few times, pressing a hand to my head. One benefit of the vision annihilating me and then quickly departing was that it didn't drain me as thoroughly. "That was intense. Maybe if what I saw just happened, the vision is stronger than the others."

Griffith frowned, but wisely refrained from openly disagreeing.

Through trial and error, I'd identified a pattern. The further away in time into the past or the future, the harder the images were to clarify. This time the images appeared as if watching a movie. They presented as crystal clear but told me nothing. "I saw a man's hand touching the sign as he passed. I'm fine."

Griffith studied me with concern furrowing his brow. "I still think it wasn't in your best interest for you to come out here after you just went through all...of that."

Before we left his house, he reiterated his lack of faith in my newest ability. He'd stated, for the millionth time and sounding an awful lot like Chance, about how I had no idea how to interpret my recently acquired gift of foresight. He insisted he feared at worst the vision could lead me into a trap.

I'd denied Hecate and hadn't chosen to follow in her footsteps to reign in the Underworld. That didn't mean she or her minions wouldn't seek another method to claim me—even if it was against my will. Bad guys didn't have to play nice.

"I'm here now. I'm fine." I studied the area, trying to locate anything else recognizable from my vision. Nothing appeared remotely familiar.

Despite the short interval of time since Chance and I found the creepy cabin, the foliage had morphed in size and shape as if we visited decades ago. I didn't think the atmosphere could've appeared more ominous. I was wrong. "This doesn't look the same as when we were here before."

Twigs snapped underneath my feet as I cautiously approached. I couldn't quite identify the difference, but something had changed. The closer we got to the cabin, the more unusual the remaining trees and plants appeared. At first glance, some resembled ordinary growth and skeletal shrubbery. Their subtle shifts from normal allowed them to blend into the background as my gaze skimmed by, but eerie enough to draw my attention to return for a closer inspection.

Other vegetation didn't bother with attempts to camouflage their abnormality. Their branches curled up and over like arms. Long, tentacle-like fingers reached toward or away from the cabin, depending upon *when* you looked. I spun to the right when something shifted in the corner of my sight. As I focused on the still scenery, a chill made me tremble. Griffith's reassuring touch did little to calm my racing heart or my growing unease, but his presence provided me with the confidence to continue rather than flee as my failing courage urged.

Thoughts of the vision and Berta enabled me to move closer. The ground rose in a way that made the growth sprouting from the trees appear to defy the laws of gravity. I struggled to maintain my balance as I crept closer. The kaleidoscope of ever-changing greenery made it difficult to discern a clear path. It was as if we viewed the area in the distorted mirrors of a fun house. I feared if I wandered too far into this section of the woods that I'd be unable to separate fact from fabrication.

The only thing grounding me in reality was Griffith. I laid my hand on his arm, drawing comfort from his unruffled manner. He stood with his hands braced on his hips, sturdier than any tree trunk. The peculiar surroundings failed to intimidate him.

"I've seen this kind of growth before near an entrance." Griffith's clipped words, and the twitch in the tense muscles along his jawline betrayed his apprehension. "These changes are the early stage. After it advances enough there won't be anything left green or standing, only rocks and piles of dirt." He sighed. "Everything gives up after a while. There's only so much fight in anything."

"An entrance to what?" I looked to him, uncertain if I wanted to know the answer. I had a pretty good idea of what he referred to with his vague reference, and I didn't like it—not at all.

Chapter Thirteen

The way Griffith studied me, and the tension lining his jaw left me with no doubt that he was determining how to explain more of the unexplainable. His hesitation revealed how much he wanted to leave me secure in blissful ignorance. No matter what his good intentions were, inevitably he would have to destroy a little more of what I considered reality.

"Just like people, the forest tries to become resilient against unnatural change. The process is like evolution. It adapts to survive. Some things do, some don't, and others...well they're changed, kind of mutated. Still a tree, but not the same anymore."

A shudder ran through me as he confirmed my concerns about the cabin. I moved closer to him. I glanced around with more scrutiny than before, with my bravado fading faster than the recent echoes of the stilled engine of the motorcycle. The woods loomed unusually quiet—not an encouraging sign. The overwhelming shade prompted much of the foliage to die well ahead of schedule. Either the lack of sunlight killed the growth, or the breeding of Oppressors. The greedy bastards tended to suck the life out of anything, not only people. "If there is an entrance, can things come out, as well as go in?"

I held up my hand, stopping his response. "Forget I asked. The answer is not important now, is it? I mean, whole hordes of Oppressors, or other unearthly creatures, won't lurk in that cabin, will they?" My forced, dry chuckle scratched my parched throat.

Griffith's expression deterred me from waiting for, or wanting, an answer. "Maybe," he said.

He knew I didn't need a response. He waited for me to come to that conclusion for myself and accept the potential risk involved. *It was go time.* I drew back my shoulder blades. I needed to act like an Enchantling, or forever feel like a cowardly imposter. I sucked in a deep breath and pressed on before he tried to change my mind. "Can you see the cabin?" I pointed to where part of the structure was visible through the dead stalks of grass.

Griffith nodded. "Yes." He braced his hands on his hips and held his shoulders more rigid than a general preparing to commence battle. His patience made my own racing heart mimic a hamster fruitlessly trying to break free from the wheel.

What I wanted to ask was if he could *feel* the cabin like I did, but I feared that might prompt him to ask more questions. He knew about enough of my oddities, no need to wave my freak show flag. I detected the close proximity of the weird funhouse long before the entity assaulted my sight. The cabin was small in stature but commanded the space it claimed. The disturbing shadowy structure penetrated my mind, poking and prodding to gain my attention. I never experienced anything remotely like this. This *thing* shouldn't have emotions. The lure was reminiscent of the way Chance led me to my family, and the disquieting way Drake had invaded my thoughts.

Drake's presence in my head had presented as

more threatening and evil, while the weird awareness of the cabin was almost like it's feeble attempt to welcome me. As if the structure longed to stretch out planks of wood to engulf me in a splintery hug. It proved about as successful as a deranged clown extending an invitation into a sewer tunnel promising fun and games for an unknown price.

We stopped and stood at the base of the small hill to face the cabin. I wiped away the damp sweat from my forehead with my sleeve. I huffed a few breaths to act as if exertion, not fear, prompted my perspiration. It was doubtful my charade fooled Griffith, but he was kind enough to pretend he didn't notice.

My cellphone confirmed a lack of service, although I couldn't imagine who I would call for help if I could. I wouldn't risk Chance, and having Griffith with me was my best bet. We were on our own. I sought his hand to link his fingers with mine. His neutral expression made me suspect he didn't experience the same unsettling draw to the unearthly dwelling.

He faced me and then placed my hands on his chest. I could feel his heart. His worry for me prompted an extra gallop to its pace. "You have to be sure. You're volunteering to rush into who knows what. We don't even know if Berta is in there. I don't know exactly who, or what, will be waiting inside, but I doubt we'll face many at once. They're predators, so they need living things to feed upon. They won't find enough surviving to draw from around here. Besides, they don't travel in groups, especially low level Oppressors. They're too volatile. They have no ability to work together."

"No problem. We make a great team. They're no

match for us," I said, with forced enthusiasm to try and lighten my unease.

Griffith raised his brows, reminding me without a word about his vow to avoid situations such as these. I assumed he might consider risking my life and saving Berta's an exception. I sighed. "Right. Just me then. Let's get this over with."

Griffith straightened and dropped my hands, effectively closing the conversation. "You can wait at the motorcycle while I check the area out. If anything goes wrong…well, hopefully you can manage the bike well enough on your own." He cringed. "Remember that my motorcycle isn't anything like the one you rode."

I'd assumed correctly. No way could he stand by and not become involved, no matter how much he didn't want to. "No, it's not, and I'm not going to wait."

Although secretly pleased that he proposed to step in and let me play the role of damsel in distress, I couldn't. His half-hearted offer of his motorcycle revealed how much the situation unnerved him. Even though he wouldn't admit to it, he loved that bike. He'd named it. I heard him whispering to *Zelda* when he washed the frame with a loving caress. If he wasn't thoroughly worried, there was no way he would offer to sacrifice his metal baby to my inept riding skills. We both knew I couldn't manage the eight-hundred-pound beast without inflicting more than one dent or disfigurement. Most likely I'd end up dropping the motorcycle on my leg, crushing my bones, and leaving me helplessly pinned to the ground to await death by a hungry Oppressor.

I shook my head. "I started this mess. You won't

have to finish it, again." Like he had to do for me before with Drake. That act left him suffering with guilt for months about his role in his half-brother's demise—and maybe forever. Neither of us wanted to go into the cabin, but sometimes you did what you had to do, not what you wanted to do.

Griffith's sigh spoke louder than any words. "You don't need to do this. I'm made for dealing with whatever awaits in the cabin. I have before, and I can do it again."

He said the words with reluctance, because he had hoped to not have to do these things again. He'd made an effort to change what he was, what he believed he was destined to do, but it seemed I kept challenging him. His fear that he might discover he enjoyed experiencing that rush of power again, if given the chance, was evident.

"Yes. I do need to do this." I touched his arm. The ropey muscles were rigid with tension. "I need to do it, much more than you. To right who and what I've wronged."

"It's not your fault." His dark eyes flashed with irritation, and the hazy fog building around his head conveyed his frustration.

"It's more my fault than yours." I stood my ground, arms crossed over my chest, crushing the two jackets against me. The hodgepodge items crammed in the pockets poked into my sides. I could be as stubborn as him, perhaps even more so.

"No. You don't need to do this, Hope." He spoke the words slowly and firmly. His intention was clear. He lifted his hands toward me, reaching for my face.

I stepped away from his false reassurance,

identifying his gesture for what it really was, a method to sway my decision. "Oh, no, you don't. Don't you dare try to use any of your hypnotic-crap to get me to agree. I mean it."

He dropped his hands when I called his bluff. "Can we at least face this together this time?" Griffith spoke as if he offered a compromise. The underlying steel determination in his eyes told me he planned to push me out of harms' way the first chance he got.

I just couldn't give him the chance.

We were both stubborn. This futile argument could go on for far longer than Berta might have. "Fine. Do you mind if I leave the motorcycle jacket here? I wouldn't want the coat to get torn or dirty, and I'm a little warm anyway." That was partially true. Today was unseasonably warm for fall, but my request had more to do with my desire to have less restriction to move quickly if necessary. I needed all the advantages I could get.

"Sure. No one will bother it." He waited as I slipped out of the jacket, leaving my lightweight surplus jacket on underneath. I could've left that as well. My anxiety worked as a furnace, ramping up my body temperature, but I didn't want to leave the ratty, old jacket. It was kind of like my security blanket. I touched the soft fabric of the sleeve, drawing comfort from the familiar item. It was one of the few items remaining from what I liked to think of as my life before arriving in this town. I couldn't think of that time as before Griffith. In some way or another, he was always a part of my life, if only in my dreams.

We started up the hill, with Griffith leading. He moved with a slow predatory stride, taking in the area with an intense confident focus. The hazy fog surrounding him danced with lights, betraying his heightened emotions.

I tried to mimic his self-assurance, but instead froze as my stomach clenched with anxiety. I struggled to focus on Berta and willed my anger to the forefront of my thoughts to prepare myself. This hadn't worked that well the last time I visited the cabin, but it was the only thing I could offer to help find Berta. Perhaps I should've practiced controlling my ability beforehand instead of practicing like it was an on-the-job training seminar, as Ruthie referred to nurturing my skills. Better preparation would've been wise. Then maybe my ability wouldn't have almost killed me when Andy sapped the life out of me. The time before that, Hecate had as well.

I was so screwed.

By the time I overcame my indecision and gained control of my rising panic, Griffith was already on the crumbling porch. His concerned expression confirmed that my attempts at disguising my unease were unsuccessful. With total disregard to replicating the caution he displayed, I broke into a jog to catch up before he could reiterate the multitude of rational reasons why I should wait outside. Being rational wasn't one of my strong points.

The flimsy steps creaked and cracked under my determined stride. I nodded to dispel his unspoken question and set a firm line to my lips. "Are you ready? Let's go."

Griffith opened the door with more force than necessary and almost tore it from its hinges. He ducked to squeeze through the doorframe. I followed. His broad shoulders blocked my view of the interior until he stepped aside. I tensed, waiting for the cabin to sense me and send its tentacles probing for my innermost thoughts. *Nothing.*

I released my breath and scanned the small room. With the foreboding sensation and underlying devious intent missing, the place only appeared to threaten tetanus from a rusty nail or an asthma attack from the heaps of accumulated dust. It felt like nothing more than an old, abandoned cabin. *Had I imagined it before?*

"I need to get some fresh air." I walked back outside, shielding my eyes from the sunlight streaming through the break in the trees to where I stood. I sighed. I was so sure. Maybe my vision was long past or hadn't happened yet. Perhaps we were too early. I could only hope. Griffith didn't question my abrupt departure. He was probably relieved that I left the inspection to him and got out of his way.

I stepped off the porch. The board on the step creaked in protest at my weight. I clutched the rail shaking under my hand, fearing I might break my neck in this run-down shit hole. I circled around the house. The back of the structure was bricked except for a single door about three feet from the ground. There was no attached porch or steps to stand on. Impulsively stepping out guaranteed a nice fall and the promise of a few broken bones. The porch had either been neglected in the building process or crumbled and fell apart from years of decay.

My skin prickled along my spine. I spun. *Nothing.* The woods loomed about eight feet behind the cabin. Roots and dangling branches appeared to creep forward, longing to close the space. The trees back here were more twisted and warped than the ones on the path. Eerie knotholes presented an uncanny resemblance to malevolent eyes. I couldn't shake the uncomfortable sensation that the thick, peeling bark watched me. *Goddess.* I was losing my mind.

A breeze picked up and the trees shuddered in unison, causing a shower of leaves. They should've been colored with the beautiful autumn shades of orange, yellow, and auburn but instead landed on the ground dead and blackened at the edges.

I studied the foliage. The growths were thicker and overlapped here more than any other section we passed. New plants sprouted and grew on top of the others and smothered the previous growths. Something didn't want me near this part of the woods. Usually that thought alone would be enough to convince me I shouldn't be there. Despite being an Enchantling, courage wasn't always my strong point, but being angry was, and I was thoroughly pissed about everything that led me up to this dead end with Berta. Determination burned a fire within me to find her and bring her back alive and unscathed.

My confidence waivered as the breeze returned and the branches of the trees scratched against each other, sounding akin to nails on a chalkboard. *Nice try.* That sound never bothered me. I took a step. The trees quieted. They appeared to hunker together to form a conspiring huddle. The wind trickled to an unclear whispering.

I took another step. Two squirrels rushed me from the front of the house and stopped so close in front of me that I nearly stepped on one. They hopped around in spasms despite their near miss with the sole of my shoe. I pulled back, fearing they might be rabid. They stilled and sat on their haunches to study me. I lowered my hands to my sides.

"Oh." Surely by now even the critters would've figured out that I'm not Destiny. I couldn't even come close to her gentle soul. "Sorry fellas, I don't have time for this."

When I tried to ignore them and continue, they ran circles around my feet, dizzying me with their speed. One would drop out and run to the road and then race to return. Then the other would do the same. I watched them with fascination, wondering what the hell their problem was other than frustration that I denied their attention.

"Ouch." One of them pulled at my pant leg, nipping through the fabric to my flesh. I pulled up the material to examine the spot. I rubbed the tender flesh, relieved the skin didn't break from the bite. Besides the weird obsession with me, these squirrels weren't acting normal. I knelt and both squirrels froze. They locked their beady eyes on me in an intent stare. Once assured they gained my attention, they simultaneously looked toward the road like some creepy zombie critters.

"You want me to leave?" Questioning the squirrels validated that I had finally lost my mind. But this response was obviously the correct one. Both squirrels scampered toward the road again and then back to me. "Sorry fellas, I need one quick peek or I'll never forgive myself. No stone unturned, okay?"

I rushed toward the woods before losing my confidence. The squirrels chattered their protest and then ran in the opposite direction, leaving me on my own. The grass and twigs snapped under my feet until I neared the edge where the ground was mostly dirt. Where nothing dared to grow. I pushed through the first trees. The thick foliage hindered my progress and tore a small section on the arm of my coat when the fabric caught on a stray branch. "Damn."

I stumbled to a stop in front of a wall of thick tree trunks. I braced my hands against the bark so I didn't run headlong into them. I leaned forward, panting to catch my breath, and then peered through a small gap between the trees. Discarded shells of cicadas lined the trees. I drew my hand back as I brushed against one and it crumbled into dust.

An orange rusty van sat concealed by the woods. A narrow, rutted path led to the spot. Layers of dirt covered the van and a bumper sticker that said, *"Horn Broke Watch for Finger."* My breath caught. I knew this van. I saw the piece of crap almost every day at Last Call.

I looked around until I found a way through the foliage. Crouching to crawl by a bush wasn't my first choice, but it was my only choice if I wanted to get to the van. The stealth I desired for my approach was lost as the bush shook to and fro from my unsuccessful attempts to squeeze through. Branches clung to me and caught in my hair.

I stood once I emerged and scanned the area. The silence remained absolute—never a good sign. I leaned to the left, peering toward the driver's seat and sighed with relief. The van was empty. The driver's window was half open. I recoiled at the stench wafting out. Careful not to touch the window sill of the van in case this later became evidence, I held my breath and leaned forward for a better view. I refused to think about what I might find, because doing so made me consider the possibility that Berta wouldn't return alive.

It pained me to think of telling my brother that she was dead. Then there was the possibility that Berta would find a way, family or not, to return to The Kitchen in the afterlife to harass me for the rest of my days. She'd force her way into mirrors in my house to criticize my lackluster skills with cosmetics or advise me on new hairstyles. I had to find her alive.

Trash from fast food restaurants littered the van floor. Every cup holder housed a can of soda, half empty cup of coffee, or another unidentifiable liquid. Dead bugs floated on top of the liquid where they stopped in for their last drink. The back of the van wasn't visible, because the last two seats were either missing or completely buried in trash. I moved to the outside rear, drawing my hands inside the sleeves of my jacket to open the double doors on the back of the old-fashioned van without leaving fingerprints.

I grabbed the handles and turned them with haste before chickening out. I threw open the doors. The stench rolling out made me stumble back and cover my nose with the sleeve of my jacket. Although I didn't associate the reek as rotting flesh—my worst fear—but rather the trash and dirt piled upon a decaying mattress. Stains and tears through the fabric confirmed it was the home, and burial ground, for more than one creature. I wrinkled my nose in disgust.

I ran back to the cabin, ignoring the scratches of the barricade of branches, and burst through the tree line. Griffith circled around the house, his pace quick. He stopped when he saw me rushing toward him, relief evident on his face. "Where the hell did you go? Don't tell me you went in the woods by yourself."

"Okay, I won't." I bent, panting from the exertion of the sprint. "I found a van in the woods, hidden within the trees. She's here, Griffith. She has to be."

He studied me, and then looked toward the woods, doubt clouded his features. "You're sure? I searched the cabin."

"Yes, it's Ritchie's van." Even though days had already passed, it felt like every additional minute sealed an unpleasant fate for Berta.

"Did you, um, did you look inside the van?" He ran a hand over his head and studied me. Starting with my hair, which had to be littered with a halo of twigs and leaves, and then settling on my face. I'm sure I'd ditched the confidence and self-assurance I arrived with and replaced it with a wild-eyed crazy woman. Griffith's uncertain expression conveyed his preference to dealing with Oppressors and other boogeymen over hysterical women.

I nodded and a few leaves fell off me. "She's not in there. A lot of other crap, but no Berta." I clutched his forearms, ignoring the way my voice raised and cracked when I said her name. "She has to be in the cabin. We should go back again. We're missing something. Just like the van, I would've never seen it if not for the squirrels showing me. There must be something hidden that we didn't see the first time."

"The squirrels?" He spoke slowly and deliberately, and then shook his head. He held up his hand. "Believe it or not, I don't want to know. I wouldn't understand, nor would I want to. But we've been through the cabin. She's not there. We would've seen something by now if she was."

I was uncertain if my hysterics put Griffith off, or the comment about the squirrels, but I wouldn't let him deter me. "Please Griffith, we need to look one more time." Something lured me away to the van. It wanted me before, when I was alone, but not with Griffith. I didn't give a shit what the sleazy supernatural sensation wanted, I needed him with me. I could handle it on my own, but having a security blanket in the form of a big, hunky Splice was helpful if this was the Underworld's way of inviting me in for tea and toast.

He sighed. "Fine, let's go before we lose what little light we have when darkness sets in."

I shared my life with darkness since day one, but I didn't believe he referenced the same thing. We returned to the cabin with less hesitation than before, our unease lessened by the amount of time we'd already spent inspecting every part. But apparently, we hadn't checked everything. There had to be something we were missing. I just knew it. There had to be.

Griffith barged through the door with less stealth than before, obviously believing a second exploration was unnecessary. Once I entered, the eerie sensation returned with less intensity than on my first visit. My unease with the oily invasion of my mind distracted me from my intent and made me want to leave immediately. The whispered word, *leave*, echoed through my mind. I froze. It wasn't my fear pressing me to leave. The cabin or whatever inhabited it wanted us gone. It'd tried to distract me all along. This time I wasn't playing.

I stopped in the middle of the small room, tensing to slow my racing thoughts, worries, and fears. I had to focus. *What didn't it want me to notice?* I closed my eyes and inhaled. There it was again. A waft of the scent of chewing tobacco that Ritchie was never without. It intermingled with the stench of death and brimstone I only associated with one thing. I furrowed my brow. The smell didn't make sense. Ritchie wasn't an Oppressor.

I surveyed the room, overlooking the broken furniture cluttering the space. There had to be more than these few ramshackle rooms. I closed my eyes again, ignoring the noise from Griffith as he tromped around, tossing things in his impatience to finish this task. He grunted as he stubbed his toe on the protruding edge of wood propped against the wall. The offending piece fell with a clatter.

I stopped looking around and looked down. Clutter concealed the floor. Pieces of all manners of fragments of wood, trash, animal droppings, and dirt littered the space…except for an area in the corner. I approached the chair. Someone's great, great grandmother had gotten their money's worth, and then some, out of the dilapidated eyesore. The dust ended near there. The rest of the floor didn't spare a place to walk without stubbing a toe or gaining a splinter, but this section was clear.

I knelt. The stench increased enough to cause my eyes to water more profusely than any onion. Having an elevated olfactory sense wasn't necessarily a good thing. The pungent scent of death and decay was never pleasant to start with, let alone amplified.

The creak of the floorboards announced Griffith's approach. "What are you doing?"

I ran my hand across the dirty floor, gaining a

splinter as I sought inconsistencies in the grain. I stood and wiped my palms on my pants. "There has to be a trap door here somewhere, except I can't find a ridge for it."

Griffith bent and ran his hands over the floor. A crack appeared in an outline of a rectangle hardly big enough for a person to squeeze through. He pushed his fingers into an edge and pulled. It opened to reveal a dark, spider-web-infested hole with a descending ladder.

I took a step back, peering into the dark abyss. The cabin suddenly looked much more appealing than whatever waited below. I looked to Griffith. He appeared less enthusiastic than I did about his discovery. It wasn't every day that your boyfriend opened the door to—goddess knows what. Just when I thought I'd figured him out. "How did you do that?"

He ran his hands over his jeans, leaving a shadow of dust on the fabric. He raised his head with a frown. "The wood recognizes me. No matter how far I bury it I can't change what I am."

The despair in his words pained me. I touched his arm, wishing I could provide him comfort. "Well, this time it's a good thing. Otherwise we would never have pried it open or found this."

He flushed and avoided my look of empathy. He straightened, shedding any further thoughts about his vulnerabilities. "Take some credit. You thought to look on the floor, not me. Besides, it doesn't mean she's down there. You should wait up here. If we find Berta, well, it might not be pleasant. A lot of time has passed."

"No. We're in this together, remember? We won't know if she's down there unless we check." I held my hand over my nose but couldn't prevent the odor from gagging me. It was difficult to maintain a kick ass persona with bile rising in the back of my throat. I'd lose all credibility if I vomited on Griffith's shoes. "Doesn't the stink bother you?"

He shrugged, oblivious to the putrid fumes. "Somewhat, but sadly I've become accustomed to it over the years."

This was a scent I never wanted to become used to. Griffith turned and lowered himself to the first step, clutching the swaying ladder in his descent. Ritchie must be much more agile than I envisioned for a man his size to descend the rickety rungs without breaking his neck.

Griffith hopped to the dirt at the bottom, eliciting a cloud of dust. I followed him, ignoring the rush of fear that once I entered, the trap door would snap shut and never release me from the bowels of this unnatural entity.

I jumped from the last step. Griffith steadied me when I stumbled into him. I turned to face a gaping cavern carved into the earth. "What in the hell is this?"

"Not hell, but close." Griffith's deep voice echoed through the space.

The ground opened in a tunnel. Lanterns hung along the walls were lit with a small flame. Their soft glow barely penetrated the inky blackness. It was daylight outside, but this hellhole didn't abide by the rules of night and day. We walked into the dead of night. I groped for Griffith's hand, grateful he came with me and that I didn't have to face this alone. If nothing else, his steady grip might prevent me from doing a nosedive if I tripped over the huge stones cast to the side.

I scanned the walls, and then covered my mouth to stifle my scream until I realized it was only my distorted reflection staring at me. A warped, hazy mirror hung on the wall beside a small shelf. The combination reminiscent of something kept for storing keys and mail upon entering someone's house. All it needed was a cross-stitched *Home Sweet Home* to complete the tacky ensemble. But who, or what, would want to live here? A mountain of discarded keys was stacked high in the corner. One of Berta's bizarre superstitious sayings rose in my mind. *A key without a lock opens the devil's door.*

Like the bizarre story of the girl falling in a rabbit hole, the width of the tunnel expanded as we progressed. I pulled my jacket tight to block the unexplained gusts of chilly air. The temperature dropped at least ten to fifteen degrees colder than outside. Our footsteps echoed loudly off the dirt walls, alerting anyone or anything of our arrival. I froze as the light breeze sounded like a loving whisper.

Honey, we're home.

Chapter Fourteen

I rushed to keep pace with Griffith. He didn't react, so I must've imagined the voice. I wouldn't allow myself to consider how much it sounded like the one from the cabin the last time I was here. Or how welcoming and inviting it sounded.

As the walls widened, the area became bright enough for me to see a little better. I stumbled when my foot rammed into a makeshift wooden floor. I glanced to Griffith. He shrugged, appearing as confused as I was as we stepped on the wood. My hope faded. The odd environment was just as unfamiliar to him. As we walked, we encountered large piles of clutter. This must be where all the washing machines deposited stolen socks, and all the other odd objects misplaced over a lifetime. Most of the rubble consisted of items no one would miss, or trash that was already discarded.

"It's like a tunnel of lost crap." Despite my whisper, my words echoed back to us off the underground walls.

"One man's trash." Griffith scanned the room, his gaze stopping on the ceiling.

"Ends up in another man's tunnel?" I altered the saying and followed his gaze.

We stood in front of a built-in wooden archway. I shuddered. My skin crawled with a ghostly sensation as if we'd arrived at the door to hell. Unfortunately, the archway meant whatever dwelled in there wouldn't have to climb out because the door was already open. "This may be the creepiest thing yet."

The wood on each side was fashioned into the form of a man. One arm dangled in greeting. Another reached up to form the arch and intertwined with the figure carved on the other side. The wide stump of the tree spread out, with no visible roots supporting it. The creepy ass thing burrowed directly into the ground.

"Is it…are they…these aren't low level Oppressors, are they? This isn't how they start? Or these weren't people petrified into wood, were they?" Hecate had resembled a medusa with her snake-like tendrils of hair, but I didn't think she had the ability to turn anyone into stone…or rather, wood. Spending the rest of my life in a dark, smelly tunnel fashioned into a tree trunk would not be an ideal way to finish my days.

I was relieved to have Griffith here for more than his strength and support, but also his knowledge to help explain the continued mysteries the forest contained.

Griffith ran his hand over the trunk of the *figure*, causing me to shudder. "No, I don't think so. These were just trees. They were probably trying to contort themselves into a form she'd desire in the hopes they might have a chance to walk the earth rather than spend their lives rooted in one spot."

I pressed closer to Griffith as we passed under the archway. I picked up my step, instinctively ducking my head in fear that one of the tree men would grab at my hair with his stick fingers. After we emerged on the other side, the walls held less dirt. Pieces of wood and plywood pressed up against them. Stones and dirt seeped around the make-shift walls. As we progressed further, brick and concrete patches were incorporated to solidify the walls better. The hodgepodge efforts at building grew more mindful the deeper we went. As if something was building the tunnel on its way out, rather than building one in. The thought was more disturbing than anything I'd seen so far.

"My goodness. The tunnel is like part of a house. It has little rooms." We stopped to face a door on the left, embedded into the wall with rocks protruding around to form the frame. What's behind door number one? I wasn't so sure I wanted to find out.

I felt like I fell down the rabbit hole, but this was no wonderland. This was closer to the gates of Hell. I reached for the knob but hesitated with my hand hovering midway. "Should we open it?"

"That's what we came here for, isn't it? I think we both know where this might lead." He gestured to the tunnel. It continued with no apparent end. The stench of desolation and decay increased the deeper we went. I hoped we wouldn't have to go much further. "Hope, we can't leave without seeing what's inside the room."

There was nothing I wanted more than to turn and leave before seeing the image of goddess knows what that waited behind this door, but I couldn't. Griffith was right. I rested my hand on the knob. Griffith laid his over mine, squeezing lightly. "Together?"

I smiled. His touch provided the comfort and reassurance I needed. I nodded. "Together."

We turned the knob. When the door swung open, Griffith jerked me against his chest and stepped aside. We tensed against the wall as one form, waiting to see if something, or someone, would emerge. Nothing did. He released me and inched forward enough to view inside the room.

"Did you ever think this might've been a good time to bring some kind of weapon?" I whispered into the shoulders blocking my view.

"I am a weapon," Griffith whispered back.

"I hope that means you're bullet proof, and resilient against sharp objects, and—"

"Shh, I think someone's in here. I see something in the mirror." He clenched his fists.

"A mirror?" Would Tessa or one of my other dead relatives choose to drop in here? I moved around Griffith to get a look in the room.

He shoved me back. A grunt escaped me when I fell on my ass on a pile of junk. Griffith stepped into the room in a fighter's stance. I braced myself on my hands and pushed to my knees. He'd lowered his arms to his sides. I stood and moved in behind him, ready to give him more than a piece of my mind for his attempt at heroics. My irritation waned once I followed his attention. "Berta?"

She slowly turned from where she was secured in an old kitchen chair. Chunks of stuffing hung from the torn padding on the plastic seat. "Hope?" Berta's voice sounded as flat as her hair. Her usual upbeat self appeared deflated and defeated without her ritual of bathing, brushes, and her arsenal of cosmetics.

She was alive. Until that moment, I hadn't realized how much doubt had penetrated my thoughts. I rushed to kneel in front of her. "Are you all right?" Roped knots bound her elbows to the chair, but they were loose and not tight enough to hold her if she wanted to escape the bindings.

She shrugged. "I guess. I'm tired, dirty, hungry,

and sick of this hole. I guess it could be worse. Why, how bad do I look?" Her gaze traveled over me and she wrinkled her nose. "At least I have an excuse, what happened to your hair?"

I self-consciously reached to pull out a few more twigs and then smiled. I was so happy that she was fine that I ignored her snarky comment. Leave it to Berta to ignore the bizarre surroundings and focus on her appearance. Luckily, the mirror wasn't within her view, or she might've been a tad more upset to catch a glimpse of her current disheveled state. "Fine. You look fine." I released the ropes, and she rubbed the red marks on her arms. "Why didn't you just untie these yourself?"

"I have, but he only left a few minutes ago. Sometimes he stops back to ask for another reading before he goes." Her eyes widened with the first signs of distress, and she dropped her voice to a whisper, "Plus, they don't like it if I try to leave."

Griffith followed Berta's gaze to the doorway. He stepped in the opening and scanned the tunnel. "Who left? Ritchie?"

Berta began to stand, but her quivering legs made her collapse back on the chair. The cushion let out a weak gust of air. "Yes."

I touched her shoulders to steady her and permitted a little hope to strengthen her. "Why?"

She frowned and looked to my hand. I withdrew my touch and shoved my hand in my pocket. "He likes to collect things. They're not going to be happy if I try to go without Ritchie."

The glittery tendrils of hope spilled from my pockets to flutter and dissipate. "But why did he take you?"

"Man, I'm so hungry I could even eat some carbs. I can't remember the last time I had a carb." She touched her hair and grimaced at the greasy lock. "Or washed my hair." She sighed and deflated, leaning over her knees. "Ritchie did it so I can read his palm anytime he wants. They made me stay because they like to keep him happy."

I tensed and looked to Griffith. The way his gaze scanned the room and hall like a predator didn't relieve my growing unease. "Wait, you said 'they.' Who else is involved?"

Berta cupped her head in her palms. "Not who; what. Whatever the hell comes up from that tunnel." Her eyes widened, and her expression turned solemn. "I'm not going out to find out. Anytime I open the door I can hear them. I smell them. So, I didn't try to go out. Heck, I won't even open my eyes if I think one of them is nearby. I'd much rather deal with Ritchie. Better the evil you know…"

I stepped with caution. Junk filled the room from corner to corner except for the small area cleared in the center for Berta. She sat in the place of honor, nestled amongst the cluster of possessions. No space was left uncovered and no surface untouched. Clutter pressed against the small bed by the wall. The edges of the dingy mattress were exposed under the lacey, frilly comforter much too small for an adult, let alone a bed. It appeared to be an adequate size for a doll. Comments I made previously about Berta resembling a living doll rose and washed over my thoughts. Never had I considered Ritchie might actually want one, or dreamed about the horror of him trying to make Berta into one.

"Does he live here?"

"I think he stays with his mother most of the time. This place is kind of like his man cave." Berta shuddered. "It's disgusting. I mean, I'm okay. I haven't died of starvation or gone stark raving mad, but close to it. It's just gross. I'd give almost anything for bleach and hand sanitizer. He couldn't have considered a woman's reaction when he brought me here. He thought I might make this a home. He said that. Is he crazy?" Her eyes widened, and their whites stood out against the smudges of dirt covering her face. "Wait, he must be nuts, even I know that. He kidnapped me and planted me here whether I wanted to stay or not. Who does that?"

A tremor ran through Berta, and her eyes misted over. "I'm ready to get out of here." She stood, and the color drained from her face. She swayed. I grabbed her waist to steady her and lowered her back to the seat. "Guess I didn't realize I got a little weak. I just need some sugar or a good sweet tea." She focused on me. "What…"

The sharp pain ignited my every nerve. I gritted my teeth as my vision grayed at the edges, giving the room a softened, vintage look. The arm of the chair supported me as my knees wobbled from inadvertently infusing Berta with a twinge of hope. I always avoided touching her, not that she wasn't already aware of my ability because of Chance's blabbing, but because it drained me too much.

Her eyes widened. She studied my hand and then my face. "So, it's true," she whispered with a frown and words laced with amazement. "No wonder Andy is always hitting you up for this stuff."

Griffith looked at me sharply at the reminder of my indiscretions and then stepped toward Berta. He rested his hands on her shoulders. "Here, let me help you." He gently tugged her from me. I released my grip and sagged over the chair, panting.

Once supported by Griffith's wall of strength and energized by my hit of hope, Berta brightened. "Let's get out of here before he gets back. I want to go."

Griffith's gaze traveled over my weakened state. "We'll wait a few minutes until Hope is ready."

I knew Berta's energy wouldn't last. She'd burn off that hit I gave her before she got out of the cabin. It was now or never. We needed to move while she had a little strength. I couldn't afford to give her much more. "Just go. Chance will never forgive me if we don't return his girlfriend safe."

I housed enough guilt without coming this far and then failing to get Berta safely out of here. "Go on." I gestured with my hands. "I'll be right behind you."

Berta didn't have to be told twice and started toward the door, tugging Griffith along with her. He frowned, his immense dislike of the suggestion evident. "But Hope—"

"For goodness sake, I banished the Queen of the Underworld. I think I can handle a creepy tunnel. We haven't seen or heard anything the entire time we've been down here and Berta said she hasn't either." I turned to her for confirmation. "Right, Berta?"

She screwed up her lips. "I did hear something the first few nights, an awful moaning sound. I thought it was a ghost coming or something like that. Although I'm not all that bothered by ghosts. I've talked to my grandmother occasionally over the years when she dropped by."

I rolled my eyes and then nodded for her to get on with the story.

"Anyway, the noise quit after the first two nights. I figured out the sound was Ritchie snoring outside the door. He told me he was afraid to leave the cabin, at first. "Cause I read his palm that day at the bar and told him a mysterious stranger would come into his life." She shook her head. "Ritchie doesn't like strangers, so he waited it out and kept making me do readings. Finally, I realized the only way to get rid of him was to tell him something positive." She shrugged. "Getting him to go didn't make much difference. I couldn't force the damn door open 'cause it locks from the outside."

I looked to Griffith. "Why aren't they hurting him? He's not an Oppressor." I tried to convey my unspoken question of why they left Berta alone. I didn't want to scare her by mentioning that the threat lurking outside of the door was much more immense than Ritchie.

Griffith pulled his lips in a thin line. His gaze flickered to Berta, but inevitably he determined no easy way to share his opinion without Berta overhearing. "He's like a Trojan horse, unsuspectingly aiding them with a means to an end. The Oppressors thrive on misery and the suffering of others, so it only makes sense that they'd promote this. He's their link to real, live people. Maybe this, Berta, I mean, is the first step. Or an agreement. We won't know until we ask Ritchie."

Our attempts at caution failed due to the tiny room lacking privacy and Griffith's weak attempt at discretion. Berta looked from me to Griffith, her eyes wide. "What do you mean an agreement?" Her voice rose with a tinge of hysteria.

"Just go, Griffith. I'll catch up."

Our eyes locked in an unspoken battle. He didn't want to leave me. I wasn't ready to go. Besides inadvertently giving Berta most of my energy reserves, once we found her the stress that held me together for the days she was missing departed and left me depleted. I just needed a few minutes. But it felt as if every minute counted while stuck underground in this hoarder freak show. I would only slow them down. They could be out of the cabin by the time I caught my breath. Easy peasy.

"Yes, let's go. We need to go." Berta bobbed her head. Her anxiety rose with each word as if she just realized the potential threat. In her weakened state, she lowered to the ground, clutching Griffith's leg.

He sighed and touched my arm. "Fine. You'll be directly behind us, right?"

"Yes. I promise." I had no intention of lingering here longer than necessary. But I couldn't let Chance down again. "Just get out of here quickly."

This was too easy. I knew it and by the uneasiness on his face I think Griffith felt the same. "If you're not out by the time I get Berta outside, I'm coming back for you."

The firm line to his jaw betrayed his unhappiness with this decision, and that he expected me to protest his statement.

"I'd expect nothing less." Our lips touched. I closed my eyes to relish the feel of him. He laid his hands on my shoulders. The light pressure steadied me. His scent comforted me and soothed my racing heart.

"You two can get a room later, let's go." Berta

tugged at Griffith's pant leg like an impatient child.

He pulled away and studied my face as if memorizing my features. With one swift move, he lifted Berta as if she weighed no more than the sacks of peanuts at the bar. He rushed out the door and strode down the hall at a rapid pace.

****

True to my word, I wasn't far behind. I peered down the tunnel, feeling like a mole seeking the sunlight. The darkness swallowed Griffith from my line of sight shortly after he left. I shuffled along the path. The stress and exertion of exploring the cabin, and the incident with Andy, revealed its toll on me in my sluggish stride. My progress was akin to a snail compared to Griffith. His predatory vision rivaled a nocturnal animal. My breath echoed off the walls and amplified in my ears. Now that I was completely alone, the feeling of isolation increased.

After what felt like an eternity, but in this warped reality was probably only about ten minutes, I made it to the exit. Relief flooded me at the thought of emerging from this hellhole. Just imagining the time Berta spent down here made me shudder.

I braced my hand on the wall and took a few deep breaths to prepare for the climb up the stairs. I grimaced. The nasty smell made me regret the inhalations.

A noise from above drew my attention. Someone had opened the trap door. I smiled. Thank goodness. Griffith must've gotten impatient and returned to get me. My smile faltered. A men's work boot, and a large ass, descended the ladder toward me.

No doubt about it, the jiggly mass of flesh wasn't

Griffith. *Shit*. Ritchie was back. I shuffled further in the tunnel, trying to avoid kicking loose stones and making too much noise. My efforts were fruitless since my steps echoed in the confined space. Ritchie paid me no attention. He was preoccupied grumbling to himself.

I stopped once I passed through the archway near the room Berta just vacated. There was a door on the other side, but a quick glimpse confirmed the space overflowed with junk. There was no room for me to squeeze in without risking permanent burial under an avalanche of trash. Ritchie wasn't exaggerating when he said he liked to collect things. I settled for pressing myself into the stone and dirt of the wall, hoping he might be too engrossed in his warped mind mutterings to notice me tucked in the shadows.

Ritchie shuffled down the hall. Unlike me, he didn't care how much noise he made. He huffed as he lumbered along. I never realized how noisy he was. It must be concealed by the volume of the bar on most days.

I held my breath. He came to a stop in front of the room where he kept Berta. He twisted the knob and peered in the room. "Bert? Where are you? Are you hiding from me?"

Although he always cherished Berta, after the recent events, the concern in his tone surprised me.

The door dragged along the ground when he forced it the rest of the way open. He entered the room. Sounds of him shuffling objects around confirmed his search for her. He must assume she was hiding amongst the clutter. I backtracked toward the ladder, hoping to exit this hole of horrors before he realized she was gone. I'd confront Ritchie and drag him back to pay for kidnapping Berta, but not in this creepy-ass tunnel. If the Oppressors were allies with Ritchie, hordes of them might emerge at any moment, leaving me at a complete disadvantage. I needed my feet firmly planted above ground to deal with them.

"Did you take her?" Ritchie yelled, his voice cracking with anger.

Fear froze me in place. *Damn.* No such luck evading him. I drew my shoulder blades together and spun to face Ritchie. I swallowed my retort because he wasn't talking to me.

His back was presented to me as he stared into the depths of the tunnel. "You promised to leave her alone." His voice echoed. "You…you said you wouldn't hurt her." His voice trembled, and he twisted his fingers in his hair. His agitation increased as he keened to the inky depths. "I need her. I don't know if I can go on without her. I don't know what to do. I need another reading. Give me my Berta."

Just who in the hell was he talking to? Rather than wait around to find out, I backed away. A protruding rock caught my heel, and I stumbled and fell with a thud. The air rushed out of me in a gasp.

"Who's there? Bert, is that you?" Ritchie turned toward me, squinting into the darkness. He hurried at the pace of a fast walk, probably having given up the thought of running years ago. When he spotted me, he stopped. Confusion clouded his expectant expression. "Hope? What are you doing here?"

"I, um." I couldn't think of one good reason why I was in Ritchie's underground home away from home.

"You took Bert, didn't you?" His brows drew together as the thought settled in his mind. "We were just fine. She liked it here." His face colored with anger. "You took her."

I pushed to my feet, brushing my hands to rid them of grime. "She's not yours to take, Ritchie. She doesn't belong in whatever this place is. You kidnapped her. That's a crime." I spoke in short sentences, hoping to make my point as quickly as possible, because his fury was escalating.

"She liked it here," Ritchie growled and bared his teeth, clenching his hand into a fist and then punching the warped mirror. As the glass shattered, the veins bulged in his forehead.

"That's seven years of bad luck, buddy." Unease trickled into me. No sense trying to convince him that Berta didn't care for her accommodations. He was beyond reason. Ritchie had never intimidated me before, but this was different. I was on his turf, literally. Plus, I'd never seen him this angry before. My best bet would be to escape this hellhole before things got worse.

Too late. A tremble ran through the tunnel. A few stones rolled across the ground. The skin along my neck prickled. I looked over my shoulder, and my jaw dropped. The shadows along the wall waxed and waned and morphed between black masses and human-like forms. They emerged from the depths of whatever fresh hell this lead to. The lanterns dimly lighting the space trembled and then extinguished as the entities approached. To help them develop a more consistent form, they rushed to feed upon something to sustain them. Me.

"Holy shit." I ran. The blackness made it difficult to keep the exit within my sights. Instinct had me digging in my pocket for my cell phone to use as a flashlight. I got a handful of tissues, lint, peanuts, and hard candy. I groped in the other pocket until I found the phone. A glance at the screen confirmed what I suspected—still no reception. I guess it would be asking a lot to have reception underground in the tunnel to hell. I suspect emergency numbers would be inundated with calls and a lack of staff willing to assist.

The phone provided a small beacon of light, but not enough to stop me from ramming into the ladder. Undeterred, I grabbed a rung. It clanked against the wall as I mounted the bottom step. Anger must've inspired Ritchie to pick up his pace. His grunting breath grew louder. He caught the back of my jacket and yanked me to the ground. My ankle twisted to the side as I landed on my back. My phone skidded across the dirt.

I bit back a yelp of pain so not to lure the Oppressors during my weakened state. Although they didn't need the sound of my distress to alert them; they could sense my emotions. When Ritchie loomed over me, I felt the Oppressors' intense craving of the desperation rising within me. My phone's dim light, and one remaining lantern shaking against the wall above me, illuminated him and cast his face into sharp, frightful angles.

I had never realized what a big man he was. His simplicity masked the inner beast frustration stirred—no different than any other male. I'd overlooked this flaw because I never considered Ritchie as a threat. That oversight might cost me my life. Once he touched me in my weakened state and began to sap my essence in the presence of the desperate low-level Oppressors, I was done.

"Who will tell me what to do?" His voice elevated in a whine. "I need my Bert—" His eyes widened, and the color drained from his face. He staggered a step away, visibly shaking.

I scrambled away to put more distance between us. Sharp stones poked into my palms. I glanced at my hand, wondering what made him back off. No glitter or black fog leaked out. That was no wonder since my emotions were immobilized by fear. The Oppressors approached. The lantern flickered as the flame fought the chilly unearthly wind. Clouds of hate and desolation washed over me, pushing and pulling with no pattern to their rhythm. I followed Ritchie's gaze. It wasn't stones poking my flesh, but the broken and discarded peanuts and their shells surrounding me. They must've fallen out of my pocket in my search for my phone.

I picked up a peanut and crushed it. Dust of the filmy husk fell between my fingers.

"No, don't." Ritchie held his trembling hands in front of him and backed away.

"Don't make me." I extended the peanut remnants like a shield and pushed myself to stand, favoring my left ankle. The Oppressors flanked him like his dark army. "I'm leaving and you're not going to do anything to stop me. Do you understand?"

Ritchie nodded, but apparently the force that was the Oppressors didn't agree to the deal. The wind picked up to a howl as they closed around me, passing him without hesitation in their eagerness to reach me.

Why didn't they feed from his fear? Even I felt the terror emanating from Ritchie. Somehow, he was immune from their thirst. I, however, was not. I scooped up more peanuts amongst a handful of dirt.

"Call them off." I shook my fist and peanut shells fell from my clutch. Ritchie eyed them as they floated to the ground. The whites of his eyes cut through the dimness. He tried to back up but the wall of Oppressors rising from the depths immobilized him.

"I said, call them off!" I didn't know if he could. But I had to count on him having some control over them, otherwise I wasn't leaving this place alive. "Call them—"

Their projected desperation seeped into me. My body trembled as I sank to my knees, tossing the peanuts at Ritchie before I collapsed. His shrill scream assured me I'd hit my target.

"I have more," I murmured as my brain fogged with thoughts of hopelessness. I fumbled in my pocket and found a few more peanuts and extended my hand.

The eagerness of the Oppressors made them bump and shove Ritchie closer as they thrashed to pass him. Ritchie's screams intensified upon being forced toward the source of his anxiety. I grabbed his pant's leg and drew him nearer. I hoped to use him as a shield from the Oppressors. I gripped the fabric as if my life depended upon it, because it did.

He hopped on one foot, trying to shake me off as if I were a rabid dog. Thoughts of all those I'd failed in the past rose to the forefront of my mind. Destiny. Tessa. Even Bob, whose job I took when he was fired after I showed up.

I didn't save them. I didn't deserve to live. I was no Enchantling. I obviously hadn't provided enough hope to anyone to make a difference. I knew the thoughts weren't my own, but the emotions unleashed with them overwhelmed me as the Oppressors unburied my deepest regrets and fears and shoved them to the forefront of my mind. They washed over me in a massive blast of desperation and guilt. The weight of my misery settled upon my shoulders, and my grip on Ritchie loosened. *Why should I continue my lackluster existence?*

I grimaced and focused on pushing one thought to the brim of my consciousness—*don't let go of Ritchie or I'm doomed.* Throughout my life, I'd danced with the threat of death more than once. Yet I survived the nuns' failed attempts to exorcise the evil within me, gave Tessa gray hair earlier than she should've had from more than one teenage adventure, and most recently in my showdown with Hecate. There was no way I was taking my last breath on earth in a filthy tunnel because I couldn't outwit Ritchie the witless wonder.

I groped blindly with my other hand to clutch a handful of what I hoped were peanut shell remnants, or trusted that at least Ritchie thought they were. I threw them on his leg. They bounced harmlessly off the fabric to the floor. He screamed. It was terrible to exploit his phobia, but I'd done worse things in my life, and his terror was my only weapon.

"Leave her!" Ritchie gasped out to the masses of oppressive hate pouring from the tunnel. Sweat streaked through the grime smeared on his face. His ragged breath confirmed he was on the verge of hyperventilating in his hysteria. He tried to back away, but I held tight. He fell to join me on the ground, but I never relinquished my grip. "I said, leave her be."

Chapter Fifteen

The walls vibrated. I clung tight to Ritchie as the fog of Oppressors advanced and retreated in a whirlwind of confusion. Their palpable dismay tainted the air. A wrenching moan howled through the tunnel. Their displeasure of being denied the chance to feast on my desolation echoed and made goosebumps rise along my arm.

Ritchie raised his fist and shook it. "Go."

Particles of dirt and stone rained down with their retreat, and the tunnel shook like a child's temper tantrum. I covered my head, fearing the tunnel might collapse and I'd be buried alive. A gust of wind chased their hasty departure.

I sensed the presence of a few remaining Oppressors. They watched and waited. The desolation that had settled within me rose and left with most of the retreating bottom-feeders. The emotion was rapidly replaced by anger that my fate lay at the hands of a misguided moron. I held on to that feeling. A festering rage filled me.

Join us.

I tensed when their chilling whispers rose from the depths. Filled with false promises, power, and revenge for all that had wronged me in my lifetime. The list was long. They unearthed old memories I'd long buried. The pain of past betrayals and taunting felt new—fresh.

I ignored the beckoning of the Oppressors as fury fueled my strength. The intensity of my anger startled me, and I feared the Oppressors may have contributed to my rage—but I couldn't stop the reckless emotion churning through me. Ritchie had refused their needs, and they weren't to be denied.

I pushed my knees under me, maintaining my grip on Ritchie's leg. My vision sharpened and cut through the darkness, offering the perks of accepting the predator within me that I could become.

Lead us.

Their whispers floated in from the depths on a chilling breeze. Ritchie's face grew slack, as if he realized the Oppressors were considering changing sides. My hair fell forward over my face in dirt encrusted clumps. I peered through my grimy locks, focusing on my target. *Ritchie.* He had drawn the Oppressors to feed on me.

He'd stopped shaking his leg, only giving an occasional half-hearted kick as defeat settled in.

I pushed my hair aside and lifted my head to study him. At first, I thought he might actually be having an allergic reaction to the peanuts, but it only appeared as if the thought drove him to self-imposed immobility. He opened and shut his mouth. No longer strong enough to scream, he emitted a weak, raspy wheeze.

I struggled to crawl, gasping with the effort in my weakened, depleted state. Utilizing his thick, stump-like legs to pull myself forward, I gained strength as my body hummed with rage. Black fog poured from my fingertips. The coils twisted and turned and increased in momentum as they sought refuge in their wanting. Once released, their desire to regain pleasure into my bleak outlook was insatiable.

The tendrils steadily wrapped around Ritchie's legs. He gasped. The unseen enemy I produced tightened the steel grip on his emotions. Ritchie blinked with confusion and gazed at his body. He wouldn't be able to see what was happening. My oppressor-like characteristic would be invisible to his eyes. But he could certainly feel the change. The black tendrils climbed him like vines, restraining him better than any rope could by linking to his emotional psyche.

He returned his focus to me, his terror for the peanuts momentarily forgotten. He stared wide-eyed and open-mouthed. Perhaps his terror mounted in response to the alien sensation he felt. His immunity to the Oppressors' abilities didn't apply to me. I wasn't an Oppressor. I was…something else.

I cocked my head and smiled as his resistance waned. "What? Didn't you think two could play at this game? Except I don't need any pets to take care of me. I can take care of myself. Always have. Always will."

Ritchie screamed as if he looked in the eyes of the devil himself…or I should say, herself. Finally, he realized the bigger threat. I was much more lethal than a peanut, or his bottom-feeding pets.

His fear taunted and tempted me, promising to rid me of all my pain and angst. No longer the victim. No more suffering. I licked my lips in anticipation. The experience with the reporter rose in my mind, and the promises Drake used to try to convince me to join him long before his demise…fear tasted better than anything.

Ritchie bucked violently until he tossed me off. I rolled into the wall, bringing a shower of dirt and stones raining upon me. He struggled to balance on his knees and crawl away, dropping to his forearms in his haste. He howled with frustration and fear. The sound hurt my ears as his cries mingled with his words and echoed through the tunnel. "You promised," he sputtered with a voice scratchy from yelling.

"I didn't promise you anything." Besides, promises were always broken, at least that was my experience. I hesitated, thinking of Griffith. I was grateful he wasn't here to see me like this. I grabbed Ritchie's legs and squeezed. I focused on taking and released my demons to feed. They rapidly surrounded him, filling every open orifice to suck the emotions from him.

"Ouch." I released my hold when I pressed down on a piece of broken glass. Pain seared through my finger. I sucked on the cut digit to ease the pain. My distorted reflection stared back at me from the broken piece of mirror. I gasped.

Finally. You are one of us.

****

I lowered my finger from my dirt encrusted lips, surprised I even recognized myself. But there were no other dirty, deranged looking women crawling through the tunnel, so it had to be me. Were the Oppressors playing mind games with me? Or was it my own thoughts confirming my worst fears? That it was already too late to save myself?

I let go of Ritchie and gently picked up the chunk of mirror. My hand shook as I held it in front of me. I sat back on my haunches. Ritchie lolled to the side, looking as if he'd curled up for a nap, but the fetal position he chose told me he was protecting what little of himself remained. *What I didn't take yet.*

My eyes flashed dark and stormy, far from their usual calm sea green. The dark haze bobbed around me and grew frantic in its urge for me to take what was mine, to finish what I started. My hair lay in snarls. The taut curls resembled a coiled snake. The veins in my neck against my pale flesh stood out against the blackness, bringing images of Hecate to my mind, facing similarities I didn't want to find, that I had long denied.

This was the reason I was alone. Why I never let Griffith get too close. My secret fear that this morbid resemblance to the evil goddess may be the true underlying reason for his fascination with me. *Why hadn't he come back for me?*

Thoughts of Berta clutching him when he carried her from the tunnel resurfaced and stirred my self-loathing. Griffith deserved better than someone like me. The sound of Ritchie's quiet crying further deepened my remorse at what I'd let myself become—everything I was against. The monster I fought was me.

"Hope, you're not alone."

I tensed until I realized the sweet voice wasn't the Oppressors. "Tessa?" My gaze darted around the empty darkness and then settled on the piece of glass I held. My blood smeared the ragged edges of the glass. The only visible part of my aunt in the reflection was her comforting gaze, but it was the only thing I needed to see.

"Ritchie is an innocent. Deep in your heart you know that. Just like you know who you are. This isn't you. You can stop it."

Her voice and image faded so quickly that I wondered if I imagined the entire exchange. If her words were only in my warped mind. "Tessa? Tessa, don't go." Silence settled and left me alone with my thoughts, Ritchie, and the undeniable presence of the Oppressors. They waited for my decision. The Oppressors assured me they wouldn't judge me. That I'd never be alone again. They waited. I only had to go to them. They would never leave me.

Ritchie's low crying drew my attention. Tears streaked down his face, leaving a trail through the dirt smudges covering his features. My fury abated as Ritchie hedged further away from me, trembling in fear. His terror and confusion stripped him, leaving him as helpless as a child. Tessa was right, he was an innocent. The Oppressors used him almost as much as they used me or Griffith. He was still guilty of keeping Berta against her will, but I didn't think his feeble mind enabled him to view it that way. He set up the little room as if it were her vacation home, and probably considered it as such. Still a crime, but not necessarily punishable by death—and certainly not by my hand.

I held up my palm, studying the blackness pouring from my fingertips. The tendrils danced, frantically eager for release after so many years of restraint. Their crisscrossing path had a disturbing resemblance to Hecate's medusa-like hair strands. I focused on my hand, trying to will the desire away, to gain control of the urge to finish what I started, and to maintain the upper hand. To get what deep down I believed I deserved.

Ritchie shifted, starting to come around a little since I'd given him a brief reprieve from my consumption. It was now or never. If he regained what little sense he had, he would most likely call back the

Oppressors. He wouldn't hold them off this time. Now that he knew the peanut shells were the least of his worries.

Take. Take.

The Oppressors urged me by preying upon the greed echoing through my thoughts and desires. After a lifetime of deprivation in almost every sense of the word, I wanted it all. The Oppressors no longer focused on Ritchie for direction. A few stealthily approached and hovered near me, obediently waiting for my lead.

No. I wasn't like Hecate. I wouldn't be. I pushed to my haunches and closed my eyes. I concentrated on Chance, picturing how my brother became so despondent compared to how he used to be. Imagining how he'd react if I let myself go. If I joined their ranks.

Ginger.

I startled. An icy chill of fear sped up my spine at the whisper. I snapped my gaze to the darkest corner of the tunnel. He wasn't there. *No.* It couldn't be him. He was gone. Griffith banished Drake. I squeezed my eyes tighter and tried to still the racing of my heartbeat, afraid of what I might see if I opened them. I wouldn't fall for the Oppressor's mind games.

I didn't want to become like that, like them. Living fueled by anger and a need for revenge for all that life denied. I'd be much worse off than Chance. I housed a lot more accumulated hate and heartache over my lifetime. My hopelessness wouldn't only affect me. It would change everything. All the years Ruthie and Tessa gave up would be for nothing. I thought of Griffith. What would he think? What would he say if he saw me in this state? I slumped to cover my face, rubbing at my eyes as if I could remove the thought. He wouldn't approve. I couldn't bear to see his disappointment.

I took a few slow breaths and opened my eyes. Everything looked the same, yet everything had changed. The insatiable need to feed my inner demons faltered and faded. A sense of peace enveloped and embraced me. The hammering of my heart quieted in my ears. The tension constricting my body and thoughts eased. For the first time, I pulled back my ability and reined in my uncontrollable desire to give or take emotions. I did it.

I picked up my phone. The flashlight continued to cast a low illumination despite the cracked screen. I looked around for something to restrain Ritchie with to keep him from fleeing—or calling back the beasts from the depths. If they realized I was myself again, I knew they'd align with Ritchie again.

Despite all the piles of clutter surrounding me, there was nothing immediately available that I could use to bind him as effectively as I had with his emotions. He lay shaking in a ball. One arm was thrown over his head. He peered under his arm, tracking my steps with a wary eye looking below the dirty flannel fabric.

I stood with hesitation, wincing as I tested the weight on my swollen ankle. Something crunched under my step. The wall provided a brace as I lifted my shoe. Pieces of glass and peanuts intermixed on the ground. I reached in my pocket and pulled out a few intact peanuts and knelt in front of Ritchie.

"Go away." Ritchie pulled back, trembling as he tightened into a ball.

I resisted the instinct to comfort him. Dim witted or

not, he'd kept Berta trapped here for days. Despite his inability to understand the extent of his actions, he'd kidnapped her, and then there was the fact that he wanted to feed me to the Oppressors.

"Listen to me. I'm going upstairs to the cabin. I don't want you to move." I spoke in short sentences to try to emphasize my request and then placed a peanut a few inches from him. "I don't want you to call your friends from the tunnel." I situated a couple more nuts in a make shift barrier surrounding him. "Or else I will be back, and I'll bring more peanuts. Do you understand?"

Ritchie nodded, fear displaying the whites of his eyes as his gaze locked on me. I wanted to believe his obvious terror was stimulated by the peanuts and not me. But his look indicated otherwise. I chose not to notice that.

I stood and hobbled a few steps on my ballooning ankle. A glance back ensured he wasn't making any move to summon the Oppressors or deter my departure. He still laid curled into a ball, quivering and watching my every move, paying no attention to the peanuts.

Even if he did flee, he could only go one way—deeper into the tunnel—because I'd be waiting outside. Some of the satisfaction of besting Ritchie paled knowing I required intimidation and fear tactics to succeed. Somehow, I thought being an Enchantling would be a little more amiable, but maybe that was just me. I doubted Destiny would've resorted to such strategies or played upon another's weakness. But she was dead. Sometimes survival meant getting your hands dirty. I hoped Griffith understood that.

I focused on the exit. Relief flooded through me as

my gaze found the ladder promising release from this hell hole. Since the Oppressors retreated, silence loomed heavy. I feared they might be regrouping and returning soon if I didn't hurry. They were determined to have me one way or another. The shadowy silence was pierced intermittently by Ritchie's sobs.

Hopefully Griffith would be waiting outside. I thought he would've returned for me by now. Although I had assured him I didn't need help. That I could take care of myself. I was just surprised he listened.

I frowned. Perhaps he was too preoccupied with Berta. She was certainly better at pumping up any man's ego, and everything else, with her exaggerated damsel in distress tactics.

I gasped when pain pierced my skull. I grimaced and grabbed my head, my old fears of migraines resurrected. Although I hadn't moved, my ears popped with the sensation of changing altitude. I steadied myself against the wall. My vision blurred. *Shit, now what?*

The pain in my head retreated, leaving an oily residue over my brain. I hadn't realized the Oppressors had penetrated and violated my mind and thoughts so seamlessly. No one had been able to do that since…

I shuddered. The sounds of the tunnel—and Griffith's shouting—amplified. I tilted my head and peered up the ladder. Griffith? The trap door rattled. *He didn't leave me.* Somehow the Oppressors obliterated the sound of his efforts to reach me—until now. They'd buried his voice with my hope by using their mind games while they oppressed my emotions. They wanted to ensure I felt completely alone, so I'd consider joining them to wallow in loneliness and despair.

They must've backed off when they realized they'd lost the fight. They wouldn't gain my alliance. A heaviness lifted from my heart when I detected worry penetrating the anger radiating from Griffith's voice. I smiled at his scarcely disguised concern.

The ladder rattled when I mounted the first step. The ascent took longer since I struggled to be careful to keep my weight off my ankle. I pushed through the trap door. It emitted a loud creak when I forced it open. The door thumped against the floor. My first inhalation of above ground air changed into a cough from the cloud of stirred dust until it floated to settle.

Before I could push through the opening, Griffith's face appeared. He fanned the air to clear the particles of filth, but the hazy iridescent fog surrounding him betrayed his own heightened emotional distress. The haze of dirt cleared enough for me to see his face. It was the best thing I'd seen all day.

He frowned to disguise his expression of relief with aggravation. "It's about time. What the hell is going on? I've been trying to open this damn thing." He struck the wooden trap door in a tired display of retaliation. "It wouldn't budge."

What the hell was right. I wasn't sure if I was ready to share that part yet, or how the Oppressors tempted me to change tactics and let me lead them, if I chose to. Everyone always told me that the choice was mine to make. I just hadn't realized how deadly the outcome of my choice might be.

Just the welcome sight of Griffith, and knowing he cared about me, made the stress of the encounter with Ritchie and the Oppressors fade. The departure of the all-encompassing stress and tension allowed me to relax and left me feeling a little giddy. The next time someone told me to go to hell I could retort, been there, done that. Well, close enough for my comfort. "Was I worth the wait?"

His gaze raked over my face with concern. "I'm tired of waiting for you. I'm done with that. Next time I'm staying with you." He reached in for my hand. His strong grip steadied my ascent.

"Next time?" I hoped there wasn't a next time. I'd prefer to call this a once and done situation. When my head emerged first through the opening, I scanned the cabin floor. It looked even more disgusting from my low vantage point. I pulled myself through the opening and scooted away on my butt before quickly closing the trap door. "Where's Berta?"

"Outside." He glanced over his shoulder, drawing his lips into a tight line. "Those strange squirrels that were with you are sitting with her. She refused to come back inside the cabin. I can't say I blame her after her experience." He grimaced. "But she hasn't shut up since I carried her out." He shrugged. "I assume she's safe enough. They'll let us know if she needs help…right?"

For him to admit that he trusted a couple of squirrels for surveillance, instead of hauling her around like a curvy, chatty sack of potatoes, was the first time he'd given any indication that he had faith in my newest ability. I suppressed a smile so Griffith wouldn't think I'd gone completely insane. "I think so. They've kind of deemed themselves as part of my posse."

A gang of what, goddess knows. By now Berta had probably provided them with a plethora of tips for maintaining a glossy coat and proper squirrel etiquette.

Heck, she might've done a reading on their tiny paws to tell them where to find the best nuts to store for the winter. I giggled, earning another troubled look from Griffith. Although perhaps she might not push her readings as much after this experience. "Oh, Ritchie is in the tunnel."

"Ritchie? How?" He furrowed his brow. "He must've snuck past me when I went to get a comb from the bike." He shook his head. "Berta wouldn't leave me alone until I did. Once she left the cabin she started to get hysterical; retrieving the comb was the only thing I could do to calm her. Are you okay?"

I dipped my head. I was far from okay, but telling Griffith about what happened in the tunnel would either make him worry more about me, or confirm I was going off the deep end. Considering everything else accepted as the norm in this town, and that he already knew the tunnel lead somewhere quite unsavory, he'd believe my story. But I would never have a moment's peace again—nor would he.

He didn't deserve that. I'd caused him and everyone else enough distress. I feared Berta's abduction may have been a ploy to bring me to the cabin. Just one more innocent falling prey to what was either my bad luck, or an alternate destiny.

If I shared everything with him, this time he might never return. He might be better off without me, but I selfishly wanted him in my life. I needed him. He was my destiny, *wasn't he?* I'd tell him when the time was right, when I was ready. If I needed to. Just not now. "I'm fine."

"Good." He met my gaze. His expression indicated he didn't quite believe me, and he knew there was more to the story, but he chose not to press me now. "I better get down there and get Ritchie before he takes off...somewhere in there."

His faraway gaze made me think he might have a good idea where the tunnel led, but he wasn't sharing. Perhaps he was right. Just like him, there were things I was better off not knowing. "Don't worry. He's not going anywhere."

"How can you be so sure? Did you restrain him? Or...hurt him?" His intense gaze sought to know if I used my ability.

I had, somewhat, but that wasn't what kept Ritchie immobilized now. I was tempted to tell him how I had used my magic, and how I had controlled it as well. Well, not at first, but I did gain control. I might have used it to intimidate a little and maybe manipulate Ritchie, but I didn't hurt anyone and that was what mattered. That it didn't have to be a bad thing, that I used my ability for good and it worked in our favor. Then perhaps he might not worry so much about the darkness dwelling deep within me. That maybe I wouldn't have to be ashamed of what I was. I opened my mouth to reply, and then I thought about that brief time without Griffith. How painful it was when he needed his space and time away from me.

"No. I had some help from a couple peanuts." Griffith's perplexed expression made me smile. We all have our secrets. I braced myself on the wall to stand, grimacing as the swelling in my ankle became painfully obvious. Griffith glanced to where the flesh bulged and overflowed in a very unflattering, rapidly discoloring lump above my shoe.

Concern washed away the disquiet filling his

features. "You hurt yourself."

"Oh, it's nothing." I tried to sound indifferent even though it hurt like a fire poker was jammed in my ankle.

"No, it's something." Griffith bent and lifted me in his arms.

I feebly protested until my ankle sung with relief as my painful weight was alleviated. I wrapped my arms around his neck and laid my head against his shoulder, grateful for his support. Like a balm his scent surrounded and soothed me. The cabin was silent in my mind, no longer calling for me but wallowing in its loss. Apparently, whatever entity spawned the vengeful wood had yet to accept that love usually triumphed over hate. "But Berta—"

"She'll be fine, and besides, there's nothing to be jealous about." He kissed the top of my head and then touched his forehead to mine.

"I didn't say I was jealous." The churning in my belly when I saw her wrap her arms around him as he carried her from the tunnel indicated otherwise.

"Really? You didn't need to, it was written all over the scowl on your face. Just shut up and let me take care of you." He bent to my lips. I couldn't tell if the ringing in my ears and the ground shuddering was from the kiss, or the cabin grieving its defeat.

Chapter Sixteen

"Do they have to do the interview today? For goodness sake, it's a holiday." I cupped my hands against the frosted windowpane in Aunt Ruthie and Uncle George's living room. I leaned nearer to peer through the make-shift border my hands had created, displaying Berta and Tom *the jerk* reporter standing on the road. My breath fogged the cool glass. It seemed Berta planned to extract all the attention she could out of her kidnapping experience.

Tom shoved his microphone in her face, and she chatted away with excessive animation as she shared her story. The scene was familiar to me, since it depicted the vision haunting my thoughts for so long. My vision was true, except for the part where Berta snuck off to spill our secrets. If Berta followed the plan we devised, the only thing she'd be spilling was a lot of misinformation to convince Tom there was nothing worth reporting in this town. At least not for his shitty newspaper which thrived on oddities and freaks. A run-of-the-mill kidnapping by a local mentally ill man wouldn't interest his readers. Especially when there was no blood shed or unusual happenings.

Each time Berta recounted the events leading up to Ritchie kidnapping her, the story grew and expanded. Most of the additions highlighted Berta's so-called heroic acts and unbelievable empathetic nature. I rolled my eyes.

This was partially my fault. I wanted nothing to do with the limelight, or to be part of a feature story in Neb Knows. I'd be relieved to see the last of the reporter and breathe a whole lot easier without him skulking around town. So, I asked for my role in her rescue to be completely extricated from the story. Berta took it upon herself to make up details to fill in the gaps.

As if sensing my stare, Berta turned to the window and waved. I dropped the curtain before the reporter noticed my engrossed interest in them, or my narrowed gaze. I was pretty sure his curiosity in me had waned, for now. I wanted to keep it that way.

Unfortunately, Officer McCrory still wasn't convinced I wasn't involved somehow. In his mind, I was always guilty until proven innocent. He hadn't shared what he thought I might be guilty of, but he never ceased looking. It was annoying, but since McCrory planted enough roots in this town to grow his own forest I didn't think he was going anywhere. I'd just have to deal with him and be on my best behavior. I grimaced, realizing the extent of that challenge.

For weeks after the incident at the cabin, Tom lurked around the house and the bar, and just about everywhere else, pestering everyone for Berta's story. I still couldn't figure out why none of the Oppressors had gotten rid of him yet. It seemed he even annoyed them to the point that sucking the hope out of him wasn't worth their time. I guess he might leave a bad taste in their mouth—or he had someone looking out for him.

The only thing ensuring he maintained his distance and didn't harass her constantly was Berta's promise to provide him with first dibs. An exclusive interview on her story when she was ready. That and a few discreet threats from Chance. To further increase Chance's annoyance, Tom never strayed far from Berta. He was a constant exasperating reminder to ensure she wouldn't forget her promise.

She insisted she owed *poor Tom* that much after how most of the town treated him. She'd told Chance this while giving me a knowing stare. Despite my starring role in her rescue, and how I managed to secure the psychological help Ritchie needed rather than imprison or annihilate him, it was obvious who she felt treated *poor Tom* unfairly. Mostly me. She still clung to the warped notion that she could smother the fear and hate in this town with her Pollyanna-like persistence. Perhaps she and Chance were more alike deep down than I realized.

Chance emerged from the kitchen to join me at the window. George's snoring increased in volume as he settled more comfortably in the worn recliner behind us. Chance craned his head to peer up and down the street. Until now, he wouldn't let Tom or anyone outside of family close enough to Berta to allow her to recount her twisted tale. Chance stalked around her like a silverback gorilla until I told him that if he didn't tone it down a little I'd think his oppressive side was starting to show. I was happy to say that it was the only potential Oppressor characteristic I'd noticed lately. Even though she still drove me crazy, it seemed Berta did bring out the best in him.

What finally made him relent to letting Berta do the interview was the realization that if she didn't tell her story, and gain her *fifteen minutes of fame*, as she liked to call it, we'd be subjected to listening to the exaggerated story until the end of time—and then some.

Plus, Tom would either make up his own embellished recount of the events, or never leave town. Right now, I didn't care what he made up. I just wanted him gone. Let us enjoy Thanksgiving. We agreed to do the interview if Tom agreed to our specifications and demands. Including insisting that no one else in my family would have any part of the interview, or be mentioned in the article, besides Berta.

We chose the holiday since we thought it wouldn't be as newsworthy, the town was a little more subdued, and maybe just to ruin the nosy reporter's holiday a bit. I know seeing the last of him was something *I'd* be thankful for. Dishes clattered in the adjoining room as Ruthie cursed and mumbled about all of George's hoarding. She sought specific plates and dishes to show off her feast on the dining room table and refused our offers of help. She insisted the holidays were her area of expertise and that she knew how the table had to look, and what she wanted to cook, and didn't want any interference. Ruthie was happier than I'd seen her in some time, so I had no intention of ruining the day by fumbling around in her way.

Chance frowned when the rooster-imprinted curtain fell from where he wrapped it around the rod to gain a better view. He scowled and shoved the fabric out of the way. "She shouldn't be out there alone."

"Don't even think about it." We'd already discussed at length how sending a clone to follow around Berta was a very bad idea. Besides freaking her and most of the town out with a newfound twin, it would only be a matter of time before ole Neb Knows figured out someone else in the family had a story worth pursuing. "She's fine. Ritchie is committed to the psychiatric hospital. Tom's not going to do anything rash with you glaring through the window. Besides, she's not actually alone, Griffith is on the porch."

I followed the decadent aroma wafting from the kitchen as if intending to peer out the door at Griffith. All I really wanted was to bask in the perfume of the meal until my pores absorbed it. Chance dogged my heels, following me.

I insisted he and I not have any involvement in the interview to avoid peaking the reporter's interest any further or permitting him to gain photographs or other stealthy recordings. I'd learned my lesson about his underhanded tactics of acquiring information for his stories. And I had no desire to see my face plastered in his paper. Chief continued to faithfully buy the printed garbage trying to charade as real news. I snuck in his office occasionally to flip through the tabloids to ensure Tom kept his word and left us out of his news.

Berta readily agreed to the arrangement, wanting to keep the attention firmly in her court. My impatience with the lengthy interview wasn't due to concern for Berta's safety, but more so that Ruthie's famous Thanksgiving dinner was going to burn, or get cold, if Berta took much longer.

The door ushered Griffith in with a gust of cold air that knocked the curtain back off the rod to sway in front of the window. I sighed when I noticed that he carried in the crustless, and most likely tasteless, healthy pie I intentionally forgot in the car.

His spinach, kale, veggie, health-food-overload disguised as actual holiday food wasn't going to fool anyone. I insisted that Ruthie liked to do the cooking, and that she would be insulted by anyone else making food. That this wasn't the way into Ruthie's heart. He retorted that he was worrying about all our hearts, and keeping them healthy, one dish at a time. He might get my family to accept him as a Splice, but trying to pry the fat, salt, and flavor out of the diet Ruthie swore by was crossing the line.

Truthfully, I just wanted the real deal for Thanksgiving dinner. All the fatty, fabulous fixings without worrying about how terribly unhealthy everything was. Wasn't that what Thanksgiving was supposed to be all about? Not checking the fat grams, cholesterol, calories, and protein stuffed into the meal or tweaking traditional fare with tasteless substitutions.

Griffith used the opportunity to check on Berta to get a closer look, provide an intimidating reminder for Tom, and to retrieve his wholesome, unwelcome contribution to dinner. He met my gaze with a triumphant smile. I frowned. No one else was going to touch that dish once their taste buds realized how he masqueraded diet food as something delicious. But there was no way I could avoid a slice of his baked abhorrence, or else I'd hurt his feelings. It figures that one of the few times it was blatantly obvious that he had feelings was when it came to experimentation with his healthy, clean cooking.

Chance abandoned his post and rushed to the door. He looked over Griffith's shoulder as if he believed Griffith toted Berta on his back. When he didn't see her, he tried to push past to get to the porch, almost knocking the pie dish out of his hand. Almost—no such luck. "Where's Berta? Why did you leave her out there?"

Griffith didn't budge, effortlessly blocking Chance's exit. After carefully setting the baking dish on the counter, he laid his hands on Chance's shoulders. When he drew back, Griffith lifted his hands, palm up, and took a step away. "Give her some space, dude. Women don't like you to hover over them all the time."

Finally. Just when I thought he didn't listen to anything I said, he went and proved me wrong. I turned to Griffith with a smile at the affectionate way he addressed my brother. Almost forgiving him for forcing his healthy habits on me. As if dying from an unhealthy diet was high on my risk factors. We both knew I was much more likely to die from other unnatural causes. "That's right. She survived right outside hell's front door for days with a mass of Oppressors for company. I think she can handle one nosey, irritating reporter."

Griffith met my gaze. As if sensing he'd accidently lowered his guard, his brief smile was replaced with his usual look of indifference. "I don't think it's the reporter we need to worry about detaining her. He's been trying to end the interview for ten minutes. Berta won't let him leave. She's not done talking." He stepped aside to allow Chance to pass, and to move the baking dish into the living room—halfway to its destination of the dining room table.

Chance ran a hand through his hair, elevating the strands to match the rooster decor. He stepped on the porch to keep a closer eye on Berta and to probably give the reporter a closer look at the stink eye he cast.

I turned to Griffith. "Do you think the reporter will believe her story?"

"I'm sure he will. But he might add his own embellishments. He was probably expecting something much more bizarre from this town. A standard kidnapping isn't all that exciting and won't bring the big headlines he's hoping for."

I touched Griffith's arm. His relaxed posture assured me that despite his reluctance to use his Oppressor skills, he accepted his role in our deception. When he carried Berta out of the cabin, he took that time to use his oppressive abilities to persuade Berta that the events occurred in Ritchie's run-down van, helping her forget all about the cabin and what lay beneath. Not only for the protection of the town and nosey spectators, but to allow Berta to sleep a little more soundly at night. I wouldn't wish the nightmares that plagued me on anyone. Griffith was right. There are some things that most are better not knowing, especially if sleep is a priority.

Initially, I protested. Not about him influencing Berta; if anyone needed to talk a little less, it was her. But because I wanted the tunnel exposed and destroyed or buried—or whatever would obliterate it from the earth and my nightmares. I still harbored uncertainty about attempting to try to forget it existed. It wasn't a good idea. Besides, that was impossible, and I refused Griffith's offer to persuade my memory otherwise. Knowing what I was up against was preferable than future unpleasant surprises in exchange for peace of mind today. "Are you sure we shouldn't go back and try to seal the tunnel somehow?"

Griffith's sigh conveyed his exasperation at having to once again repeat his explanation, but his sympathetic gaze let me know he understood my frustration. "I wish it was that easy. But you know, better than most, that you can't bury evil. It just finds a way to dig itself back out and rear its ugly head. There would be a new tunnel. A different door. There always is. It's better that we know where the entrance is. Trust me. It's an advantage for us."

So, as I suspected, the war against evil—my war—would never be over. The best we could hope for was having the upper hand and shifting the balance in our favor. I planned to enjoy today and each day, since I didn't know what tomorrow had in store.

My distress must've been evident, because lacking the appropriate comforting words, Griffith did the next best thing and wrapped me in his arms. His masculine scent mingled with the delicious aromas from the kitchen, making me feel more than content. I leaned into his shoulder and closed my eyes with a sigh. Just like his Trojan horse healthy pie, on the outside, everything was perfect. On the inside, it was a different story, but I was the only one aware of that. I'd spent years burying fear, uncertainty, and misgivings, and I didn't intend to stop digging now.

I hadn't told him about the whisperings of the cabin and how a few times I thought its persuasive voice still called to me, waking me from my sleep. How sometimes my curiosity peaked with an overwhelming urge to return to see where the tunnel lead. To let all my inner ugliness hang out and have it accepted and embraced.

Griffith had finally come back around. We were together again. He accepted me. There was no need to scare him away again with my irrational contemplations. I assumed they were just nightmares and if not, they were something I preferred to keep to myself.

"The table is perfect. I knew just how I wanted it to look." Ruthie bustled in from the dining room, untying her apron and tossing it on the couch. It landed on one of the dolls, covering the creepy glassy-eyed stare. "Is that girl ever done talking? Dinner is about ready, and I know it's going to be delicious—"

Griffith released me and stepped away as if I'd burned him when Ruthie stopped short in the kitchen, but it was just Ruthie's heavy look of disapproval scalding him. She might tolerate and even accept Griffith for what he was, but approving of him for me was a different story. He drew in his shoulders, but his large frame still made him appear out of place and awkward in her tiny kitchen. As he squirmed under her scrutiny, he bumped the wall shelf overcrowded with figurines, ceramics, and trinkets.

Ruthie gasped when one teetered and fell.

Quick reflexes enabled Griffith to catch the hideous rooster knick-knack moments before it hit the floor and shattered. He replaced it gently and stepped closer to me. He appeared so pleased to have saved the ugly ceramic from demise that I refrained from mentioning that it might not have been much of a loss.

It amused me how Ruthie could intimidate the hell out of him. Griffith was a Splice feared by most of the Oppressors. His mother disowned him, and he banished his own brother for me. He'd literally been to the Underworld and back, yet still this old witch knew she made him tremble. But I knew most of what he feared was her disapproval.

I placed a comforting hand on his arm and smiled at him. I felt some of his tension dissipate. Griffith followed my lead and slowly slid his arm around my waist. I didn't miss how Ruthie followed his arm with her gaze and a slight frown, but she didn't complain. She only made a muffled, unintelligible sound. We were making progress. No matter what Ruthie thought, Griffith was family, too.

Chance and Berta came into the kitchen. Stinker streaked past them, making a beeline toward the living room before they banged the door closed behind them. Chance appeared much more relaxed now that the reporter was gone and Berta was safe inside the house with him. He helped Berta hang her coat and then ran his hands down her arms in a loving gesture. I was pleased to see him happy again.

"Much longer and I would have burned dinner." Ruthie opened the oven and bent to peek. Her ample hips crowded us, and we stepped away.

"Wouldn't be the first time. Watch you don't burn your buns." The mirror reflected with Tessa's amused face, and the sound of her tinkling laugh warmed my heart.

Ruthie startled, and she let the oven door shut with a thud. The trinkets rattled but held their ground on their posts on the shelves. "Lands' sake, sister. How about announcing yourself before you pop in like that and try to scare me to death? You probably just want to make sure I don't get to enjoy all my labors of love on this meal." Ruthie's smile betrayed the jest in her comment.

"Don't worry, Ruthie. I think you're good. I'm sure you know how to make dinner," I assured her. Even Stinker's signature smell was obliterated by the festive scents emanating from the oven. The smell was heavenly. This was no frozen or reheated dinner. I wished that Tessa could be here to enjoy the meal, but I supposed having her here in spirit was good enough.

George snorted as he woke from his nap on the recliner. "Did someone say dinner? Is it time to eat? How come nobody woke me?" He waddled into the kitchen while rubbing his round belly and smacking his lips in anticipation. With everyone crammed into the small kitchen, there was nowhere to move. Ruthie lined the counter with the prepared courses.

I carefully picked up one of the casserole dishes with potholders and turned to take it to the dining room. George barricaded my way.

"Don't tell Ruthie, but I snuck a piece of that pie Griffith brought." He winked, and a few green crumbs that might have been spinach or kale fell from his mustache. "Pretty tasty, but it sure didn't fill me for long. What was in that? Maybe you can share the recipe with Ruthie."

Griffith and I exchanged a glance when George moved to let us pass with the food. There was no way he would block our passage when we were bearing dinner. I shook my head slightly. Indicating this wasn't the time to tell George just what that pie was composed of, despite the flicker of hope I glimpsed in Griffith's eyes. He probably envisioned bonding with Ruthie by sharing his healthy recipe. Trying to change the eating habits of a man who thrived on a diet mostly composed of sugar, sugar, and more sugar should be a gradual process...or not at all. "It's a secret recipe, George."

This might fall into that category of things that Ruthie and especially George were better off not knowing. They might be able to deal with Oppressors, dead spirits, a Splice, and newfound family members, but slipping health food into their hundred-percent unhealthy diet might just push them over the edge. Griffith might never break that barrier again.

Once Griffith and I set the serving platters on the dining room table, I leaned back against him and surveyed the room. Chance and Berta filtered in with additional dishes while Ruthie and George brought up the rear. Tessa popped into the mirror to criticize Ruthie's placemats. Apparently, placemats depicting cross-stitched rooster replicas weren't an acceptable replacement for a turkey scene on Thanksgiving. Ruthie playfully argued back about personal preference and long-honored traditions while arranging the platters.

Stinker tentatively approached Tercet until she was certain the little finicky feline wasn't going to flee. Then she curled up beside her in the corner. Bonding together to scout for any fallen table scraps.

I smiled. My heart couldn't be fuller. It wouldn't matter if Ruthie burned all the food, or if the desserts tasted like cardboard. All this time I thought I was missing out on the food for this holiday, but really, I was missing something else entirely. The best part of today and every day was being with my family and friends. Even Berta was starting to grow on me. It wasn't the food or the decorations that made a day special, it was the people who shared it with us.

A word about the author…

Maureen Bonatch grew up in small town Pennsylvania and her love of the four seasons—hockey, biking, sweat pants and hibernation—keep her there. While immersed in writing or reading paranormal romance and fantasy, she survives on caffeine, wine, music, and laughter. A feisty shih tzu, teen twins & her alpha hubby keep her in line. You can find Maureen trying to be witty on her website or slewing sarcasm and fun on Facebook.

http://www.maureenbonatch.com
https://www.facebook.com/maureenlbonatch/
http://www.maureenbonatch.com

Thank you for purchasing
this publication of The Wild Rose Press, Inc.

For questions or more information
contact us at
info@thewildrosepress.com.

The Wild Rose Press, Inc.
www.thewildrosepress.com

To visit with authors of
The Wild Rose Press, Inc.
join our yahoo loop at
http://groups.yahoo.com/group/thewildrosepress/